DISCARD

WHEN MY HEART JOINS THE THOUSAND

WHEN MY HEART JOINS THE THOUSAND

A. J. STEIGER

An Imprint of HarperCollins*Publishers*

HarperTeen is an imprint of HarperCollins Publishers.
When My Heart Joins the Thousand

For information address HarperCollins Children's Books, a division of HarperCollins Publishers, 195 Broadway, New York, NY 10007.

www.epicreads.com

Library of Congress Control Number: 2017938997

ISBN 978-0-06-265647-6

Typography by Michelle Taormina

17 18 19 20 21 PC/LSCH 10 9 8 7 6 5 4 3 2 1

❖

First Edition

To Joe

WHEN MY HEART JOINS THE THOUSAND

AUTHOR'S NOTE

I was first introduced to the world of *Watership Down* as a child, through the 1978 animated film, which captures the brutality as well as the hope and beauty of the original book. I fell instantly in love with its world and characters. Decades later, I find its power undimmed.

Rabbits are survivors. Faced with a world of predators, they adapt, struggle, fight, and persevere. As individuals they are weak and short-lived, but as a species they are mighty. They represent the will to live, the deepest instinct burning within every creature of this world.

Alvie, too, is a survivor. Her emotional connection to rabbits—and to *Watership Down*, specifically—is the thing that first brought her to life in my mind, and a touchstone I returned to through revision after revision.

For that, I owe a tremendous debt of gratitude to Richard Adams. He passed away in 2016, but his legacy will endure for generations. Far more than a fantasy, *Watership Down* is an anthem of life. It reminds us of our deep and intimate connection to the earth, to animals, and to each other.

For rabbits, the process of courtship and mating combined takes about thirty to forty seconds.

I am not a rabbit. If I were, my life would be simpler in many ways.

"Are you sure about this?" Stanley asks. "You can still change your mind, you know."

I tug twice on my left braid. "If I didn't want this, I wouldn't have asked." Though I didn't expect him to say yes.

We are in a motel room with an ancient, rattling heater and a factory painting of a windmill. Stanley sits on the edge of the bed, fidgeting, his crutch leaning next to him. His hands are clasped tightly in his lap.

I take a few steps toward him. He lifts his hands, then stops. "No touching, right?"

"No touching," I reply. That's the agreement. I touch him. He doesn't touch me.

His pulse beats in his throat. I count twenty beats in ten seconds. One hundred and twenty beats per minute.

This is, I suppose, very sudden. Technically we just met for the first time today. But I want to try. Just once. This should be instinctive. Any animal can do this. Surely I can, too. Even I am not that broken.

Slowly I reach out and take his hand in both of mine. He makes a sound like he's about to sneeze—that sharp intake of breath. I study his fingers, which are long and slender. I don't like being touched, because it hurts, but when I'm the one controlling it, it's bearable. "You know," I say, "all whiptail lizards are female. They reproduce themselves by cloning. Females will mount each other to stimulate egg production."

He doesn't say anything, just looks at me.

"With seahorses, the sex roles are reversed. The female injects her egg into the male, and he carries and bears the young."

Stanley places his free hand on his stomach.

"Emperor penguins have only one mate per breeding season. The mated pair can locate each other by their distinct calls. The male stays in one place and bugles to the female until she finds him. They bow to each other, stand breast to breast, and sing."

"They sing?"

"Yes."

I wonder—what am I? A rabbit, a penguin, a hyena, a gibbon? Something else entirely? The only thing I know for sure is that I don't identify very well with humans.

"Are you sure about this?"

It's the second time he's asked that question, but maybe he's right to ask it. I wonder if I've gone crazy. This could easily turn into a disaster.

"Let's proceed," I say.

CHAPTER ONE

Three weeks earlier

During certain times of day, my apartment smells like rancid Gouda. Apparently no one else in the building has noticed. I've written four letters to Mrs. Schultz, my landlady, but I stopped when I learned she was putting them all in a file folder marked CRAZY, which I happened to glimpse when I went down to her office to pay my rent.

So now, when the smell gets too intense, I just go to the park and play online Go on my laptop.

It's October 5, 5:59 p.m. The temperature in the park is roughly fifty-six degrees. Silence fills my ears. When I listen more deeply, I can hear the sounds woven into it—the dull roar of distant traffic, the *shh-shh* of leaves in the wind, the whoosh of my own blood through my veins—but no human voices.

I pull up the hood of my sweatshirt, which offers the dual advantage of keeping my ears warm while hiding my face, giving mc a sense of privacy. All around me, the park is quiet and still, an expanse of sleepy green grass. A few maples have already started to drop their bloodred leaves. Nearby, a small pond glimmers. *Anas platyrhynchos* glide across the water, and the heads of the males gleam like carved emerald studded with bright onyx eyes. When they rear up, wings spread, the iridescent blue-black of their speculum feathers catches the light.

I glance at the empty bench by the pond and check the time on my cell phone. I am waiting for the boy with the cane.

Every day, at precisely six o'clock, a boy about my age—perhaps a few years older—emerges from a salmon-colored building across the street, limps to the park, and sits on the bench. Sometimes he reads. Sometimes he just watches the ducks. For the past three weeks, this has been his routine.

When he first started coming here, I resented his encroachment on my territory. I didn't want to talk to him—I dislike talking to people—but I didn't want to abandon my park, either. So I hid. After a while, something shifted. He became a part of the scenery, like the ducks, and his presence ceased to annoy me. The clockwork regularity of his visits became—almost comforting.

Sure enough, at six o'clock, the door opens, and he emerges, looking the same as ever: slender, pale, and not too tall, with light brown hair that looks like it hasn't been trimmed for some time. His open blue windbreaker flaps in the breeze. I watch him make his way to the bench, leaning on his cane. He sits. I turn away, satisfied. Leaning back against a tree, I open my laptop, prop it against my knees, and start a game of Go with a random opponent.

The boy is unaware of my presence. I'm careful to keep it that way.

By the time I leave the park, it's almost night. On the way home I stop at the Quik-Mart, grab two packages of ramen, a loaf of white bread, a jug of orange soda, and a cellophane-wrapped vanilla cupcake.

I buy the same thing every time, so I know exactly how much it costs: six dollars and ninety-seven cents. I count out exact change before approaching the counter and quickly slide the money, along with my purchases, toward the clerk.

"Anything else?" he asks. I shake my head.

My apartment is just down the street. It stands on the corner, a squat brick building with a single scrawny tree out front. A blue condom hangs from one of the topmost branches like a tiny flag; it's been there as long as I can remember. Amber shards of broken glass glitter on the pavement.

As I approach the door to the lobby, I freeze. A thin, balding, fortyish man in round glasses and a sweater vest is waiting for me outside, briefcase at his feet, arms crossed over his chest.

"Dr. Bernhardt," I blurt out.

"Glad I caught you. I've been buzzing your apartment. I was about to give up."

I clutch my groceries to my chest. "Our meeting is on Wednesday. It's Monday. You're not supposed to be here."

"I needed to reschedule. I called you several times, but you never answer your phone. I realize you hate surprises, but that being thc case, maybe you should try checking your voice mails now and again." His tone holds a slant that I've come to identify as *wry.*

Dr. Bernhardt is a social worker. He's also the reason I'm able to live on my own, despite being a minor.

"So," he says, "are you going to let me in?"

I breathe a tense sigh and unlock the door. "Fine."

We enter the building and climb the threadbare steps to the second floor. The hallway carpet is a faded shade between beige and blue, with a dark, sprawling stain that could be a spilled drink or dried blood. Like the tree condom, it's been there ever since I moved in. Dr. Bernhardt wrinkles his nose as he steps over it, into my apartment.

He surveys the inside. A pair of unwashed jeans lies on the floor next to a pile of sudoku books. A half-empty glass of orange soda stands on the coffee table with crumbs strewn around it. A sports bra lies draped over the top of the TV.

"You know," he says, "for someone who loves order and routine, I'd think you would be a little more concerned about hygiene."

"I was planning to clean before you came over," I mutter. Messes don't bother me, as long as they're *my* messes. The chaos of my apartment is familiar and easy to navigate.

As I enter the kitchen, an earwig scuttles into the sink and vanishes down the drain. I drop my purchases onto the kitchen counter, open the refrigerator, and slide the orange soda inside.

Dr. Bernhardt peers over my shoulders, surveying the contents of the fridge—a paper carton of leftover Chinese food, the moldy remains of a ham sandwich, a tub of Cool Whip, and some mustard. He raises his eyebrows. "Is there anything in here with nutrients?"

I shut the door. "I'm going grocery shopping tomorrow."

"You really ought to buy a fruit or vegetable once in a while."

"Are you obligated to report on my eating habits."

"Remember, rising inflection for questions. Otherwise people can't tell when you're asking them something."

I think the sentence structure makes it obvious, but I repeat myself, placing emphasis on the last two words: "Are you obligated to report on my *eating habits*?"

"No. I'm just giving you a piece of advice. You do realize that's part of my job?"

"Are you asking me a question."

"It's rhetorical." He walks into the living room. "May I sit?"

I nod.

He lowers himself to the couch and laces his fingers together, studying me over the rims of his small, round glasses. "Still working at the zoo?"

"Yes."

"Have you given any thought to the possibility of college?"

He's asked me this a few times, and I always give him the same answer: "I can't afford it." And I'm unlikely to get a scholarship, since I dropped out of high school—not because I was failing any classes, but simply because I hated being there. I have a GED, but most colleges view an actual diploma as superior. "Anyway, I like my job at the zoo."

"You're satisfied with your current situation, then?"

"Yes." At least, it's preferable to the alternative.

Before I got this apartment, I stayed in a group home for troubled teenagers. There, I shared a room with a girl who chewed her fingers bloody and woke me up at odd hours by screaming in my ear. The food was terrible, the smells worse.

I ran away on three separate occasions. On the third, I was caught sleeping on a park bench and was dragged to court for vagrancy. When asked why I kept running, I told the judge that homelessness was preferable to living in a place like that. I asked her to grant me legal emancipation—which I had been researching—so that I could live on my own.

She agreed, but only under the condition that someone check up on me regularly. Hence, Dr. Bernhardt became my guardian, at least on paper. He's obligated to meet with me at least twice a month, but outside of that we have very little to do with each other, which suits me fine.

Still, there's always an awareness in the back of my mind that he has the power to send me back to the group home. Or worse.

"May I ask you a personal question, Alvie?"

"If I say no, will that make a difference."

He frowns at me, brows knitting together. He's frustrated. Or maybe hurt; I can't tell. I avert my gaze. "Fine. Ask."

"Do you have any friends?"

"I have the animals at work."

"Any friends who can talk? And parrots don't count."

I hesitate. "I don't need any."

"Are you happy?"

It's another rhetorical question; obviously I'm not what most people would describe as happy. But that has nothing to do with anything. Happiness is not a priority. Survival is. Staying sane is. Pointing out that I'm not happy is like pointing out to a starving homeless man that he doesn't have a sensible retirement plan. It might be true, but it's entirely beside the point. "I'm stable. I haven't had a meltdown for several months."

"That's not what I asked."

"I don't understand the point of this question, Dr. Bernhardt."

He sighs. "I'm not a therapist, I know, but I *have* been charged with looking after your well-being. I realize you like your independence, but I'd feel a lot better about your situation if you had at least one friend to rely on. When was the last time you actually started a conversation with someone outside of work?"

Until now, he's been content to ignore my social life, or lack thereof. Why is it suddenly an issue? I rock back and forth on my heels. "I'm not like other people. You know that."

"I think you overestimate how different you really are. Maybe to start with you could, I don't know, try a chat room? Online communication is often easier for people with social difficulties. And it might be a good way to meet people with similar interests."

I don't respond.

"Look. Alvie. I'm on your side, whether you realize it or not—"

That's a line I've heard before, from many adults. I've long since stopped believing it.

"—but the way you're living now . . . it's not healthy. If things don't change, I'll have to recommend to the judge that, as a condition of your continued independence, you start seeing a counselor."

Panic leaps in my chest, but I keep my expression carefully neutral. "Are we done."

He sighs. "I suppose we are." He picks up his briefcase and walks toward the door. "See you in two weeks." As he steps out into the hall, he pauses, glancing over his shoulder. "Happy birthday, by the way."

The door closes.

After he's gone, I stand in the center of the room for a few minutes, waiting for the tightness in my chest to subside.

I unwrap the cupcake I bought from the convenience store, set it on the coffee table, and stick a candle on top. At exactly 7:45 p.m., I light the candle and then blow it out.

One more year to go, and I won't have to deal with Dr. Bernhardt or any interfering adult from the state. All I have to do is make it to eighteen without losing my job or missing rent. Then I'll be fully emancipated. I'll be free.

CHAPTER TWO

At the Hickory Park Zoo, there's a sign standing next to the hyena exhibit: *Happy? Sad? Mad?* And beneath that, in smaller letters: *Attributing human feelings to animals is called anthropomorphizing. Instead of asking, "What is it feeling?" ask, "What is it doing?"*

I see this sign every day when I come to work. I hate it.

Elephants grieve for their dead. Apes can learn to use sign language as skillfully as a five-year-old human child. Crows are magnificent problem solvers; in laboratory experiments, they will use and modify tools, such as pebbles or short pieces of straw, in order to obtain food. When animals do these things, it's rationalized away as instinct or a conditioned response. When humans do these same things, it's accepted unquestionably as evidence of our superiority. Because animals can't vocalize their thoughts and feelings, some people assume they don't have them.

I sometimes fantasize about breaking into the zoo at night, stealing the sign, and throwing it into the nearest river.

I sit on a bench in my khaki-colored uniform, eating a bologna sandwich with mustard, the same thing I always eat on my lunch break. The hyenas snuffle around inside the cave-like enclosure, scratching at the rock-textured walls. Kiki, the dominant female, is chewing the bars.

A woman hurries past me, dragging a chubby little boy along with her. He's around seven years old and eating an ice-cream cone.

"Hi!" the mother trills, smiling. Her mouth is wide and smeared with candy-red lipstick. "Can you look after him a few minutes? I'm going to use the restroom." She dashes off before I can say anything.

The little boy stands, squinting at me, ice-cream cone in hand.

What is she thinking, leaving her child alone with a total stranger? For all she knows, I could be a pedophile. Or a hungover idiot who would just watch, mouth hanging open, while the child crawled into the hyena enclosure. I'm not, but that's beside the point.

"Hi," the boy says.

I have no idea what to say or do, so I just keep eating, watching him from the corner of my eye to make sure he doesn't run off.

He licks his ice cream. "Are you, like, an animal trainer? Do you get to teach them tricks and stuff?"

"No. I just feed them and clean their cages."

He points at Kiki, who's still chewing the bars. "Why is he doing that?"

I swallow a mouthful of sandwich. "It's called stereotypy. It's a nervous habit, like nail biting."

"So he's like a crazy hyena?"

"No. Repetitive behaviors like that are common in captive animals. It's a normal response to an abnormal environment." As an afterthought, I add, "Also, that's not a he. Her name is Kiki."

"No way. He has a thing. A *penis.*" He enunciates the word carefully, like he's not sure I've heard it before.

I take another bite of my sandwich and mutter through a mouthful of bologna, "That's not a penis."

He scrunches up his freckled face. "Then what is it?"

"A phallic clitoris."

"A *what*?"

"Female hyenas are unusual in the animal kingdom. They're larger than the males, and dominant, and they have a clitoris the size of—"

I stop talking as the boy's mother, red faced and tight lipped, grabs his hand and drags him away.

"Mom," the boy says loudly, "what's a clitoris?"

"It's a kind of bird," she mutters.

"That's not what the lady said."

"Well, we're going to have to talk to the lady's supervisor, aren't we?"

A drop of mustard falls from my bologna sandwich and lands on the cobblestones between my feet. I take another bite, but the bread is paper-dry in my mouth. It sticks in my throat.

That afternoon, before the end of my shift, Ms. Nell—the owner of Hickory Park Zoo—calls me to her office. She glares at me from across her desk, drumming her lacquered nails on the arm of her chair. Ms. Nell is stout and short haired, and her outfits always hurt my eyes. Today her jacket is a blinding pink—the same color as Duke, the parrot who sits in a cage in the corner of her office. There's a bare spot on his chest where he's pulled out all his feathers, also a nervous habit.

"You know why you're here, don't you?" she asks.

I shift in my chair. "Because of something I said. But I was just answering—"

"Alvie."

I stop talking.

"I *know* you ain't as dumb as you act sometimes." She only says *ain't* when she's very agitated. It makes me nervous. "You ought to have enough sense to know that you don't start explaining the birds and bees to a kid you've just met. Particularly not while his mother's in earshot."

"I was explaining hyena anatomy. It's part of my job to answer any questions the guests have about the animals. You told me so."

She closes her eyes briefly and squeezes the bridge of her nose. "Cut the crap."

From his cage in the corner, Duke the parrot squawks, "Cut the crap."

I stare at my feet. "I'll apologize to the boy's mother if you want me to."

"No. You'd probably make things worse."

I say nothing, because she's right.

"You know," she says, "this isn't the first complaint I've gotten about you."

I tense. "Please give me another chance. I'll—"

She holds up a hand. "Relax, I ain't gonna fire you. But I want you to keep your fool mouth shut around the guests. Stick to feeding and cleaning."

I hesitate. "What if someone asks me a question."

"Pretend you're deaf."

"How do I do that."

"I don't know. Start signing." She moves her hands around like she's making an invisible cat's cradle, or maybe casting a magic spell. "Like this."

"I don't know sign language."

"Fake it," she snaps.

I nod, afraid that if I argue, she might change her mind.

Though I've been working here for over a year now, I'm well aware that my position is precarious. I have less than two hundred dollars in savings. I make just enough to cover rent, groceries, and car payments, and if I fail to fulfill my financial responsibilities, I'll become a ward of the state once again. It has occurred to me that, if I'm not able to successfully live as an adult, a judge might even declare me incompetent, resulting in a permanent loss of my freedom. Given my history, it's not entirely outside the realm of possibility. I might end up trapped in a place like the group home, not just until my eighteenth birthday but for the rest of my life.

I can't lose this job.

That evening, after changing out of my work clothes, I go to the park with the duck pond and sit in my usual spot under the tree.

After a while, I check my watch. It's 6:05, and the boy with the cane isn't here.

I don't like the fact that he's late. I'm not sure why that should bother me, why I should care at all, but after the unsettling, unexpected meeting with Bernhardt and the lecture from Ms. Nell, I feel like my world has been knocked askew. This is one more incongruity, one more sign of discord.

I pace for a bit, sit on the grass, and pick at a hole in the knee of my left stocking. I keep picking, widening it, until the boy finally emerges from the door of the building. I dart behind a tree and peek out as he limps across the street, toward the park.

He seems different today, somehow. He moves slowly and stiffly, like he's in pain, as he sits down on the bench. He's facing away from me, so I can't see his expression.

I wait, watching, holding my breath.

At first, he doesn't move, just stares straight ahead. Then his head drops into his cupped hands and his shoulders shake in silent, shuddering spasms.

He's crying.

I hold very still, not breathing. After a few minutes, his shoulders stop shaking, and he sits very still, slumped. Slowly he stands. Then he takes his cell phone out of his pocket and throws it into the pond. The splash startles several ducks, who fly away with a chorus of quacks.

He limps out of the park. For a while, I don't move.

I retrace his steps to the salmon-pink building. Beyond the glass double doors is a lobby with a TV and a fake potted plant. I touch the rough brick wall, slide my fingers over the glossier stone of the sign outside the door, and trace its chiseled letters. ELKLAND MEADOWS.

I don't have my laptop with me, so I flip open my phone. It's a TracFone—I pay by the minute, so I'm very careful about when and how I use it, but it *is* internet enabled. A quick online search reveals that Elkland Meadows is an assisted-living facility for people with brain injuries or degenerative neurological diseases, and I wonder for a moment if he's a patient there. But this isn't an outpatient clinic. That leaves only one conclusion: he's visiting someone.

When I walk to the edge of the pond, I see the phone's silver curve in the mud, winking in the sunlight. I don't want to reach into the water—I don't like water—so I hunt through the grass until I find a stick with a hooked end, and I use it to fish the cell phone out of the pond. On the back, printed on thin white tape, are the words PROPERTY OF STANLEY FINKEL. Below that is an email address.

It seems a little silly, putting his contact information on the phone. If he's so concerned about it getting lost, why did he throw it away? I press the on button. The phone flickers once, then dies. I'm about to toss it back into the pond, but something stops me. After a few seconds, I slip it into my pocket.

CHAPTER THREE

It's late.

I'm sitting on the mattress in my bedroom, legs crossed in front of me, eating Cool Whip from a plastic tub with a spoon. A glob falls onto my shirt; I scoop it up with one finger and suck it clean. The lights are off, the room illuminated only by the faint glow of my laptop, which rests on my pillow. I am playing Go.

Abruptly Dr. Bernhardt's voice invades my thoughts: *If things don't change, I'll have to recommend to the judge that, as a condition of your continued independence, you start seeing a counselor.*

I make a stupid move, and my opponent captures several of my stones. Irritated with myself, I quit the game and close the laptop. I don't feel like sleeping, so I retrieve my yellowing, dog-eared copy of *Watership Down* from the shelf, open it, and begin reading. I try to fall into the familiar rhythm of the sentences. *The primroses were over. Toward the edge of the wood, where the ground became open and sloped down to an old fence and a brambly ditch beyond, only a few fading patches of pale yellow still showed . . .*

I've read the book countless times. Returning to its world of intelligent rabbits and their struggle for survival is a comfortable ritual. But tonight, my thoughts keep wandering. I close the book with a sigh.

Dr. Bernhardt doesn't understand, and I can't explain it to him. He thinks my aversion to human contact is just fear of rejection. It goes so much deeper.

Inside my head, there's a place I call the Vault. I keep certain memories there, sealed off from the rest of my mind. Psychologists call this repression. I call it doing what's necessary to survive. If I didn't have the Vault, I'd still be in the institution, or on so many heavy-duty medications I'd barely know my own name.

When I close my eyes and concentrate, I can see it in front of me—a towering pair of metal doors at the end of a long, dark hallway. The doors are strong and solid, with a massive bolt lock holding them shut, protecting me from what lies on the other side. I spent several years constructing this place, brick by brick, forming a sort of mental quarantine unit.

If Dr. Bernhardt forces me to go to counseling, the doctor will pick and pry at those doors and try to dismantle the fortress I've built to protect myself. Psychologists think the solution to everything is to talk about it.

My hands are shaking. I need to reduce my stimulation.

If I had a bed, I would hide beneath it, but there's only my mattress on the bedroom floor. So I go into the bathroom, curl up in the empty bathtub, and cocoon myself with blankets. I wrap them tightly around me, covering even my face, so that there's only a small slit for air. The pressure helps. Alone, in darkness, I breathe.

Quiet, enclosed spaces have always felt safe. When I was in second grade, my teacher, Mrs. Crantz, put a cardboard box around my desk and cut a small window out of the front so I could only see straight ahead. Because my gaze wandered, she thought I was distracted by my surroundings, that the box would help me pay attention. She didn't understand that I was lost in my own thoughts. Cut off from the outside world, it was easier to withdraw inside myself. I spent my time drawing mazes and three-dimensional hexagons in my notebook, which was more fun than listening to Mrs. Crantz read *Little House on the Prairie* in her droning, nasally voice. Then one day, she tried to take away the box, and I screamed. When she put a hand on my shoulder, I kicked her in the knee. She hauled me to the principal's office and called my mother.

Mama arrived wearing sweatpants, her hair still damp from a recent shower. In my head, I can see her now, sitting in the principal's office, gray eyes wide, fingers clenched tightly on the strap of her purse. "Alvie," she said quietly, "why did you kick your teacher?"

"She grabbed me," I replied in a small voice. "It hurt."

"I barely touched her," Mrs. Crantz protested. "It couldn't possibly have hurt."

But it had. Lots of things hurt me—bright lights, loud noises, itchy dresses—but no one ever believed me when I told them. "It burned me," I insisted.

"Burned?" Mrs. Crantz frowned.

The principal cleared his throat. "Ms. Fitz . . . perhaps you should take your daughter to see a behavioral specialist."

Mama's brow creased. "A doctor? But why?"

"She's been having difficulty at school for some time now. I can give you a number to call, if you wish." He slid a card across the desk. "Please understand . . . we're just trying to help. For now, maybe you should take her home."

I sat in the chair, head down, hands fisted in my lap.

As we drove home, Mama was quiet, staring straight ahead. Little pieces of her hair caught the sun, turning brighter red. "Does it hurt when *I* touch you?" she asked.

"No. Not when you do it."

Her stiff shoulders unstiffened. "I'm glad." She was quiet again for a while.

It was hot in the car. Sweat glued my shirt to my back. "Why does the principal want me to see a doctor. I'm not sick."

"Maybe not, but . . ." She bit her lower lip. "Maybe we should go. Just to be safe." Her eyes were watery from the bright sunlight. "I love you very much, Alvie. You know that, don't you?"

The musty smell of blankets seeps into my awareness, pulling me back to the present. Suddenly the fabric around me doesn't seem protective so much as constrictive. I gasp, overcome with the feeling that I'm suffocating. I jerk upward, clawing free.

Moonlight from the tiny window gleams on the tiles, illuminates the pattern of cracks in the walls and the spots of rust blooming on the tub.

I slump, leaning my head against the wall. My throat thickens briefly, and I choke down the feeling. Mama is gone now. Dwelling on the past won't help anything. I push the memory of that day back into the depths of my mind, where it belongs.

Focus. Isolate the problem: Dr. Bernhardt wants me to have a social life. But he can't hold me accountable if other people avoid *me*, so if I can just present him with some evidence that I've been making an effort, maybe he'll leave me alone.

The phone I retrieved from the pond is still sitting on my coffee table. I retrieve it and study the information on the back.

Stanley Finkel. The name of the boy in the park, the boy with the cane. What would I say to him, anyway?

It doesn't matter, I remind myself. I open my laptop, log in to my email and plug Stanley's address into the "to" box. I type the first question that pops into my head: *What do you think of the Copenhagen interpretation?*

Stanley will probably assume the message is spam. And even if he doesn't, he has no idea who I am, so why would he care?

I stroke the touchpad, dragging the cursor toward the corner of the screen to close my email program. But before I can, a new message appears in my inbox: *Hi, ThousandEnemies. :) That's an interesting handle. Uh, do I know you?*

I sit, frozen. Sweat trickles down my sides, tiny cold beads. He asked me a question; I should at least answer it. I send: *No.*

How did you get my address?

It was on your phone. I found it in the park. It doesn't work anymore.

A pause. *Oh. Well, that's fine. I'm overdue for a new one, anyway.*

So, what's the Copenhagen interpretation?

I didn't expect him to respond at all. I take a few minutes to compose myself, and then I respond, fingers flitting rapidly over the keys: *It's a common interpretation of quantum physics. It holds that quantum particles don't conform to one objective reality, but instead exist as multiple probabilities. Only the act of observing or measuring those particles causes them to collapse into a single reality. The thought experiment known as "Schrödinger's cat" is the most common example. In it, there's a cat in a box. The cat's life or death depends on the behavior of a subatomic particle. If the particle spins in one direction, a flask of poison gas is opened. If it spins in the other, the flask remains sealed. According to the Copenhagen's interpretation, while the box is closed, both exist as possibilities, so the cat is both alive and dead. Only when the box is opened does a single reality emerge.*

I hit send. My palms are damp, so I rub them on my shorts.

His reply comes a minute later: *Well, that's definitely one of the more unique conversation starters I've heard. People usually say something about the weather. Or sports. Though, come to think of it, I never know how to respond to that, either.*

Of course. He doesn't want to hear about quantum theory. People usually don't.

Do you want me to leave you alone? I send.

No, he replies quickly. *You can talk to me about Copenhagen all night if you like. Hey, you want to sign on to Gchat? It'll be easier.*

Fine. I sign on.

So what's your name? he types.

I suppose there's no harm in giving him that information. *Alvie Fitz.*

Alvie, huh? Like that guy from the Annie Hall *movie?*

It can be a girl's name, too.

Oh. You're a girl?

I'm female, yes.

I like it, he sends. *Your name, I mean. It's better than mine, anyway. I mean, Stanley Finkel. It sounds like a skeevy game show host or something. Also it rhymes with "tinkle." Which, needless to say, made grade school a blast.*

It sounds like a normal name to me.

Well, thank you. :) And then: *I have to ask. How did you come across my phone?*

I saw you throw it into the pond. There's no response. I wait. *Why did you throw it away?*

Several minutes pass without a reply, and I begin to wonder if he's gone. Then a new message appears: *I didn't think I'd need it anymore. I was being stupid. It doesn't matter now.*

I'm not sure how to respond, so I don't. After a minute, another line of text pops up: *Alvie? Thank you.*

For what?

Nothing. I just wanted to say thank you.

I can't remember the last time someone has thanked me. It's a strange feeling.

I have to go, I say.

I close my laptop. For a while, I sit, staring into space. My heart is beating faster than normal.

CHAPTER FOUR

I don't sleep much that night. Variations from my routine always upset my sleeping schedule, and the past few days have been full of aberrations.

Finally I drift off on the couch and wake to the glare of sunlight through the curtains. The light brightens and spills across the floor, illuminating the shabby blue-gray carpet, the cluttered stacks of books and newspapers in the corners of my living room. The rancid cheese smell permeates the air.

I pry myself off the couch and plod to the kitchen, where I start a pot of strong coffee. My shift starts in less than an hour. I need to get ready for work.

I brush my teeth, comb and re-braid my hair, and wash myself with a rag and a pot of soapy water. I don't like showers or baths, but it's possible to stay clean without them—not to mention I waste less water this way. Even hair can be washed in the sink. It just takes a little longer.

It's cold out, and it takes me a few tries to start the car. I turn the key, and there's only a dry click and a faint wheezing sound. I try a few more times, and the engine sputters to life.

At work, I clock in and walk down the cobblestone path. There's a prickling itch in my skin, like an allergic reaction, as I pass the sign about anthropomorphizing.

I'm on feeding duty this morning, so I retrieve bags of trout and squid from the walk-in refrigerator in the storage shed; cut the slippery, pinkish-gray meat into tiny chunks; then feed it to the two river otters. Afterward, I give the gibbons their fruit. The gibbons are a mated pair named Persephone and Hades. This, I believe, is intended as irony.

The pale golden female leans down to pull my braid, and I let her. The touch of animals has never bothered me the way human contact does.

I move on. Inside a large, barred enclosure, a red-tailed hawk named Chance perches on the branch of a fake tree. He's the zoo's first hawk, acquired from a wildlife rehabilitation facility a few weeks ago. His eyes are a clear, light copper gold, somewhere between the color of champagne and a worn penny.

I unlock the door, very slowly, and remove a dead mouse—sealed in a little plastic bag—from my pocket. My hands are covered by thick protective gloves, the same khaki color as my uniform. I remove the mouse from its plastic sleeve and hold it by its tail. "Breakfast," I say.

Chance's yellow toes clench on his perch. His claws are long and black, very sharp—weapons for seizing prey and puncturing vital organs. But his hunting days are over. He flexes the stump, which is all that remains of his left wing.

I open the cage door, place the dead mouse inside, and nudge it toward him with my foot. Chance cocks his head, eyeing the rodent, but doesn't move.

Since he arrived, I've been spending a lot of time with him. He's still skittish around people. All wild-born animals are, at first . . . and since Chance has been through a severe injury, he's easily agitated. If he were human, his condition might be called post-traumatic stress disorder. A zoo probably isn't the ideal environment for him, but since he's stuck here, he needs to adjust to the presence of humans. It will take time, but I've already made progress. In the beginning, he would go into a panic whenever anyone entered his cage. One day, perhaps, he'll take food from my hand—but for now, I'm just trying to get him to eat in my presence.

The mouse lies on the dirt floor between us.

Chance hops down to the cage floor, snatches the mouse, and climbs back up to his perch, using his wing stump for leverage as he grips the branches with his talons. I'm impressed at his adaptability.

"What happened to that bird, anyway?"

The familiar, nasally voice grates like sandpaper on my brain. I turn to see Toby—a newly hired part-timer—standing with a can of grape soda in one hand. His long face is speckled with acne, and a few straggly strands of brown hair hang out from under his cap.

"He was injured in the wild," I reply. "Probably by a coyote or a fox. His wing was badly broken and had to be amputated."

Toby raises his soda can and takes a long slurp. "That sucks," he says. "Nothing more depressing than a bird that can't fly."

"I can think of a few things more depressing than that. The Holocaust, for instance."

Toby laughs, loud enough to make me flinch. "True." He takes another swig and wipes the back of one hand across his mouth. "Hey, can I feed him?"

I bristle. Toby mostly works the concession stand and changes the garbage bags; he's not qualified to deal with the animals. "No."

"Why not?"

"Because he's not used to you."

"So what? It's not that complicated, is it?" Toby knocks on the cage bars. "Hey! Hey, birdy!"

Chance shrinks away.

I tense. "Don't do that. He perceives sudden movements as a threat."

Toby grins, showing a pair of oversized incisors. "Relax. I'm just messing with him. Don't you have a sense of humor?"

I want to ask him how he'd feel if a noisy giant locked him in a cage and then started banging on the walls. Would he find *that* funny? "You should be working," I say. "You're not supposed to have beverages while you're on the clock."

"I'm on my lunch break." He digs around in one ear with a pinkie, then glances at his watch. "Guess I should go clock back in. Be seeing you." He walks away.

I breathe in slowly, then out. I doubt he'll last another week. Ms. Nell has no patience for slackers; it's one of her more admirable traits. I just have to wait until he gets fired.

I fetch another bag of dead mice from the storage shed and go to feed the snakes in the reptile house. On the way, I pass a young couple lingering near the hyena enclosure. Their arms are draped around each other. The boy whispers something into the girl's ear, and she giggles and kisses him.

Watching people share affection with each other in public has always made me uncomfortable. But now, for some reason, I can't look away. They both look so happy. They make it seem so easy, so natural.

The girl notices me staring, and the smile fades. Her lips form the word *creep.* She takes the boy's hand and leads him away, and I'm left standing alone. A dull heat spreads over my forehead and the back of my neck, burning in my ears.

Creep.

The world falls away, and I am six years old, approaching a group of girls on the playground during recess. My heart skips, and there's a hard little nut lodged somewhere behind my belly button. The girls are giggling and talking together. As I approach, they fall silent and turn to stare at me. Their smiles disappear.

My legs quiver. I twist my shirt and grip one braid, pulling until I feel the tingling pressure in my scalp. When I open my mouth, the words come out all in a rush: "Hi my name is Alvie Fitz can I play with you."

The girls exchange glances. They're talking without words, beaming silent messages with their eyes, something I have never learned how to do.

A blond girl turns to me with a wide smile. "Okay, let's play a game. It's called 'puppy.' Since you're new, you can be the puppy."

I keep pulling on my braid with one hand and twisting my shirt with the other. "How do you play."

"Get down on your hands and knees and start barking."

The tightness in my stomach loosens. That's *easy.* I drop down to my hands and knees. "Ruff-ruff! Ruff-ruff-ruff!"

The girls giggle. I bark louder and faster, and they laugh harder. I pant and roll over, then I start to dig in the wood chips with my hands, and they practically squeal.

More kids are gathering now. Someone throws a stick and calls, "Fetch, girl!" I pick it up in my mouth. More laughter. Excitement flutters inside me. I never knew it would be so easy to make friends.

One girl looks at another, rolls her eyes, and twirls a finger around her temple.

I freeze. The stick falls from my mouth. I've seen people do that before. I know what it means.

A large group of children stands around me, staring, mouths open. My chest hurts. I'm breathing too fast, but I can't stop.

Whispers echo in my ears. *Weirdo. Freak.*

I drop the stick and start to run. I run off the playground, away from the school, but I can still hear their voices, echoing over and over inside my head.

Back in my apartment, I grab a box of Cocoa Puffs from the kitchen, sit on the couch, and turn on the TV. I scoop out handfuls of dry cereal and eat them as I watch a rerun of *Cosmos.* My gaze strays to the laptop sitting on my coffee table.

Has Stanley sent me another email since last night?

I turn off the TV and sit, turning a Rubik's Cube over in my hands. I twist the rows of color this way and that, not really trying to solve it, just focusing on the smooth plastic under my fingertips, the *click* as a section snaps into place. My gaze wanders, again, to my laptop.

Talking to someone online should be safe enough. As long as I'm careful about keeping my distance, confining the conversation to non-risky topics, what harm could it do?

I pick up my laptop and open my email. Sure enough, there's a message from Stanley.

So, the cat in the box, the one that's alive and dead . . . I mean, is that really how the world works? Like things don't become real until we observe them? But what does that mean for us?

I sign on to Google Chat. He's there, waiting. A funny, hollow feeling fills my stomach, like the swooping sensation of being on a roller coaster.

He asked me a question about physics. That's something I can understand, something I can deal with.

Schrödinger's cat is just a thought experiment. Originally it was meant to illustrate the absurdity of the Copenhagen's interpretation, but some people take it seriously.

Are you studying this stuff? I mean, are you a physics major, or something?

I'm not in college. I'm seventeen.

I bet you're in AP courses. :)

I don't go to school, I reply.

A brief pause. *Homeschooled, then? My mom homeschooled me for a few years. Some people can be judgy about stuff like that, but I don't think there's anything wrong with learning from your parents.*

I don't have parents.

Another pause. *I'm sorry,* he sends.

Why are you sorry?

No response. I shift my weight, wondering if I said something wrong. I don't often talk about my situation with people—the fact that I have no living relatives, at least none close enough to take me in—that my mother died when I was eleven, that I never even knew my father. The few times I *have* mentioned this, it's usually resulted in sudden silence followed by a rapid change of subject.

Then more text appears: *I know how tough it is, being on your own.*

My heart lurches. *You lost your parents, too?*

Kind of. I mean, my dad is still alive, but we don't talk much. I'm nineteen, so I can live by myself now, anyway. I'm getting by. But still, it's not easy. It must be even harder for you.

He's alone. Like me.

My body rocks lightly back and forth. My hand drifts to my left braid and starts tugging. I recognize the anxiety mounting within myself; I need to steer the conversation to safer topics. *I do all right,* I send. *Anyway. You don't need a teacher to learn about physics. Anyone can look up the information if they take the time. And a library card is a lot less expensive than college.*

Lol. Well, I am *a college student, so I can vouch for that,* he replies. *I'm not studying physics, though. I'm kind of a humanities guy. I'm taking neurobiology for my science requirement because I thought it would be all about how we think and what makes us human, but it's more like, "memorize these 50 different processes that are involved in eye movement." Pretty boring stuff.*

It doesn't sound boring. I like reading about the brain. It helps me make sense of human behavior.

There's a lot about the brain that we don't understand, though, isn't there?

I tell myself that I'm only going to stay online for a few more minutes.

We talk about perception and the nature of reality, which shifts to a discussion about truth and how much of what we believe is simply because other people have told us to believe it. That, in turn, transitions into a conversation about the lies adults tell to children.

We tell each other our respective childhood reactions to finding out that Santa Claus is just a story. He cried; I was indifferent because the idea of a magical, omniscient fat man breaking into my house every Christmas Eve never made much sense to me in the first place.

I tell him how, as a little girl, I was told that oatmeal sticks to your ribs—which is not exactly a lie but an expression, something you're not meant to believe literally. As a child, it took me a while to understand the difference, and to this day I can't eat oatmeal because I visualize all those sticky white clumps coagulating against my heart and lungs.

I learn how, when he was little, his mother told him that thunder means the angels are bowling, and that the crescent moon is God's fingernail.

I reply that the moon is a ball of iron and rock, and that it's getting farther and farther away from us all the time. It moves away from Earth by a distance of 3.8 centimeters each year. We are losing it.

You know, you're kind of a pessimist, he remarks.

It's just a fact, I reply.

But 3.8 centimeters is hardly anything. That won't make any difference, will it?

Probably not for millions of years. The human race may not even be around then. But nonetheless, the things we think of as permanent are not. Eventually the sun will expand, engulf our entire solar system, and then die.

There's a pause. *It's beautiful tonight,* he sends. *The moon, I mean. Can you see it from your window?*

I look. It's nearly full; there's a misty ring of light around it. *Yes.*

If it's going away, he says, *we should enjoy it while it's here.*

Clouds glide slowly across the moon. The world goes dark, then bright again, bathed in a ghostly glow.

You don't have to stay up with me, you know, he sends. *I know it's late. You probably have to get to bed.*

I glance at the clock. 4:00 a.m. *You're an insomniac, aren't you?*

Lol, guess you found me out. Yeah, I'm not eager to go back to tossing and turning.

I know what he means. There's no worse feeling than being alone and unable to sleep at four in the morning, with the *tick-tick-tick* of the clock echoing in your skull. *I'll stay up with you, if you want,* I offer, surprising myself. But the truth is that I want to keep talking to him. It's a curiously addictive experience.

I appreciate that. But I don't want you being exhausted tomorrow on my account. I should probably at least try to sleep, anyway. I've got class in the morning, and I don't want to be a zombie.

I'll send you some alpha brain wave recordings, then. They're supposed to be for meditation, but I use them when I'm trying to sleep. Sometimes they help.

Cool. That's really nice of you. :)

Not really. It won't take much effort on my part.

Well, thanks anyway.

I upload the recordings and send him the links, then sign off. For a while, I sit there on the couch. The moon shines through the curtains. It's very bright. I rise, spread my fingers and press my palm against the window, over the pearly sphere, as if I can capture its light.

CHAPTER FIVE

A dead mouse lies nestled in the palm of my gloved hand. Slowly I stretch out my arm.

Chance cocks his head, peering at me. I can see my reflection in the glass-like, convex curve of his cornea. In one swift movement, he snatches the mouse, pins it beneath his long yellow talons, and pulls out a string of bloody meat with his beak. A thrill of triumph runs through me. It's the first time he's taken food from my hand.

A hawk's claws can exert over one hundred and sixty pounds of pressure. They're designed to lock into prey and hold it immobile. Even without his wing, he could seriously hurt me. But he won't—not unless I make a sudden move and frighten him. He's grown to trust me a lot more over the past two weeks. I'm looking forward to telling Stanley about my success.

It's strange, how routine my conversations with him have come to feel—how quickly and easily he slipped into my life.

Chance finishes his lunch and yawns. The feathers on his throat are a creamy yellow brown, speckled with black. When he preens his one wing, the sunlight shines through his pinfeathers, turning them almost translucent.

I check my watch. Lunchtime for me, too. After stripping off and disposing of my gloves and washing my hands, I retrieve my bag lunch from my car and make my way to the main office building where the break room is located. In the hallway outside, I freeze. There are people inside the break room; I can hear them talking through the door. I recognize the voice of Toby and one other coworker, a young man with a unibrow whose name I can't remember.

"I dunno, man," Unibrow says, "she's pretty weird."

"Well, it's not like I'm gonna ask her out or anything," Toby replies. "I'm just sayin', she's got a nice ass. I'd hit that."

"But isn't she, like, autistic or something?"

"What, so she can't fuck?"

"Gross," Unibrow says. "You're sick, man."

Toby laughs.

I back quietly away, retreat from the building, and lean against the wall outside. My heart is beating a little too quickly. There's an unpleasant, squirmy sensation under my skin—the sense of violation that always comes from overhearing people talk about me behind my back. My appetite has evaporated, so I throw out my sandwich, grab a broom and dustpan, and start sweeping the path.

After work, I go straight home. Since I started talking online with Stanley, I've stopped going to the park. He doesn't come there anymore, and without him, it feels empty.

It's Wednesday. My meeting with Dr. Bernhardt is at four o'clock.

This time, I'm not caught off guard, so I straighten up my apartment before his arrival, dousing every surface with Lysol and shoving the dirty laundry into the closet. I buy a bag of oranges so he can't complain about the lack of fruit or vegetables in my kitchen.

"You know," he says, "you could offer me a seat. Or something to drink."

"I assumed that you'd sit if you felt like it and that you'd ask for a drink if you wanted something."

"Yes, but it's polite to offer."

I take this as his way of saying he wants something to drink. I wish people would be more direct. "I've got water, coffee, and orange soda."

"Just water, thanks."

I fill a glass and set it on the coffee table, and he sits, peering at me over the rims of his glasses. "So," he says, "how have you been?"

It's a routine question, and I usually answer *fine* without elaborating. But after last session, I feel like I need to be more specific. "I met someone."

He raises his eyebrows. "You mean . . ."

"We're just talking online," I reply quickly. "We've been discussing quantum theory. Among other things." I pour myself a glass of orange soda.

"So, are you going to tell me anything about this person? How old is he? Or she?"

"Nineteen. He's a student at Westerly College."

"And?"

I take a swig of soda. The fizz tickles going down my throat. "He's . . . interesting. I like talking to him." Even admitting that much feels strange. "But we've never met face-to-face."

"Text-based companionship is better than none at all. In any case, I know this was a big step for you. And it sounds like you and he have some common interests."

"I suppose. He doesn't have a very advanced knowledge of physics. And he turns everything into a metaphor. Sometimes a thing just is what it is."

"Even so. It's encouraging that you've started getting outside your comfort zone." For the next twenty seconds, he's silent. He seems to be thinking about something. At last, he takes a deep breath. "Alvie . . . do you still want to be emancipated as soon as possible?"

Of course that's what I want. I've wanted that from the beginning. Still, a moment passes before I answer, "Yes."

"I want you to think about it, about what it would mean for you. You'd be an adult, which also means that you'd be responsible for all your own finances. You wouldn't receive any help from the system."

I'm not receiving any help from the system now. But I've always known that a safety net existed, that if I lost my job and my apartment, I wouldn't end up on the streets. Even if I was miserable there, the group home meant a roof and regular meals. "Why are you saying this."

"I talked to Judge Gray recently. She's prepared to review your case again."

The words send a jolt through my system. I hadn't expected it to happen this soon. The plan was for me to keep seeing Dr. Bernhardt until I turned eighteen. What's changed?

"To be honest," he continues, "I'd prefer that you stay under supervision for another year. I see no need to rush this. But the decision's not up to me."

My mind is empty, white static.

"Alvie? You don't have to do this, you know. You can wait."

This is what I wanted. Isn't it? "I'll do it." I take a breath. "When—when is the appointment?"

"One month from now. In the meantime, I can help you prepare. We'll go over any questions she might ask you. And, obviously, I'll put in a good word for you. But Judge Gray is the one who'll make the final call. You'll have to convince her that you're capable of living independently, that you're mentally and emotionally ready for it."

My hand drifts to my left braid, and my fingers curl around it, pulling. I catch myself and drop my arm to my side.

All I have to do is present the judge with evidence that I'm a functional adult. I pay my bills. I show up to work on time. That's all that matters, isn't it?

Dr. Bernhardt seems to be waiting for me to say something else, so I say, "Okay."

"Right, then." He takes a sip from his glass of water, which he's barely touched—why did he ask for it if he wasn't thirsty? He stands and turns toward the door. "I'll see you in two weeks so we can start preparing—same time okay?"

I nod. Before he steps out, he pauses and looks over his shoulder. "I'm glad you made a friend."

The door closes behind him.

Friend. Is that what Stanley is to me?

That night, when I sign on to Google Chat, Stanley isn't there. I wait a few minutes, then a few minutes longer. Something is wrong. Stanley *always* signs on at eight o'clock.

An hour goes by. I pace around the apartment. My chest feels tight, as if there are invisible bands around it, constricting a little more with each passing minute. Briefly I consider signing off and never signing back on. After all, I originally started talking to him just to get Dr. Bernhardt off my back, and that's no longer an issue.

But I've grown accustomed to my nightly conversations with Stanley. He's now a part of my life. I don't like that I've come to anticipate his presence. It feels dangerous.

Finally a message pops up on the screen. *Hey. Sorry I'm late.*

I should probably act like this isn't a big deal, like it doesn't affect me. But I've never been good at faking indifference. *Where were you?*

It's kind of a long story.

I have time.

The words *SFinkel is typing* flash across the screen, disappear, appear again. He does this sometimes, as if he's composing responses and then deleting them.

I broke my fibula in biology class today. Fell against a desk. I realize that sounds completely ridiculous, but I'm a klutz, so this kind of thing has happened to me before. It's just a hairline fracture, but they kept me at the hospital for hours, and I had to practically start a fight with them to avoid getting X-rays. Anyway, I'm feeling okay now. They gave me Percocet for the pain. Great stuff. Sends you right to la-la land. They put it in a little bag with a smiley face and everything.

I reread the words. *You're not okay,* I send.

What?

When you say "okay," it always means "bad." When you're actually okay, you say "great."

There's a brief pause. *If I may be completely honest, I feel like shit. It's not even the pain. I just really hate hospitals. Can I call you? I'm a little loopy right now. It's easier to talk than type.*

His typing seems fine. I start to rock back and forth.

Until now, my conversations with Stanley have felt abstract, disconnected from everything else in my life. Even if I know what he looks like, I've only interfaced with him from behind the safety of a screen, and he's never pushed for more. Now he *wants* something. If I talk to him on the phone, it will change things.

My own breathing echoes through the silence, a little too loud and fast.

Alvie?

You can call me, I send. *But I'd prefer to respond through text if that's acceptable to you.*

After a brief delay, he asks, *Why?*

The request must sound strange to him. I suppose I could just tell him I'm mute, but I have no faith in my ability to lie convincingly. *I feel more comfortable communicating through text. It's easier for me.*

Well, okay. If that's what you want.

The phone rings once. Twice. I pick it up.

"Alvie?" His voice sounds more or less the way I expected, young and a little uncertain.

I'm here, I type. It takes a little longer with one hand.

"Um. Hi."

Hello.

A few heartbeats of silence pass. "So how was work today?"

Passable.

"Well, that's good. I mean, I guess passable is good. It's not bad." He lets out a small sigh. "God, I'm so out of it right now. So, uh . . . how are things outside of work?"

I've been reading about multiple worlds theory.

"Oh?"

I start to type out an explanation of universal wave function, but before I can finish, he says, "I'd really like to meet you sometime. In person, I mean. If you found my phone, you must live in the area, right? I thought maybe . . . we could have lunch, or something."

My heart drops out of my chest. Or at least, that's what it feels like.

"I won't pressure you," he continues. "I know you're a really private person. But I'd like to know what you're like in real life. Not that this isn't real, but. You know."

My vision momentarily grays out, and my hearing goes fuzzy. When it comes back, he's saying my name, his tone urgent. "Alvie? Alvie, are you there? Please say something."

The phone is slick with sweat, pressed against my ear. I'm breathing too hard. Too fast. I feel a little nauseous.

He keeps saying my name.

"I . . ." My voice emerges flat and hoarse. "I have to go." I stab a button with my thumb, ending the call. Black spots swim across my vision, and I shut my eyes, hugging my knees to my chest.

In a flash, I see the doors of the Vault before me. A faint rumble emanates from within.

My chest feels strange, as if a yawn's gotten stuck inside it. My jaws clench. A dull pain throbs behind my left eye and shoots down my neck. I recognize the beginnings of a panic attack. I go to the tub and wrap myself in blankets, but it doesn't help—not this time.

No one has ever died from a panic attack.

In ten minutes or so, it will be over.

I just need to get through it. I repeat the well-worn phrases to myself as I gasp for breath.

When the attack dies down I'm left shaking and bathed in a thin, icy layer of sweat. I extract myself from the covers, kneel in front of the toilet, and retch.

Hand shaking, I wipe my mouth with toilet paper. It's been months since I've been that bad.

For a brief moment, I think about calling Dr. Bernhardt. Maybe he can put me in touch with someone who'll prescribe me some sedatives—something to numb me, to take the edge off. But I can't deny the sinking dread that fills me whenever I think about setting foot inside a doctor's office.

When I was fifteen, fresh out of foster care, I had a mandatory psychological assessment with an old woman who emitted a pickled, salty smell, like olives, but the session was very short and perfunctory. I spent most of it staring at the wall and answering her questions as vaguely as possible, wanting to get it over with. I'd already had far too much interaction with doctors and other medical professionals when I was a child. None of them ever truly helped me.

The first time I ever saw a counselor, I was in third grade. Her office was filled with dolls and puppets. There was a Feeling Wheel with colors labeled HAPPY and SAD and MAD and CALM. During our first session, she tried to teach me how to smile.

"A smile is an easy way to be friendly," she told me, pointing at her own rosy, dimpled cheeks. "Like this. Now you try."

I bared my teeth.

"That's . . ." She cleared her throat. "That's very good. Here, why don't you practice in front of the mirror?"

I tried again.

"Now, one more time. Try to relax."

"Apes will show their teeth as a sign of submission," I told her.

She blinked her bright eyes at me and tilted her head. "Well, that's interesting. But remember, people aren't apes."

"Yes, they are. Humans are primates, just like chimps and bonobos."

"Let's try that smile one more time, shall we?"

That week, at school, there was another *incident*, which was what the grown-ups called it when something bad happened. A boy started following me in the hallway between classes, rolling marbles in his pencil box, because he knew the sound drove me crazy. I felt like the marbles were rolling around in my head, clattering off the walls of my skull. I told him to stop, but he didn't. I tried to ignore him. He kept following me, rattling the marbles louder and louder and chanting, "Robo-tard, Robo-tard" in a singsong voice. Finally I spun around and backhanded him across the face. I got detention for two days.

"Now, let's talk about that situation," the counselor said during our next meeting. "How could it have gone differently?"

I sat in my chair with my arms crossed and my gaze fixed on the floor. "Just make them stop hurting me."

There's a pause. "That's not really what I do, sweetie. You can always talk to the principal or teachers—"

"I do. They won't stop it, either."

"For now, let's talk about what happened with that boy. I know he started it, but you can't control what other people do. You can only control what *you* do. So, tell me—what could you have done, besides hitting him?"

"Kick him," I muttered.

"That's not what I mean."

Why did everyone act like it was *my* fault when the other kids bullied me? Why was I always the one who had to change?

For the rest of the session, I refused to talk, and she sent me home early. When it came time for my next appointment with the rosy-cheeked counselor, I hid in my room. I had decided that if grown-ups weren't going to help me, I'd rather they just left me alone.

I surface from the haze of memories, turn on the sink, and wash the sour taste of vomit out of my mouth.

When I check my email, there are several new messages from Stanley.

I run my finger over the touchpad, dragging the cursor to the first message to open it—then stop. I'm not ready; I need to clear my mind, to reestablish my center of control.

I close my laptop.

My stomach is rumbling—I haven't eaten since breakfast—so I heat up a bowl of instant ramen and flip through channels until I find a nature documentary.

Polar bears amble through the snow. As I watch them, I feel my muscles untensing, my heart rate slowing. Animals' lives are simple. Eat, play, mate, survive. They don't have to worry about rent, or work, or strange, complicated, confusing feelings. I slurp up some noodles.

On the screen, two polar bears are mating. The female's eyes are narrowed to slits, her teeth bared, her tongue poking out—in discomfort or pleasure, or maybe both—as the male mounts her from behind.

I realize I have stopped chewing and the noodles are sitting in my mouth, a soggy lump.

The male polar bear finishes, withdraws, and wanders away.

The female lounges on the snow and yawns, pink tongue curling. My mind flashes back to the couple I saw at the zoo two weeks ago—the easy, natural physical contact between them, the way they looked at each other, as if nothing else existed. I wonder if they have sex.

That's not something I'll ever be able to do. How could I? I don't even like being touched.

But all animals—including humans—are hardwired to reproduce. It's basic instinct, along with eating and defecating.

I'm still human. Aren't I?

The thought triggers a memory of the overheard conversation between Toby and Unibrow—Toby's leering comments, his companion's shocked reaction—*Gross. You're sick.*

Of course, I would never mate with Toby. He's an idiot and a bully who treats animals like things. In fact, it is hard to imagine a less appealing person. But it irritates me that Unibrow seemed to find his attraction to me so repulsive. Does he assume that just because I'm different, I'm incapable of having a sexual relationship with anyone? That I'm unable even to feel desire?

Is he right?

The thought is like a flea burrowing into the back of my brain, itching, refusing to be ignored.

CHAPTER SIX

When I finally open my email, the next day, there's another new message from Stanley: *If you don't want to meet, we don't have to. We can just keep talking online. I don't want to lose this. Just let me know you're okay.*

For several minutes, I sit, staring at the message. He's offering me an escape route, a way to retreat back into our safe, text-based relationship. I should take this opportunity—should tell him that there's no possibility of us meeting. We can go back to our long, late-night conversations about existence.

But now that the sense of panic has faded, I allow myself—cautiously—to contemplate the possibility. What if I *did* meet him?

I run the various scenarios through my head, like computer simulations of battle strategies, but it all comes down to two major possibilities. Number one: I panic or say something stupid. Humiliation ensues. I slink home and resume my monotonous but safe life of solitude. Number two: somehow, incomprehensively, it goes well, and he wants to meet me again.

The second possibility scares me far more than the first. But what unnerves me most of all is that—in spite of my fear—a part of me still wants to meet him. Now that the idea has been planted, it won't leave me alone.

I pick up my Rubik's Cube and fiddle with it, twisting the rows of color, turning it over and over in my hands as my thoughts turn along with it. I empty my mind of emotion, transforming myself into a cool, efficient computer, and pour in all the data.

Something clicks.

I email Stanley: *Meet me tomorrow in the park at six o'clock.* I close the laptop without waiting for a response.

That night, I lie awake, staring at the ceiling, my mind cycling through everything that could possibly go wrong.

But I've made up my mind. I'm going to do this.

I take an over-the-counter sleeping pill, and a dull fog settles over me, but still, I don't drift off. Instead, images begin to creep through my head, things I haven't thought about for years.

People say that the past can't hurt you. They're wrong.

Humans experience time as a linear progression of cause and effect, as if we are all ants walking along an endless string, always moving forward, never back or sideways. We think that the past disappears as soon as we leave it. But that's not necessarily true. Some theoretical physicists believe that space-time is more like an infinite sea with all points existing simultaneously.

In short, the past is alive. It's happening.

CHAPTER SEVEN

I am nine years old. Jessamine Coutier, a girl in my class, is having a birthday sleepover party, and I've been invited.

I don't know why. Jessamine isn't my friend. In fact, I've heard her saying bad things about me at school. The invitation smells like a trap, and I don't want to go, but Mama begs me. "This will be good for you," she says. "You'll have a chance to make some friends. Please, just give it a try."

So I go.

For most of the party, the other girls ignore me. When it comes time for us all to go to bed, they lay out their sleeping bags on the floor of Jessamine's bedroom and stay up, talking and giggling together while I count the stripes on the wallpaper. The sugary strawberries-and-bubblegum smell of their shampoo and ChapStick invades my nose, itching. It's a girl smell; a *popular* smell.

"Okay," Jessamine says in a whispery giggle, directed at everyone but me. "Now everyone has to say *which* boy they'd kiss—"

More laughter, punctuated by squeals.

I notice the plush frog on Jessamine's bed. "You know," I say loudly, "some amphibians will shed their skin and then eat it."

The girls fall silent.

"They do it to conserve protein."

No response.

"I'm going to the bathroom now." I get up.

As I come back, walking down the hallway toward the half-open bedroom door, I hear whispers from within. I stop, holding my breath.

"You guys shouldn't make fun of her. She's half-retarded. Kristen told me."

"How can you be *half*-retarded?"

"She's actually, like, *freakishly* smart. She knows all this stuff no normal person would ever know. She's just a weirdo."

"You know, her mom's kind of weird, too. And she doesn't even have a dad."

"Well, my mom said her mom *drank* when she was pregnant with her, and that's why she turned out that way."

"Drank what? Alcohol?"

"Duh. What did you think I meant? Milk?"

They giggle.

"*Shhh.* I think she's back."

"Oh *crap.*"

I walk into the room, put my hands on my hips, and say, "Mama doesn't drink. It's nothing she did. This is just how I am."

They fidget, looking at the floor. For once, they're the ones avoiding eye contact with me.

My head is hot. It's suddenly hard to breathe. I want to forget this whole stupid sleepover and go home, but if I do, they'll all start talking about me again. So I turn off the lights, flop down on my sleeping bag, and say, "I'm going to bed."

For a few minutes, no one says anything. Then they start whispering. I put my hands over my ears, but I can still hear them. The fruity bubblegum smell of Jessamine's bedroom fills my nose and crawls down my throat, and I start to gag.

I hate their smell.

When I can't stand it anymore, I creep to the bathroom and throw up the pizza and cake I had earlier. It comes out in foamy strings, with swirls of pink and yellow frosting still mixed in.

It's raining outside and my house is two miles away, but I don't care. I walk all the way home. The air smells heavy and wet, and the lawns and trees are thick, jungle green.

Drenched, shivering, I pound a fist on my front door.

When Mama answers, she's in a blue bathrobe, her eyes puffy with sleep. "Alvie, what . . . oh my God. Honey, you're soaked. What happened?"

Without answering, I walk into the house and curl up in a ball on the couch. She sits next to me and gingerly lays a hand on my shoulder. Normally Mama's touch doesn't hurt, but I feel raw, like all my skin has been peeled off; I flinch. Her hand falls to her side, and she sits there, helpless, as my body shakes and shudders with near-silent tears.

When I look up, I see that Mama's crying, too.

She wipes tears from the corners of her eyes, and smiles weakly. "I'm sorry. I . . . I thought this might . . . I thought if they just got to know you a little better . . ." Her voice quivers, then trails off. "I'm sorry."

I don't know why she's apologizing.

I sit up, pull my knees to my chest, and huddle on the couch. Rain drums against the window. The walls in Jessamine's house have pictures of her family smiling and laughing together. Our wall just has a faded calendar tacked above the TV—a picture of a beach with palm trees. Jessamine's house has lots of pretty things in it, too, like little statues and vases and mirrors with silver frames. I wonder if houses are supposed to have those things.

But who even decides that?

I sniffle, wipe my face again, and chew my thumbnail. After a few minutes, I lean toward her. "Mama. Can I tell you a secret."

She looks at me, eyebrows scrunched together.

"Jessamine has BO. It was so bad I couldn't sleep. That's why I left."

Mama blinks. Her mouth opens, forming an O. Then she bows her head so her hair hangs in her face, and her shoulders shake, and for a moment I think she's still crying. Then a breathless wheeze escapes her, and I realize it's laughter.

I let out a little choking hiccup. Then I start to laugh along with her. I think about the cake I threw up, frothy and pink and yellow in the spotless porcelain toilet, and I realize that I might have forgotten to flush before I left, and for some reason that makes me laugh harder. We laugh and laugh, and before I know it we're holding on to each other. I cling to her, my head against her shoulder, as if we both might be swept away in a gale of crazy, breathless laughter.

Finally she pulls back, flushed and breathless and smiling, with tears in her eyes. "We'll go out tomorrow," she says. "We'll have our own party. With no smelly Jessamine."

The next morning, she takes me out for pancakes at my favorite restaurant, the Silver Dollar. As we sit, eating, she says, "You know, it might help if you went back to counseling."

I poke my pancakes with a fork. I'm still seeing a psychiatrist—Dr. Evans—but she just gives me medication to keep me calm at school. I stopped seeing my last counselor months ago. "I don't want to."

"You were getting better," Mama says. "You were learning to . . . how did she put it? 'Adapt to social norms.' If you kept at it, I'm sure you could make a friend. It would be good for you to have at least one friend."

What good is friendship, I wonder, if I have to pretend to be someone else? "I don't want to go back. I don't need any friends. I just need you."

Her face changes for a second. "I won't be around forever, you know."

"But you'll be around for a long time. Right?"

"A very long time." She tries to smile, but it looks strange, like there are wires hooked into the corners of her mouth, pulling.

After breakfast, we go shopping, and she buys me a little yellow candle in a clay jar. It smells like honey and vanilla and clover, but the smell isn't too sharp, so it doesn't make my nose itch. I keep the jar long after the candle has burned down to nothing. Even years later, particles of the scent still cling to its sides, and sometimes I bury my nose in the jar and breathe in deeply.

CHAPTER EIGHT

The digital clock on the floor next to my mattress reads 5:42.

It's time.

I put on a faded Pink Floyd T-shirt, along with my usual black skirt and black-and-white striped stockings. Most of my clothes, aside from my work uniform, are frayed and faded. I shop mostly at thrift stores and Goodwill, and because it's difficult for me to find comfortable clothes, I tend to keep them until they literally fall apart.

I walk to the park. The pond is gray and empty of ducks; the air is still and cool. Stanley is sitting on his usual bench, facing away from me. His hair is almost curly, I notice. In the back, where it's longest, it falls into loose waves.

I don't know what gives me away—maybe he hears a twig creak under my foot—but after a few minutes, he raises his head and looks over his shoulder. My heart lurches into my throat. Quickly I lower my head. Sweat dampens my palms as I slowly approach and sit down next to him, not looking up.

"Alvie?"

I cross my arms over my chest. "Hello."

He's wearing khakis and a polo shirt under a blue windbreaker, and he has a crutch tucked under his right arm instead of his usual cane. His cast peeks out from beneath his pant leg. After a few seconds of silence, he draws in an unsteady breath. "I was worried you wouldn't show up."

"I said I would."

"Yeah. You did." He holds out a hand. "It sounds strange to say 'pleased to meet you,' but, well . . . hi."

I hesitate before grasping the proffered hand, then let go quickly, as if I've touched a hot pan. If he's offended by my discomfort with touch, he doesn't show it.

"You know," he says, "it's funny. You look just the way I imagined."

For the first time, I meet his gaze. And I can't stop staring.

His eyes are blue. Not just the irises. The sclerae—the whites—are tinted a misty blue gray, like the interior of a seashell I once found on the beach. This is the first time I've been close enough to see, and for a few seconds, I can't breathe. My voice comes out as a thin whisper. "Your eyes—"

There's a subtle change in his face, a stiffening of the muscles, and I stop.

I should say something else. I reach for words, but nothing comes.

When I talk to someone, I have to run my answers through various filters in my brain to see if they're appropriate. Online, the frequent pauses in my speech aren't a problem, but this is different. I'm sitting next to Stanley, the person I've been talking to every night for the past couple of weeks, and I have no idea what to say.

I start to rock lightly back and forth on the bench. I can't help it. One hand drifts up to tug on my left braid. Several yards away, near the base of a tree, a rabbit grazes on yellowed grass.

And then the babbling starts.

"You know," I say, "lots of people think rabbits are rodents, but they're not. They're lagomorphs, along with hares and pikas. Lagomorphs are herbivorous, where rodents are omnivorous, and lagomorphs have four incisors in their upper jaw instead of two."

He blinks.

The words run out of me in a stream, filling the silence the way air will rush in to fill a void, and I can't stop: "Another thing about rabbits. They have no paw pads. They have a layer of thick fur to cushion their feet instead. They're one of the few mammals with paws but no pads." I keep tugging on my braid. I know that I look and sound completely crazy, but I can't help it. The more nervous I am, the worse it gets.

The rabbit lopes another yard away and continues grazing obliviously.

He clears his throat. "That's . . . um . . ."

"'All the world will be your enemy, Prince with a Thousand Enemies.'" My voice comes out singsongy, like I'm saying a nursery rhyme. "'And whenever they catch you, they will kill you. But first they must catch you.'"

Silence.

It's over. It's barely been five minutes, and already I've ruined this. Maybe I should just get up and walk away, spare him the discomfort of making an excuse to leave—

"*Watership Down*," he says.

My body stops rocking; the breath freezes in my throat.

"That book about the talking rabbits," he continues. "That's what it's from, isn't it? That quote? The sun god says that to the rabbit prince. What's his name, again?"

"El-ahrairah," I murmur. I look at him from the corner of my eye, clutching my arms. "You've read *Watership Down.*"

"A long time ago. Is that where the name in your email address comes from? ThousandEnemies?"

"Yes."

He smiles. "I thought that sounded familiar, but I couldn't figure out why. I loved that book."

I look down at my feet, fidgeting. Then I take my Rubik's Cube from the pocket of my hoodie and twist it around. I know it's rude to play with a puzzle while you're talking to someone, but having something to do with my hands keeps me calm. If I didn't carry this thing around, I'd probably have taken up smoking by now.

"You know," he says, "usually *I'm* the quiet one. I mean, when I'm talking with my coworkers, it's not a conversation so much as them telling me things while I nod along. I like to think that's because I'm a good listener. But sometimes I feel like I could be replaced by a mannequin and not have it affect the conversation much."

I hunch my shoulders and continue twisting around the Rubik's Cube. "Do you feel that way with me."

"No."

The cube rests motionless in my hands.

Fading daylight reflects off the planes of his angular face, with its sharp features and high cheekbones. His hair is not exactly brown, I decide. It's more muted gold, the color of wheat. His eyes briefly meet mine, then his long eyelashes sweep down, hiding them, and a light flush creeps into his cheeks.

The rabbit lopes a few yards away from us and keeps nibbling at the grass. He watches it. "I've always wondered . . . what do they eat in the winter? Rabbits, I mean. The grass and leaves are all dead then, right?"

"They eat bark and dried grass," I reply. "They also consume their own feces. Food is partially digested and expelled directly from the cecum."

"That's . . . interesting."

I pick at the edge of one thumbnail. "It's called cecotrophy."

"I'm kind of glad humans don't do that."

I slip the Rubik's Cube back into my pocket. The last traces of daylight are fading from the sky. There's only a thin orange sliver of sunlight on the horizon, shining through the branches. Stanley's long, thin hands are folded over his crutch. "I'm glad I got a chance to meet you."

There's an odd flutter, like a moth trapped in my chest.

The last wisp of sunlight disappears. The air feels very still, and there's a hollow sensation in my stomach, as if I'm looking off the top of a tall building. And I realize—if I'm going to ask him, it has to be now. If I put it off any longer, it won't happen.

"Do you like sex," I ask, staring straight ahead.

There's a long pause. "Do I . . . what?"

"Like sex," I repeat, enunciating the words slowly. My arms are crossed over my chest.

"Uh . . . why do you ask?" His voice sounds a little unsteady.

"Because," I reply, still staring ahead, "I was wondering if you would have sex with me."

When I finally look at his face, his eyes are wide and a little unfocused. A few beads of sweat stand out on his forehead, and he dabs them away with his sleeve. "Y-you mean . . . are you talking hypothetically? Like if we were on a desert island or we were the last two people in the world after a nuclear war or—"

"I'm asking if you want to have sex with me tonight."

His mouth opens and closes several times. "You're serious."

"Do I seem like I'm joking."

"You want to have sex with me," he repeats. "Tonight."

"Yes." I wonder if I've done something wrong, if I asked incorrectly. Or maybe he's just disgusted at the idea. I sit motionless, shoulders hunched, arms crossed.

His grip tightens on his crutch. He takes a deep breath and rubs his brow. "Sorry. I just—didn't expect this."

My breathing quickens. I take the Rubik's Cube from my pocket and start playing with it. *That look.* I've seen that look before. The voices of former classmates echo in my skull. *Weirdo.*

I twist the Rubik's Cube faster. My fingers are slick with sweat.

It slips from them and bounces off the ground, and I don't pick it up.

He hasn't spoken for almost thirty seconds. I feel sick to my stomach. "Go on," I whisper. "Say it."

"What?"

"I'm a freak." My voice comes out stiff and tight. This is bad. I have to get out of here before the situation worsens. I lurch to my feet and begin to walk.

"Wait!"

I keep walking.

He's still calling my name, following me. Soon, he's panting for breath. His footsteps are unsteady, broken by the muffled thump of his crutch. What is he thinking, running after me with a broken leg? I turn around just in time to see his foot slip on the muddy grass, and then he's falling.

Before I have time to think, my body reacts. I lunge forward and catch him. He slumps against me, gasping. His heart bangs against his ribs. It feels like a small animal trapped in a box, beating itself against the side in its struggle to escape. I can't remember the last time I've been close enough to feel another person's heartbeat.

"Are you okay?" he asks, breathless.

"Yes," I reply, just as breathless. I think it's strange that he's asking *me* that when he's the one who tripped.

I realize that the lengths of our bodies are pressed together, and panic flashes through me. I pull away, pick up his crutch, and hand it to him, all without looking at his face. Then I turn and keep walking, but he catches my wrist. My whole body goes rigid at the shock.

I look at his fingers, pressed against my skin. My breath comes short and sharp. My nerves are blazing, tingling; his fingerprints are soaking through my skin, down into my bones, into my DNA.

I speak, my voice low and hoarse: "Let me go."

"Alvie."

"Let me go."

"You're not a freak," he says firmly.

Suddenly my feet are rooted to the spot.

He looks down at his hand, still locked around my wrist. Slowly—as if it takes an effort—he uncurls his fingers, one by one. I clutch my hand against my chest, the skin still tingling where he touched. But I don't run away.

My fists unclench. A wave of dizziness rolls over me, and I am left feeling like the wind has been knocked out of my mind.

"Let's talk about this," he says. Then, more softly: "Please."

We return to the bench and sit. I grip my knees, shoulders tense, gaze fixed on my faded black sneakers. "If you don't want to have sex with me, you can say so. I won't be offended. That—that isn't why I reacted that way. It's just—the way you were looking at me—" I take a breath. "Never mind."

He bites his lower lip. His knuckles are white on his crutch. "Listen. I . . . it's not that I don't *want* to. But I didn't expect you to just ask. People usually go on a few dates first."

"People have one-night stands."

"Yeah, but this is different. We're not two strangers hooking up in a bar."

"Yes or no."

Several times, he opens his mouth as if he's about to say something, then closes it again. "Let me take you out to dinner," he says at last.

Dinner. That seems manageable. Slowly, cautiously, I nod. "Where."

"Is there anyplace you like? I don't know too many nice restaurants, but I think there's a French place around here that's supposed to be good."

I've never had French food. There's only one restaurant I go to, a small diner a few blocks from my apartment that serves pancakes twenty-four hours a day. "Buster's."

"Really?"

I nod.

"Okay. Buster's it is."

My Rubik's Cube is still on the damp grass. I pick it up and clean it off on one edge of my hoodie. It's just as well that we're going out to eat, because I have some questions I need to ask him. I'm still not sure if this is going to happen. He hasn't exactly said yes, but he hasn't said no, either.

CHAPTER NINE

When Stanley and I arrive at Buster's, we're the only people in the restaurant, aside from an elderly couple sitting in a corner booth. A five-foot-tall sculpture of the restaurant's mascot—a winking beaver in a chef's hat, holding a stack of syrup-covered pancakes on a tray—stands next to the door.

I order Swedish pancakes and Stanley orders eggs Benedict. The waitress fills our coffee cups.

"If we're going to do this," I say, "I have a few conditions."

"Conditions?"

I take a swig of my coffee. "First, I don't like to be touched."

"But then, how can we . . ."

I clarify: "When another person touches me, I find it very uncomfortable. But as long as I'm the one doing it, I'm generally fine. So I'll have to be in control the entire time. Is that all right with you."

His brows knit together. "Why don't you like to be touched?"

I study the red-and-white-checkered tabletop. There's a smear of dried, hardened ketchup on the wooden edge of the table. "No reason. I've always been this way."

He doesn't reply, but I can feel his eyes on me.

The food arrives. I take a bite of my Swedish pancakes. As I chew, I watch him. The fact that we're talking about this indicates that he is, at the very least, seriously considering my proposition. My head buzzes oddly. Sights and sounds are all faintly distorted, as if I'm surrounded by a ball of water. I focus on breathing and chewing.

Finally he speaks: "If that's what you're comfortable with, then that's okay with me."

The muscles in my chest loosen, letting me breathe again. I nod. "Thank you."

He sips his coffee, and I notice a slight tremor in his hand. The fingers of his other hand drum rapidly against the table. He picks up his knife and fork and starts cutting his eggs Benedict.

"Also," I say through a mouthful of pancakes, "I want to know about your kinks."

His posture snaps upright. His fork stops halfway to his open mouth, and a piece of egg falls off. "My what?"

I swallow, washing the pancakes down with another swig of coffee. "Kinks." I speak as distinctly as possible. "Turn-ons."

Color floods his face. "You want me to tell you about my sexual fantasies?" he asks, the volume of his voice rising.

At the other end of the restaurant, the elderly couple turns their heads toward us, frowning and peering over the rims of their spectacles.

He glances at them, winces, and lowers his voice. "Do you always ask about this stuff on the first date?"

I can't answer that, because this is the only date I've ever been on. But I see no need to tell him that. "Aren't you supposed to ask questions during a date."

"Questions like 'What's your favorite song?' or 'Are you a cat or a dog person?' yeah."

"If we're going to have sex, I need to know what does and doesn't arouse you. I don't like going into any situation blind."

"It's just . . . I'm really not used to talking about stuff like this with, well, anyone." He swallows. I notice that he hasn't actually eaten any of his eggs; he just keeps cutting them into smaller and smaller pieces. They're practically liquid on his plate. "We're just going to do the usual thing, right?"

"If by 'the usual thing' you mean intercourse, then yes."

On the other side of the restaurant, the plump silver-haired woman shakes her head and whispers something to her husband. Stanley glances at them again, then rests his elbows on the table, covers his face with his hands, and peers out at me between his splayed fingers. "I'm sorry," he whispers. "I can't talk about this. Not here." He stops and takes a slow, deep breath. "I don't think you really grasp how much this is messing with my head. I mean . . . look at me."

I look. I'm not sure what I'm supposed to see.

He continues, the words spilling out in a stream: "Maybe in the back of my mind there was this tiny little hope that, if today went well, you might decide to see me again. And then if we kept seeing each other, maybe someday we could become more than friends. But I thought that even if you were willing to give me a chance, a lot of other things would happen before we even started *talking* about sex."

I study my pancakes, but suddenly I don't feel hungry. The fork hurts my hand, and I realize I am gripping it too tightly.

"Hey . . ." His voice softens, and his brows draw together. He starts to reach out, then stops. "May I?"

I hesitate, then nod. He lays a hand over mine and squeezes. An electric current ripples through me, a thousand tiny painless pins pricking my skin, but after the initial shock, the sensation mellows into something . . . almost pleasant. Warm. I look at his long, pale fingers resting against mine.

I wonder how I can contemplate having sex with him when the slightest touch is overwhelmingly intense. Maybe I'm deluding myself to think that this is possible.

"Alvie? Breathe."

My lungs are aching. I exhale the breath of stale air in my lungs and draw in a fresh one. "Yes or no."

He doesn't ask what I'm talking about. He doesn't need to.

He takes his hand off mine and bites his lip again. "I want to do this right."

The bubbles swirl slowly on the surface of my coffee, forming tiny galaxies. "What do you mean."

He squares his shoulders. "I want to court you."

Court. The word feels quaint and old-fashioned. It conjures an image of ladies in bonnets and white dresses, holding umbrellas, while men in suits bow to them and help them into horse-drawn carriages. Somehow I don't think that's what he has in mind. "Be more specific."

"Just stuff like this. Talking. Spending time together. Going out for dinner or movies or mini-golfing. Anything."

For a moment I find myself considering it. Except I know better. "That's not possible."

"Why?"

I lower my head. "I can't explain." I'm only going to do this once; I've decided as much. This isn't about having a relationship. I just want to try it, to prove to myself that I *can*, and doing it with Stanley makes more sense than propositioning some random stranger on Craigslist. He's young and male, so statistically speaking, he's probably interested in sex. Last night, when I analyzed all the facts, it seemed like a win-win.

"Look at me," he says.

I raise my head, and his eyes search mine. My scalp tingles, and a tiny chill trickles down my spine. He looks at me so intently. I don't know what he sees there or what he expects to see. But I let him look.

"Please . . . tell me the truth," he says very softly. "Is this really what you want?"

I don't understand why he seems so unsure about that. It should be obvious, shouldn't it? I'm the one who asked. "This is what I want."

For a long moment, he says nothing. I don't know what he's thinking. He closes his eyes and breathes in slowly. "Then . . . yes."

Vertigo swims over me. *Yes.* He said yes. I'm going to have sex with Stanley Finkel. Tonight.

"Do you still want to know about my turn-ons?" he asks.

"I would appreciate the information, yes." Remembering his reaction, I add, "But you don't *have* to tell me."

He chews his lower lip. He keeps doing that. He's going to make himself bleed if he's not careful. "How about I answer one question?"

I consider. "All right. Tell me one thing you like, then. One thing you find attractive."

"About you, or . . ."

"Anything."

"I guess . . ." He fiddles with his silverware. "Ilikethosestockingsyou'rewearing."

The words come out in a rush. I have to pause to untangle them. "My stockings." I frown and glance down at them—black-and-white striped and a bit too large so they bunch in folds around my ankles. There's a hole in the left knee. I never thought of them as sexy. "Really."

"I just think they're cute."

I nod. "I'll keep them on, in that case."

He's blushing again. He crosses his arms over his chest, and his fingers press into his biceps hard enough to whiten the skin around his nails. "The thing is . . . I'm . . ."

I wait.

"Never mind." He smiles, a quick tightening of his facial muscles. "Is this the part where I say 'my place or yours?'"

I haven't actually considered *where* we're going to do this.

I think about my apartment: the piles of clothes on the floor, the naked walls and balding carpet, the barren refrigerator with the moldy lump in the corner that was once a ham sandwich and which I haven't thrown out yet because I'm afraid to touch it. I decide I don't want him to see my apartment. But the idea of being in someone else's place is even more overwhelming, like being in a foreign land where I don't know the laws or the language. "Neither."

"Where, then?"

"There's a motel nearby. I can drive us there."

"We're doing this like a real one-night stand, huh?"

"I don't know," I say. "I don't know how one-night stands usually happen. But I think a motel would work better."

He lowers his gaze. His smile has faded. "If you say so."

I wonder what he was about to say earlier, before he stopped. It must have been *something.* I think about asking. But then, if he didn't bother to finish his sentence, it can't have been that important.

CHAPTER TEN

Last night, in preparation for my time with Stanley, I downloaded about ten gigabytes of pornography. I already knew the biology of sex, but not the technique, the various positions and angles.

In large doses, hard-core porn becomes boring very quickly. Once you fast-forward through the dialogue and mute the music, it comes down to watching two sweaty strangers endlessly pumping, thrusting, and sucking. There's something mechanical about it.

Through my viewing, I discovered that, with enough lubricant, you can fit almost anything any*where*, and apparently some women enjoy being spanked by a man in uniform. But in the end, I came away from it feeling like I hadn't learned much at all.

In the motel room, there are blue carnations on the wallpaper in bunches of twos and threes. Two-three. In ancient China, it was believed that certain numbers held sexual significance. Prime numbers were masculine, and twenty-three was considered especially potent because it's the sum of three consecutive prime numbers. My age, seventeen, is also a prime number, and the sum of the first four primes.

"Alvie?"

My gaze jerks toward Stanley. He's sitting on the edge of the bed, fiddling with his crutch. He clears his throat. "I, uh. I'm not sure how I'm going to do this without touching you. I mean, I'll try not to. I'll keep my hands on the bed. But—"

"If it happens by accident, I'll deal with it." I trust him not to do it on purpose, which is more than I usually trust anyone. "Just be careful."

"I will." His voice turns softer. "I promise." He's still fully dressed. Maybe he's waiting for me.

I start to peel off my shirt.

"Wait," he says. I stop.

A flush creeps into his cheeks. "People usually kiss before they start taking off their clothes."

I tilt my head. "You want to kiss me."

His blush grows brighter. "I, uh—was that a question?"

"Yes."

"Sorry. It's hard to tell with you." A pause. "Do *you* want to?"

I think about this for a moment. When I see people kissing on TV, they always look like they're trying to eat each other's faces, and they make wet slurping sounds that remind me of a plunger sucking a blockage from a toilet. "I'm okay with just getting undressed."

He fidgets. "You know, maybe we should turn up the heat. It's pretty cold in h—"

I remove my shirt. Stanley clutches the edge of the bed like he's about to fall off.

My hands tremble slightly as I undo the clasp of my bra, and it drops to the floor. His pupils dilate, and his Adam's apple bobs up and down as he swallows. "Wow." His voice comes out soft and breathless. I'm not sure what's so amazing. They're just breasts. All girls have them.

"They're small," I remark.

He blinks. "Huh?"

"My tits."

"They're not. Small, I mean."

I look down. "It's just a fact."

"No, they're perfect. It's just . . ." A short, nervous chuckle. "It's a little surreal hearing you say 'tits.' It's like hearing Mr. Spock say 'motherfucker' or something."

I shrug.

"They're beautiful." His voice softens. "You're beautiful."

The words make me uncomfortable, make me feel naked in a way that just taking off my bra didn't. He shouldn't say things like that.

The air in the motel room is cool against my skin. Goose bumps rise on my arms and breasts, and my chest heaves as I struggle to control my breathing. I don't know if I am aroused, exactly, but I am very aware of my body, even more than usual. I feel the roughness of the carpet under my stockinged feet, the weight of my bones, and the whisper of blood rushing through my brain, my heart. My breathing quickens, and pressure builds inside my chest.

My hands are still trembling. Am I afraid?

I'm not worried about the mechanics of it, which are fairly simple. I tried it with my fingers last night, and while there was some stinging, the pain was no worse than bumping into a chair in the darkness on the way to the bathroom. No—I'm afraid that I'll say something or do something that will ruin this, and he'll turn away from me in disgust. Or that I'll panic.

But I'm not going to change my mind. Not now.

I stand there, naked from the waist up, and say, "Undress."

He fiddles with the first button of his shirt. Then he starts to reach for the lamp cord, to turn off the light.

"Don't," I say.

He freezes.

"I need to see what I'm doing."

The muscles of his throat move as he swallows. "Okay."

Uncertainty steals over me, the network of wires and strings pulling tight inside my body, and I wonder—again—if he doesn't want this, after all. Maybe he's changed his mind. Maybe he's disappointed by my boyishly flat chest or my knobby collarbones. I've never thought much about my body and whether someone might consider it attractive, but looking at it objectively, there isn't much of interest.

Then I look down at his pants and see the bulge straining against them.

For a few seconds I just stare. A tremor runs through me. Not fear. Excitement.

It's proof. He's not doing this just because I asked it of him, or because he feels sorry for me. He wants this. He wants *me.*

My own breathing suddenly sounds very loud and unsteady.

I notice him staring at my breasts. He notices me noticing and looks away. "You want to touch them," I say.

"Yeah." His voice comes out thick and hoarse, like he has a sore throat.

My head is buzzing. I'm suddenly very warm. "Go ahead."

"You're sure?"

I nod.

He gulps, raises his hands. Lowers them. Then takes a deep breath and raises them again.

The first touch is like jumping into a cold pool on a hot summer day. For a few seconds, it's unbearable, and then the shock fades, and I'm floating. I watch, holding my breath, as his fingertips graze my breast. His thumb brushes over one nipple, then rubs in a slow circle, and there's a pleasant flutter somewhere deep inside my body.

I'm off-balance, my head spinning. Already, my nervous system is starting to overload. I need to pull back.

I grip his wrists and push his hands down. He clutches the coverlet. I close my eyes and breathe in slowly, finding my center of control. The world steadies around me, and my eyes open.

"Lie down," I say, "on your back."

He stretches out on the bed and lies stiffly, arms at his sides, legs together. I put my hand on his crotch.

His hips jerk, his mouth opens, and his eyes go soft and glassy. "Holy shit," he blurts, then bites his lip. "Sorry."

I pull back. "Did I hurt you."

"No. Just surprised me. It—it felt good."

I reach for the top button of his shirt. Immediately he tenses up. He starts to lift his hands. "Hands on the bed," I order, breathless. He clenches his fists on the sheets again. I undo another button.

"Wait," he blurts out. "I don't have any condoms."

"I brought one." I fumble through the pocket of my hoodie, which is draped over a chair, and pull out the small foil-wrapped packet that I purchased from a convenience store earlier. "You don't have a latex allergy, do you."

He shakes his head.

"Good." I lay the packet on the coverlet and reach out to undo another button.

"H-hang on. Let's not rush this."

I freeze, not quite touching him. "What's wrong," I ask.

The muscles of his face tighten. "Nothing."

I don't move. Am I doing something bad? Lightly—very lightly—I touch his thigh. I brush my finger over the tiny metal tongue of his zipper, then tug it down a half inch. He remains perfectly still. I tug it down a little farther, and his eyes slip shut. A sheen of sweat gleams on his forehead.

Once I start, I don't know what will happen. I don't know how it's *supposed* to happen.

When I speak, my voice trembles a little, despite my effort to hold it steady: "I've never done this before, so you'll have to let me know if I do anything wrong."

His eyes snap open. "What?"

I realize at once that I've made a mistake. I bite my tongue.

"What did you just say?" he asks.

"Nothing." I start to pull down his zipper, but he catches my wrist. I flinch.

He releases me, but immediately he sits up, looking at me directly. "You're a virgin?"

"That's irrelevant."

"Please. Just tell me."

I don't know what will happen if I tell him the truth, but I can't lie. I've never been a good liar. So I don't say anything.

He covers his face with his hands. "Oh my God," he whispers.

I wait for a few seconds, but he doesn't say anything else. My chest is tight and uncomfortable. "Do you want to keep going," I ask.

He lowers his hands slowly. "I'm sorry. I can't do this. I thought—I mean, in the park, when you asked me if I wanted to . . . I thought you *must* have done it before."

My chest isn't tight anymore—it's empty. Numb.

I'm almost relieved. This is a world I know and recognize, a world where the doors of human contact are closed to me. The reason doesn't matter. The point is, it's over. I turn away.

He says my name, but I don't look at him. I pick up my bra and slip it back on.

He stands and reaches out to me. "Wait. What are you—?"

I step away. "It's all right. I'll go."

I pick up my shirt. My whole body suddenly feels stiff, and it hurts to move, but I put the shirt on anyway. My head is buzzing oddly. I need to get out of the room. I need to go home, crawl into the bathtub, and wrap myself in blankets.

He says my name again, louder, but his voice is muffled, as if I'm hearing it through several feet of water.

I walk toward the door. He blocks my path. His unzipped pants start to slip down his thin hips, and he hastily zips them back up. "Listen to me! Please. If I'd had any idea this was your first time—"

"I don't see why it matters."

"Of course it matters! What sort of person do you think I am? Did you really think I'd just—" He stops, face flushed. "Maybe I should have told you."

"Told me what."

His jaw tightens. The flush in his face grows brighter. "I've never done this, either."

I stare. Somehow it never occurred to me that he might be as inexperienced as I am. He's older than me, for one thing. And while he might be an introvert, he's definitely not autistic; his speech comes too easily, too fluidly. Suddenly I don't know what to think or how to react. I never even paused to contemplate what this experience might mean for him. Or rather, I believed that he'd simply take advantage of the opportunity, assuming he didn't find me too unattractive.

"You're a virgin," I say, though that's already been made clear.

He looks away. "I know. It's ridiculous."

I study his expression, trying to glean something from it. "Why."

"Why have I never had sex, or—?"

"No. Why do you think it's ridiculous. You're only nineteen."

He sighs. "Well, you know how it is. Guys aren't supposed to be virgins. We're supposed to lose it like two minutes after we hit puberty, and if we don't, there's something wrong with us."

"That's absurd," I say. "There's obviously nothing wrong with you. You're normal."

He laughs. It's a strange sound—empty and monotone. "Normal, huh?" His voice is low, like he's talking to himself.

"Yes. Aren't you."

He ignores the question and starts to place his hand on my arm. I flinch, and he withdraws. I cross my arms over my chest and study the pattern in the carpet. For a moment, neither of us moves.

"Sit with me," he says. "Please?"

I tug one braid. "Be careful. About touching, I mean."

"I will."

We sit side by side on the edge of the bed. My hands are clasped tightly in my lap, the skin around my nails whitened from the pressure. I don't know where to go from here. The plan has gone completely awry, and I never came up with an alternative strategy, aside from just leaving and going home. This is uncharted territory.

"Will you do me a favor?" he asks quietly.

I swallow, trying to moisten my dry mouth. "What."

"This will sound weird, but just look at me for a minute. Tell me what you see."

I look.

His hair is a bit mussed, and his shirt collar is crooked, but aside from that, he looks the same as ever. We're very close; close enough that I can see the little ripple patterns in his irises, like the veins in marble.

Eye contact is too intimate—it feels like we have our hands in each other's guts, feeling around where it's tender and bloody—but I force myself to hold his gaze.

"I see you," I say. "I see Stanley Finkel."

He averts his eyes. I have a feeling that wasn't the answer he was looking for, but I don't know what else to say.

When we finally leave the motel, it's almost midnight. I drive him back to the lot where his car is parked, and I park next to it. The engine idles. The pale green glow of the dashboard bathes his face. "I want to see you again," he says.

I know he's not talking about text-chatting. My hands are locked tight around the steering wheel. "I can't."

"Ever?"

I close my eyes. "Trust me. It's better if we just keep talking online."

"I don't understand. If it's something I said or did—"

"It has nothing to do with you."

"Then why?" he whispers.

He's not going to give up, I realize. Even if we go back to Gchat, it won't be the same. This was a mistake.

"Listen," he continues. "I know you're self-conscious about being—different. I know that's why you didn't want to meet at first. But I don't mind."

My breathing space has shrunk down again, confined to a tiny cavity inside my chest. Everything is hot and tight inside. I hear a sound like scraping rocks in my head—my molars grinding together—and I force the words out between them: "You don't know how fucking different I am."

A light drizzle patters on the roof of the car; the only sound. Droplets slide down the windshield, casting shadows that trickle down his cheeks.

"I'll be in the park again tomorrow," he says. "Same time."

I don't answer. I wait until he gets out of the car and gets into his own car. Then I drive away. A dull rumble echoes up from the Vault, and I shudder. I don't ever want to look inside.

It's horrible, and dark, and filled with the roar of water.

CHAPTER ELEVEN

Dawn creeps in through my curtains and spreads across my walls. I glance at the clock. 6:17 a.m. I haven't slept.

I'm lying on my mattress, my T-shirt sticking to my sweaty skin. I sit up and peel off the damp cotton. My fingers tremble as I pick up my Rubik's Cube and twist it around.

I keep replaying the details of last night in my head. The memory of Stanley is a constant itch under my skin. Particles of him are swimming through my blood, my brain. Whenever I close my eyes he is there, in the darkness behind my eyelids.

I didn't even have sex with him, but somehow he got inside me anyway.

Stupid. So very, very stupid for me to think I could meet him and not suffer any repercussions. I broke every rule of my personal code, and now I'm paying the price.

I push the thoughts away, drag myself to my feet, and shuffle into the bathroom to splash some cold water on my face. I need to get ready for work.

***

"Hey!"

I turn, squinting. I've just finished mucking out the gibbons' cage. Toby is leaning on his broom and dustpan, his jaws working a bright purple wad.

"You aren't supposed to chew gum during work hours," I tell him.

He smirks. "What, you gonna report me?"

Maybe in his mind, he's being cool. Perhaps this is even his backward way of trying to flirt, like a little boy pulling a girl's pigtails. I'm not amused. "Spit it out," I tell him.

He spits the gum into his palm and sticks it on the underside of a drinking fountain.

Briefly I consider dumping the bucket of gibbons' feces and rotten fruit rinds over his head. I'd be fired, of course, but it would almost be worth it. "Is there something you wanted to say to me," I ask.

He tips up the brim of his khaki-colored cap and flashes a chipmunk-toothed smile. "Ms. Nell wants to see you."

When Ms. Nell wants to see me, it usually isn't good. Of course, it's always possible that she wants to promote me. Possible, but not likely.

I arrive in her office and sit down. She squints at me. "Are you sick? You look like a dog's dinner."

I shift in my chair. She's used this expression before. It means I look bad, though I'm not sure what that has to do with dog food. "I didn't sleep well. That's all."

She taps one oval-shaped, Pepto-Bismol-pink nail on the desk, then shifts to a familiar, lecturing tone that signals I'm going to be here awhile. "You know, I'm trying to run a respectable business here. People all told me I was crazy to believe that I could turn a profit with this rinky-dink zoo. 'No one makes money on zoos anymore,' they said. But I proved 'em wrong. I bought this place when it was about to close down for good, gave it a fresh coat of paint and some new animals, put out some ads, poured in a few buckets of good old-fashioned elbow grease, and now Hickory Park is turning a profit for the first time in years. *Decades.* Do you know how I did it?"

She just told me in detail how she did it, but I recognize this game by now. "How," I ask.

"One word: *reputation.* Reputation is everything. You think people come here to see animals?"

"Yes. I mean, no."

"If people want to see animals, they can do it at home, in billion-pixel high-def, just by turning on a damn nature show. And on TV, the animals are doing interesting things. Here, they just sit around picking fleas off their furry balls. You think anyone wants to look at that?"

I consider pointing out that most of the animals here don't have the opposable thumbs necessary for that particular activity, then decide to let it slide.

She continues: "Our guests come here for the *experience.* The whole package. We're competing with movie theaters, with sporting events, with any other damn thing people can do on a

Saturday, and that means we've got to *deliver.* If guests come in and see you looking like a bucket of crap, the experience suffers."

Exhaustion creeps over me, making my body heavy. She keeps talking, but the words slide through my mind without leaving a mark. My vision wavers, and the world swims.

After a moment, I realize Ms. Nell is saying my name over and over. Her voice seems to slow, as if someone's playing a recording at half speed—*Alviiiiie . . . Aaaalviiiie.* I can see the words floating through the air, shining faintly, like they're traced in silver paint. My gaze follows them with detached interest.

"Hey!" She snaps her fingers.

My vision jolts into focus. "What."

She frowns, but her eyebrows are tilted down at the outside corners. That usually means someone is worried, not angry. "You *sure* you're not sick?"

I shake my head. "Just tired." And preoccupied.

Duke the parrot lets out a sudden squawk from his cage, and I give a start, almost jumping from my chair.

Ms. Nell's frown deepens. "Maybe you ought to go home early. Get some rest."

I open my mouth to protest—I feel calmer here than I do in my apartment—but I recognize the futility of argument. So I close my mouth, nod, and push myself to my feet.

At home, I sit on the couch, fiddling with my Rubik's Cube. I close my eyes and focus on the smooth, cool plastic under my fingers. This is just another puzzle. If I can find a way to stop thinking about Stanley, my problems will be solved.

I open my laptop and type *stopping obsessive thoughts* into the search engine. I scroll down through the results and start clicking on links. I do more searches. The rapid-fire click of keys echoes through the silence; a comforting sound. My gaze latches on to a name.

Bupropion. It's an antidepressant, but it's also used to treat addictions. And attraction, after all, is just another form of addiction. It activates the same centers of the brain as cocaine.

The thought stops me. *Am* I attracted to him? I remember being disappointed when he wouldn't let me take off his clothes. I enjoyed touching him. Maybe I *am* capable of attraction, after all—and now I'm trying to put an end to it. Ironic.

I've always avoided prescription medications, but I'm not against taking pills so much as seeing doctors. There are ways to buy prescription drugs online, but most of them aren't strictly legal, and I'd rather not take the risk.

Again, I consider the idea of calling Dr. Bernhardt and asking for his help. I don't like it, but at this point, I'm desperate enough to try almost anything.

I flip open my cell phone and scroll through my list of contacts, which includes him, Ms. Nell, Stanley—my gaze lingers on his name—and an old employer whose number I never bothered to delete. I select Dr. Bernhardt's name and call.

He picks up in the middle of the second ring. "Alvie?" He sounds utterly baffled. I've never actually called his cell phone before.

In the background, a man's voice says, "Who's that, Len?"

"Hang on," he mumbles. I hear footsteps, then he asks, "Is everything okay?"

"I have a favor to ask you."

"Uh . . . of course. Go ahead."

"I need some bupropion."

There's a pause. "You realize I'm not a psychiatrist, don't you? I have a doctorate in sociology."

"I know that." Already, this is starting to seem like a bad idea. "I just thought . . . maybe you knew someone who had some samples, or . . ."

"In the past, you've been very adamant about *not* going back on medication, or seeking any kind of help, for that matter. Why now? Why bupropion?"

I grit my teeth. If I want his help, I'll have to give him some sort of explanation. That much is clear. "It's sometimes prescribed to people who want to quit smoking or who can't stop playing video games."

"So have you taken up smoking, or are you addicted to video games?"

"Neither." I guess I could have just lied about that and said yes to one or the other, but I'm no good at lying, and I hate doing it, anyway. "I'm addicted to something else."

"What?"

I shift my weight on the couch. "It's nothing illegal. So why does it matter."

"Because even if I *could* write you a prescription myself, which

I can't, it would be irresponsible of me to hand out pills like candy without even knowing why you want them. So what are you addicted to?"

"It's a person," I mumble.

"A person," he repeats.

"There's a person I can't stop thinking about. Someone I met recently."

After a few heartbeats, he replies, "Was it a bad experience?"

"No. It went better than I expected, actually."

"So why do you want to stop thinking about it?"

"Because I'm showing clear signs of obsession. I got *no* sleep last night. My reflexes are shot. I almost got into an accident driving to work this morning. If this continues, I'm going to lose my job, and I don't want to lose my job. I like being around the animals. I—"

"Alvie, it's all right. It's all right. Calm down."

Only then do I realize my voice has escalated to a shout. I exhale a shuddering breath and slump on the couch, limp, like a broken puppet. "Sorry." This is bad. I'm slipping, losing control. "I should go."

"Wait. I can help you schedule an appointment with someone, if that's what you want."

"I'd prefer not to."

"Then I'm afraid there's nothing I can do." Another pause. "Is this the same person you mentioned to me before? The one you were talking to online?"

"It doesn't matter." My throat tightens. "Sorry to disturb you." I hang up.

I shouldn't have called. Why did I do that? If Dr. Bernhardt thinks I'm unstable, he might tell the judge that I'm not ready for emancipation. I could lose my chance.

For a while, I try unsuccessfully to nap. After an hour or so, I roll out of bed and throw on my hoodie.

It's almost six o'clock. Stanley said he would be waiting for me in the park.

I could, of course, just not show up. I could stop going online, ignore his emails, return to my safe, isolated little life. That would probably be smarter.

But I can't do that to him. After the kindness he's shown me, I at least owe him some kind of explanation.

I pull up my hood and walk down the sidewalk with my hands shoved into my pockets and my breath pluming in the air. The days are getting shorter and chillier, and the horizon glows red with sunset. I breathe in deep, feeling the prickle of cold air in my lungs, and release it through my nose.

When I arrive at the park, he's already there, sitting on the bench, wearing a gray fleece jacket. My heart lurches. Even from this distance, I can see him shivering. I duck behind a tree, press my back to the rough bark. Take a deep breath. I am going to tell him now, tonight, that this has to end. What he wants is something more than I'm capable of giving.

I need a minute to get myself under control before I face him, so I turn away and force my legs to move. My steps are stiff and jerky, mechanical, as my feet take me away from him and across the street. I slump against a wall and close my eyes, more sweat beading on my forehead. My hand slips into my pocket and grips the Rubik's Cube. I turn it over and over, focusing on the cool smoothness.

A shadow falls over me, and I tense. When I look up, I see man in a police uniform. He's enormous, with broad, round shoulders and a bushy walrus mustache. "Everything all right, ma'am?" he asks, thumbs hooked into the loops on his belt. I thought policemen only did that on TV shows.

I step away from him and start to rock back and forth on the balls of my feet, my hand still in my pocket. Men in uniforms make me nervous. If a regular person is bothering me or asking questions I don't know how to answer, I can just walk away. But walking away from a policeman can result in being arrested. "I'm fine," I mutter, and take another step backward.

His thick eyebrows bunch together, and he frowns. "Mind telling me what you're doing here?" His tone has changed, hardened. He's suspicious.

"I'm standing."

"Yes, I can see that. I'll ask you again. What are you doing?"

I lower my head, breathing rapidly. I know I'm making it worse—acting nervous, avoiding eye contact, like I'm up to no good. But I can't help it. "Nothing." I keep fiddling with the Rubik's Cube, without taking it from my pocket.

"It sure looks like you're doing something."

I try to think of an answer, but my head is full of static. My legs itch with the urge to bolt, but if I do, he'll chase me. "I don't know why you're asking me these questions." My voice shakes. "I don't know why people won't just leave me alone."

He takes another step toward me, and I take another step back. "What's that you've got in your pocket?" He holds out one meaty hand. "Let's see it."

I don't want him taking my Rubik's Cube. I don't like anyone touching my things. My skin crawls at the thought of him turning the cube over in his hands, getting his fingerprints all over it, violating it. He might decide not to give it back. I hunch my shoulders. "Go away."

He speaks slowly and evenly: "Place your hands against the wall."

I feel sick.

"Place your hands against the wall," he says again.

When I don't obey, he grabs my wrists and shoves my hands against the wall. My whole body goes rigid. The touch sends a sharp jolt through me, like a hot poker raking down my spine. His fingers are burning my skin. "Let me go."

"Keep your hands there, where I can see them—"

I can't stop myself; I start to struggle. I kick. When he pushes me against the wall, I scream.

"Get your hands off her!"

For a second or two, I don't recognize Stanley's voice. I've never heard him speak so loudly or forcefully.

The policeman looks up, blinking. "Excuse me?"

"I said let her go!" Stanley shoves himself between me and the policeman, shielding me with his body. His face is flushed and shiny with perspiration as he holds up his cell phone. "I've already dialed 911. All I have to do is hit send."

The policeman glances at his crutch and scowls. "This isn't what you think it is," he says. "Step aside."

"I'm not going to just stand back and let you assault her!"

"I'm not *assaulting* her, for God's sake, I'm trying to do my job." The man draws himself up, looming over Stanley. He's nearly six inches taller and probably a hundred pounds heavier. "Now for the last time, put your phone away and step aside. Or this is going to get ugly." The color drains from Stanley's face, but still, he stands his ground. The man reaches for something at his belt.

"Wait!" I blurt out, and plunge my hand into my pocket. The man tenses and starts to pull out his gun. In the same instant, I pull out the Rubik's Cube.

He freezes and blinks at it. His expression goes blank. Then he shoves the gun back into its holster. "Let me see that."

I hesitate. Resisting will just make things worse—for Stanley as well as me—so I hand him the cube. He turns it over in his hands, poking at it like it's some mysterious alien artifact, then hands it back to me. His expression is rigid, but his cheeks redden slightly. He clears his throat. "Well, apparently there's been a misunderstanding." He crosses his arms. "Why didn't you just take it out when I told you to?"

I don't answer. I don't know what to say.

He frowns. "Is she re . . . mentally challenged, or something?"

"No," Stanley says.

"Well, then what's her problem?"

"You're scaring her."

The man glares at Stanley, then at me. He breathes a heavy sigh. "Fine. Whatever." He shakes his head, muttering under his breath as he turns his back to us, then gets into his car and drives away. I clutch the Rubik's Cube against my chest.

Stanley starts to reach out, then stops. "Are you okay?"

"Yes." I'm still feeling shaky and weak and a little nauseous, but it will pass. It could've been worse. *Would've* been, if he hadn't shown up. "What about you."

He smiles, though his face is still pale. "Fine."

"You don't look fine."

"I have a thing about large, intimidating men yelling at me." He wipes his brow with one sleeve and sags against the nearby wall. "I'll be okay in a minute."

This is my fault. A dull heat spreads across my brow and seeps down into my ears and cheeks.

He takes a deep breath, closes his eyes, and lets it out slowly. "Do you want to sit down?"

I hesitate—then nod.

We walk over to the bench in the park and sit, side by side, not quite touching.

"That was nuts," Stanley says. "I mean, you weren't *doing* anything. You were just standing there."

I shrug. "I look suspicious. That's just how it is. Lots of people have to deal with this kind of thing."

"That doesn't make it okay."

I look at him from the corner of my eye. He stood up for me. He took a risk for my sake. Not many people have done that.

"Thank you," I say, the words awkward and unfamiliar in my mouth.

"You're welcome."

For a few minutes, neither one of us says anything. I can't read Stanley's expression. His fingers are clenched tight on his crutch, the knuckles almost white. I avert my gaze, my throat suddenly, painfully tight.

"Look at me," he whispers. "Please?"

His eyes are bright in the dimness, almost luminous. They seem to soak up the faint light and reflect it back, like a cat's; the bluish-gray whites are opalescent. "I understand, you know," he says. "Why you're scared. This whole human-interaction thing isn't exactly easy for me, either."

He thinks he understands, but he doesn't. There's so much more to it. So much I can't even begin to tell him.

I'm still twisting the Rubik's Cube, spinning the rows of color, but my mind won't focus; I'm undoing the progress I've made, scattering the rows into tiny squares, jumbling it into a mass of incoherent color.

"I was never any good at those," he says, distracting me. "Rubik's Cubes, I mean. I had one as a kid, but I wasn't able to solve it."

"They aren't really that hard. You just have to be patient."

"May I try?"

I hesitate, then hand it to him. He starts to twist it. His slender, long-fingered hands are fascinating to watch, almost hypnotic.

"Start by solving the white side," I advise.

It takes him a while, but eventually, he manages to complete one section. He hands it back to me, leaning a little closer in the process. His eyelashes are very long and dark, in contrast to mine, which are short and almost invisible because they're the same pale red as my hair. I lower my gaze and clutch the Rubik's Cube against my chest.

"You like puzzles," he remarks. There's no inflection at the end, so it's probably intended more as an observation than a question.

I reply anyway. "I find them calming."

He smiles a little. "Sometimes, when I'm stressed out, I distract myself by solving riddles. I guess that's kind of the same. Like a puzzle in your head. There's one from *Alice in Wonderland* . . . 'Why is a raven like a writing desk?' I thought about that for a long time before I learned that it was supposed to be unanswerable."

"I never liked riddles much. They're too ambiguous. A puzzle only has one solution, even if there are many different ways to get there." I lock a row of colors into place on my Rubik's Cube. "A raven and a writing desk are similar in any number of ways. They're both made of matter, for one thing. They're both heavier than a blade of grass."

"Sure, but a *good* riddle has only one right solution, and it seems self-evident once you know it. There's that moment where things kind of snap into focus."

I hesitate. "All right. Tell me one."

"Here's an easy one. What has hands but can't clap?"

"A corpse."

He winces. "A *clock.* Jeez."

"Well, my answer fits, too."

"Yeah, but . . ." He lets out a little sigh. "Okay, here's a better one. There's a house with four walls facing south. A bear is circling the house. What color is the bear?"

I twist the cube harder. "How is anyone supposed to answer that. Those two things aren't even remotely connected. Anyway, there's no way a house could have four walls *all* facing south. That's impossible."

"Is it?"

"Obviously. Unless—" I frown, thinking. "Unless it's at the North Pole. Which means . . . it's probably a polar bear." Realization clicks into place. "The bear is white."

"There you go."

I make a noncommittal sound in my throat. "All right. I see what you mean. But that one was more of a logic problem than a riddle."

He chuckles quietly. "Maybe."

It's strange, how easily we slip back into conversation after everything that's happened. I've missed it.

An image floats up behind my retinas: Stanley sitting on the bench alone, crying. "Stanley . . . do you remember the day you threw your phone into the pond."

His smile fades. "Yeah. I remember."

"Why did you do that." I asked before, once, and he just said he was being stupid and that it didn't matter. But there must be a reason.

He folds his hands together. "My mom had cancer," he says. "She had it for a long time. After a while, it spread to her brain.

And they couldn't operate. They—they said that if they took out the tumor, she would probably be a vegetable. No awareness. She didn't want that."

There's a small sharp pain somewhere between my heart and throat, like a fishhook has caught inside me.

"She knew she wouldn't be around much longer. So she went to Elkland Meadows, and they made her comfortable. That's what they do there." The moonlight makes the bruise-colored circles under his eyes darker, the hollows in his cheeks more prominent. "One day, the pain was really bad, and they asked her if she wanted to stay awake or just sleep for whatever time was left. She said she wanted to sleep. So we said good-bye. I threw away my phone because there seemed to be no point in keeping it. I mean, who was I going to call?"

A faint trace of daylight lingers in the sky, but the moon is already out. It slips behind a cloud, then emerges, wreathed in a silvery-white halo. Black-and-pearl-colored dusk shadows stretch across the grass.

"I'm sorry," I say. They're the only words I have.

"It's okay," he replies.

But it's not. Words aren't enough.

I start to reach out. Stop. Then I close the gap between us and take his hand. His fingers twitch, then curl around mine. His hand feels bird-fragile, the bones long and thin, the skin fever-hot. He squeezes my hand lightly.

"You never told me." The words fall from my numb lips, into the cold air. "Why."

“It didn’t seem fair to unload all that on you. And I didn’t want to scare you away. I mean . . . you’re kind of my only friend.”

That word again. Feelings stir beneath my skin: uncomfortable feelings, like there are thin wires running into the center of my rib cage and something is tugging at those wires, sending vibrations into my core.

“I guess that’s a weird thing to admit out of the blue, isn’t it? But yeah. I’m kind of a loner. Which is a slightly cooler-sounding way of saying ‘nerd with no social life.’”

I can’t process this. “You talk to other people at your school. Don’t you.”

“Sometimes. But it’s not the same. We talk about what TV shows we like or what music we listen to. We don’t talk like this.”

I don’t respond; I’m struggling to control my breathing.

“I guess I just unloaded. Exactly the way I didn’t want to. God. Sorry.”

He’s always apologizing.

“I’m not even nice to you,” I say.

“Sure you are. More than once, you stayed up with me until four o’clock in the morning because I couldn’t sleep. Remember?”

“It’s not like I had anything better to do.”

“Every time you show me a kindness, you downplay it like this. Why are you so worried about being seen as a nice person?”

“I’m not a nice person.”

“We’ll just have to disagree on that.”

I let his hand slip from mine. My fingers are suddenly cold. “I don’t know how to do this,” I murmur.

"Do what?"

"This. Everything."

He gives me a tiny smile. "I guess we can just play it by ear." He bites his lower lip. "Do you . . . do you want to get lunch tomorrow?"

"I have work."

He lowers his gaze.

"We could have dinner instead, maybe."

His breath hitches. "Really? I mean, great. That sounds great."

"Do you want to go to Buster's again. Or someplace else."

"Actually I was wondering . . . would you like to come to my place?"

I blink and turn toward him. For a few seconds, I'm too surprised to respond.

"I'm actually a pretty good cook," he adds.

What does it mean, that he's inviting me? What would it imply, if I accepted? "We're just going to eat dinner," I say. "We're not going to have sex."

Color rushes to his cheeks. "Well, yeah. I mean, no. Of course."

"Which is it," I ask.

"That was a question?"

"Yes."

"Sorry. So . . . you're asking me if I . . ."

"I like having clearly defined boundaries," I say. "I've never been in this situation before, so I need to know what your expectations are."

His face is bright red now. "I just want to cook dinner for you.

Honest. I wasn't planning on making any moves. After last night, I thought we should take things slow."

I pick at a loose thread of my sleeve. "Just be friends, you mean."

"If that's what you want."

Is that what I want?

Things are so much simpler with animals. With human beings, everything is so complicated and ambiguous. There are people who remain friends without ever having sex. Then there are friends with benefits, people who have sex but don't bother with the other aspects of a relationship. And then, of course, there's romance, which is something I don't understand at all.

This feels dangerous. I should say no; I should retreat, regroup, try to figure out what all this means.

"Yes."

A wide smile breaks across his face, and suddenly—despite my misgivings—I'm glad I agreed. "Great. I'll email you the directions."

I nod.

We look at each other, and I find myself preoccupied, once again, with those uncanny eyes. Blue within blue. I've never seen anything like them. I want to ask, but the words stick in my throat.

"You know," he says, "I just figured it out."

"What?"

"Why *is* a raven like a writing desk?"

I furrow my brow. "Why."

"Neither is made of cheese."

I blink a few times. "Well, now you're just being silly."

"But I made you smile." His voice softens. "You've got a nice smile, you know."

I touch my lips, surprised. I hadn't realized I was smiling.

Later, sitting on my couch, I open up my laptop. *Blue sclerae.* I plug the words into the search engine, and a list of medical sites pops up. I click on a link and start reading.

Blue sclerae can result from loss of water content, which causes a thinning of the tissue, allowing the underlying dark choroids to be seen.

I scroll down to causes. There are forty-seven possible medical causes listed. Among them are skeletal disorders, chromosome and ocular disorders, and high urine excretion. I think about calling Stanley to ask if he urinates a lot, then quickly reject the idea and go back to scrutinizing the possible causes listed on the website. Sometimes, it says, there is no specific cause. It might mean nothing.

I close the browser window. Probably I'm overthinking it.

CHAPTER TWELVE

When I pull up in front of Stanley's house that evening, my movements feel automatic, as if my mind has become disconnected from my body. Which maybe is a good thing, because in my mind, I don't feel prepared for this.

His house is small and blue, with a brick chimney, a neatly tended lawn, and a single car—a nondescript gray import—in the driveway. There's a row of azaleas beneath the window, though they're no longer in bloom.

I'm wearing a black T-shirt with a graphic of a small white bunny bearing bloodstained fangs over the words NO ORDINARY RABBIT. He answers the door wearing a burgundy sweater, and he's swapped his metal crutch for a cane carved from dark reddish wood—mahogany, maybe. "Hi." His voice cracks a little. He clears his throat and tries again. "Hi. Come in."

I slip my shoes off on the mat and take a few cautious steps into the living room. It's small and clean and smells faintly of cinnamon. The armchair and the couch are upholstered in brown corduroy. It looks very soft. I resist the temptation to run my hands over it and instead ask a question that's been on my mind for a while: "Does anyone else live here."

"No." He averts his gaze. "This was my mother's house. She left it to me."

On a bookshelf stands a clear plastic terrarium, a network of colored tubes and little round houses filled with wood shavings. A small brown gerbil is running on a wheel.

"That's Matilda," Stanley says.

"Do you give her things to chew on," I ask.

"Balsa wood, mostly."

"They need that. Their teeth never stop growing."

"Yeah." A pause. "So, uh. You hungry? I could start dinner. Or I could show you the rest of the house. Though there's not much to see—"

"Show me."

He leads me down a short hall. We pass a closed door, and I pause. "What's in there."

His expression shifts, just for a half second. I wonder if I will ever learn to read his face. It feels like watching a computer screen with code rapidly scrolling past in long green lines, too fast for me to make sense of. "Just an extra bedroom."

I follow him to the end of the hall, through another door. He flicks on the light. "Here's my room," he says.

The bedspread is blue and very old, threadbare, with a pattern of yellow moons and stars faded to near invisibility. His computer, sleek and new, sits on a plain yellow pine desk. There's a shelf next to the bed filled with model planes in every color, shape, and size. More model planes hang from the ceiling. I count thirty-two in all.

I touch the bedspread, lean down, press my face against his pillow, and breathe in. It smells like lemons. "I like your fabric softener," I say, my voice muffled by the pillow. Then it occurs to me that he might not like me shoving my face against his bedding. "Sorry," I say, straightening. "I should have asked permission before doing that." Then again, asking, *Can I smell your pillow?* probably wouldn't be considered normal, either.

So far, I'm not doing very well.

"It's okay," he says. "Really. If I seem a little uncomfortable, it's not you. It's been a long time since I've had a guest."

This is new to him, too. Somehow, the thought relaxes me.

I tilt my head back, studying the planes hanging from the ceiling. "Did you make these."

"Yeah. I started building models when I was a kid, and I just never stopped. I guess it's a little silly. I mean, a grown man with a room full of toy planes."

"I like them." I start to reach for a dark green World War II–era fighter, then stop. "Can I touch this."

"Sure."

I lift the plane. It has a row of shark's teeth and a pair of eyes painted along the nose. Most planes painted in this style are meant to look menacing, but this one is smiling. I trace the curve of its mouth. Then I turn it over, examining the joints. There's a snap, and the wing comes off in my hand. I freeze.

Stanley winces. "Whoops," he says, as if he's the one who did it.

I stare at the broken-off wing. "I—I don't know how that happened. I thought I was being careful. Sometimes it's hard for me to judge how much pressure I'm applying—"

"Don't worry about it." He takes the plane and its wing from my numb hands and sets the two pieces on the desk.

I cross my arms, sticking my hands under my armpits, where they can't do any more damage. "I'm sorry."

"I'll glue it back on. It's just a toy, anyway." He touches the plane gently, like it's an injured child. "No big deal." He smiles but doesn't quite meet my eyes. "I should get dinner ready. You can watch some TV in the meantime, if you like. It shouldn't take long."

I follow him out of the bedroom.

In the living room, I sit stiffly on Stanley's living room couch, listening to the *clank* of metal and the *hiss* of sizzling butter from the kitchen.

"The remote's on the coffee table," he calls.

I turn on the TV and flip past talk shows and sitcoms, looking for a nature or science program. There aren't any playing at the moment, but I find a channel showing a medical documentary on brain surgery. I watch the surgeon's bloodstained, white-gloved fingers slicing through the dura mater with a scalpel, probing the glistening, gray-pink folds of the cortex.

Stanley steps into the living room. "Dinner's—oh Jesus." He pales and covers his eyes with one hand.

I change the channel.

He peeks out between his fingers. "Can you really watch that stuff before eating?"

"It's informative." I've never understood why so many people hate looking at the inside of the human body. We walk around all day with blood and organs inside us. It seems silly to be horrified by something so commonplace.

He lowers his hand, still looking a little pale. "Well, the food's ready."

I follow him into the tiny kitchen. There's a white cloth on the table, along with two flickering candles in silver holders. In the center of the table is a platter covered with a silver dome-shaped lid. He lifts off the lid.

"You made pancakes," I say, surprised.

"I wanted to be sure it was something you'd like. I got five different flavors of syrup." He waves a hand toward the row of glass bottles on the table: strawberry, blueberry, butterscotch, maple, and banana.

I can't find my voice. There are moments when I wonder if he can possibly be real, or if I made him up. But I don't think my imagination is that skilled.

His smile fades. "You don't like it? I could make something else—"

"No. This is good."

The tension eases out of his shoulders, and we sit down to eat. The pancakes are warm, tender, and chewy.

"So," he says, "why rabbits?"

A forkful of pancakes freezes halfway to my mouth. "What do you mean."

"Well, I mean, I know you like animals. But it seems like

you're especially interested in rabbits." He gestures toward my shirt. "You've talked about them before, and you quoted *Watership Down* when we first met."

No one's ever really asked me about this. The answer is something I don't know how to put into words. I swallow a mouthful of pancakes and say, "I just like them."

"I've been rereading that book," he says. "I'd forgotten how political it is. I mean, the whole thing with the fascist bunny . . . Woundwort? Is it a metaphor for Nazi Germany?"

I start cutting my pancakes into hexagons. "I never really thought of it as being political. I just saw it as what it was, I guess. It's about surviving."

My knife slips and clatters against the edge of the plate. I give a start and quickly pick it up again.

"You don't have to worry, you know," he says. "I'm just glad you came over."

Apparently my nervousness is more obvious than I thought.

"And I think your way of reading is better, really," he continues. "I mean, just accepting things as they are. When you're always analyzing, it can take away from the experience. I guess I've just taken too many English classes."

It occurs to me that I don't even know what his major is. Our conversations online were always more abstract, focused on thoughts and feelings rather than day-to-day life. "Is that what you're studying. English."

"Journalism. But it's tough to make a living at that, especially these days, when so many people get their news online, from blogs and stuff. I'm thinking about switching majors to computer science, becoming a programmer."

"Do you enjoy programming."

"Honestly? Not really. It's kind of dull. But I'm decent at it." He shrugs. "How are the pancakes?"

"Very good. Better than Buster's."

He beams.

Once I'm finished eating, I pick up my plate, though I'm not sure what to do with it. At home I mostly eat takeout. My only dishes are a few plastic bowls, which I just rinse out in the sink. Or, more often than not, stack in the sink and ignore for a few days.

"I'll take care of those," he says, "don't worry about it. Do you drink coffee?"

"Coffee would be good."

He starts filling the pot. As it percolates, I say, "I need to use the bathroom."

"First door on the right."

I find it easily, but when I come out, I don't return immediately to the kitchen. I linger in the hall, staring at the open door to Stanley's bedroom. I walk toward it. Inside, the broken plane smiles at me from his desk. I can see the slot where the wing is supposed to go. I pick it up and try to stick the wing back on. It won't stay.

I should just leave it alone. If I keep fiddling, I'll probably make it worse.

I set the plane down and start to turn away, then notice the bottom drawer of his desk is slightly open. Inside, I glimpse the spine of a book. I can only see the lower half of the words forming the title, but there's something familiar about their shape. My stomach gives a lurch, like I'm looking off the edge of a tall building.

I should leave now. It would be better if I did.

Instead, I curl a finger around the edge of the drawer and tug it open, revealing the full title. *The Complete Guide to Asperger's Syndrome.*

There's more than one book in there. There's a whole stack.

I pick up the first book. Then I set it on the desk and pick up another, then another. They're all about the same subject. I open one.

Asperger's is a form of autism characterized by social and communication difficulties, atypical use of language, and obsessive interests—

I flip through the pages, my fingers leaving faint, damp sweat marks on the paper. Certain lines and sections are highlighted or underlined. I turn page after page, but it's hard to read. My vision keeps blurring. I come across another underlined section.

One of the most dysfunctional characteristics of Asperger's is an inability to empathize. Due to the lack of this fundamental trait, many sufferers remain friendless and isolated well into adulthood. People with Asperger's can seem locked inside themselves, trapped by their own limited social skills. Establishing a relationship with one can take extraordinary patience—

Is that how he sees me? As a broken thing? Is this the manual he plans to use to fix me?

The book slips from my fingers and lands on the floor with a muffled *thump*.

"Alvie?"

He's standing in the doorway, leaning on his cane. He takes a few cautious steps forward. "Are you okay?"

My chest hurts. "I should go." I walk stiffly past him, through the door and down the hall, into the living room. I can't look at him. The blood bangs behind my eyes.

Stanley follows me. "Wait. Tell me what's wrong." He blocks my path.

"I don't need your pity." I squeeze the words out through clenched teeth. "Now get out of my way."

"Do you seriously think someone like me is spending time with you out of pity?"

The question catches me off guard.

"You could have chosen anyone, you know," he says. "Anyone you wanted. For your first time. You're a beautiful, intelligent young woman. Do you not know that?"

He's making fun of me. He must be. "Shut up," I mutter. "I saw the books in your desk."

His cheeks color. "I bought those books because I wanted to understand you better. That's all. I don't think there's anything wrong with you. I never did."

I cross my arms, tightly gripping my own elbows.

"Sit down," he says. "Please?"

I hesitate, then sit in the chair. He eases himself onto the couch, across from me.

"When did you figure it out," I ask. "About me."

"I, uh. I kind of suspected right away."

So, it's that obvious. Maybe I shouldn't be surprised. "There was a part you underlined. About empathy."

His brows knit together. "What— Oh, that? I underlined it because it seemed wrong to me. I mean, you're one of the kindest people I've ever met."

Kind. Where does he get these ideas? When have I ever done anything kind? "They're talking about cognitive empathy."

"What's that? I don't remember the books using that phrase."

"It's the ability to read, analyze, and predict other people's emotions. That's what I . . . what people like me tend to struggle with."

The idea that autistic people don't feel compassion is just an ugly stereotype, but it's a viewpoint I've encountered even from some professionals, despite obvious evidence to the contrary. For instance, Temple Grandin—probably the most well-known autistic person alive—designed a more humane type of slaughterhouse for cattle, one which keeps them calm and stress-free up until the end. She cared enough to reduce the unnecessary suffering that so many animals experience for humans' convenience. How could anyone not see that as compassion?

"One of the books said that a lot of people with Asperger's aren't even aware that they have it," Stanley says.

I rub my thumb absently against the brown corduroy of the couch. "I'm aware."

For most of my childhood, my diagnosis was PDD-NOS—pervasive developmental disorder not otherwise specified. They changed it to Asperger's when I was fourteen. In the next volume of the DSM, the Asperger's diagnosis was dropped, so technically my condition doesn't even exist anymore; if I ever go back to the doctor, they'll presumably have to find some other label to stick on me. The specific words don't matter. I'll always be this way.

"I don't like being sorted and categorized," I say. "I am who I am. I shouldn't *need* a word for it. I don't understand why I can't just . . . be. Why everyone has to—" I breathe a small sigh, frustrated with my inability to explain.

Silence stretches between us. When he speaks again, his voice is soft, like he's talking to himself, almost. "At times like these, I really wish I could give you a hug."

I consider this for a moment. It's been years since I've hugged anyone. The few times it's happened during my teenage years have been without warning and against my will—usually foster parents who didn't understand my boundary issues—so it was generally a stressful and unpleasant experience. But with Stanley, it might be different. He's always gentle and careful, so I know he wouldn't squeeze the breath out of me. But the thought still makes me uneasy, for reasons I can't entirely put into words.

It occurs to me, then, that Stanley might himself want the reassurance of physical contact, independent of whether I find it pleasurable. "When was your last time," I ask.

"What, hugging?"

"Yes."

"Um." His gaze shifts away. "It's been a while."

"Okay," I say.

"Okay?"

I sit next to him on the couch. "We can try it, if you want."

He raises his eyebrows. "You're sure?"

"Just do it."

Slowly—very slowly—he slides his arms around me. When I don't flinch, he pulls me closer, but his grip remains loose so I can get away if I want to. I sit, tense, focusing on my own breathing. His hand rests on my back, between my shoulder blades. Gradually the tension recedes. I hook an arm awkwardly around his waist. Even through his sweater, I can feel how thin he is. His body is a collection of sharp angles, his spine a line of tiny knobs. And there's something else—a long, bumpy ridge running across his back. My fingertips wander down the length of it. "What is this from."

A few seconds pass before he replies. "When I was a kid, I used to go ice-skating. I was good at it. Then when I was ten, I slipped and broke my scapula. They had to open me up to put all the fragments back in place, and for months I slept on my stomach because my back was full of surgical pins."

The thought makes my own back ache. "That sounds bad."

"It was the worst."

I raise my head to look into his eyes. Our faces are very close together.

Ordinarily I'd be panicking by now, overwhelmed by the flood of touch and closeness, but there's no fear, no sense that I'm losing control. It's just warm. When I rest my cheek against his sweater vest, over his heart, I feel the movement within, like a small living creature. "You smell like a library," I murmur.

"I hope you're okay with that."

I close my eyes. "I don't mind." I wonder why I'm letting him do this, how he slipped under all my carefully constructed guards like a rose thorn under a fingernail.

Deep inside my brain, a warning bell clangs. *Too close.*

Outside, the wind howls. A wet mixture of snow and sleet slides down the windowpane. Winter, it seems, has arrived early this year.

Carefully he inches back, extricating himself from my arms, and I'm surprised to feel a small pang of disappointment. "I didn't know it was supposed to storm," he remarks.

"It wasn't. The weather report said 'cloudy.'"

"Guess weathermen don't know everything."

A branch scratches the window.

"The roads are going to be nasty tonight," he says. "You're welcome to stay."

My gaze jerks toward him.

"Only if you want," he adds quickly. "I know just coming over was a big deal, so if you're not comfortable with that, I understand. I just thought—"

"I'll stay." My acceptance surprises even me. "I should go to bed soon, though."

"Okay. Sure." He looks into my eyes, and I have the feeling he's getting ready to say something else. He bites his lower lip and looks down.

He gives me a fresh toothbrush in a new package, along with

a set of his pajamas, and goes to bed. I change in the bathroom. The pajamas are too big on me, and I have to roll up the pant legs and sleeves.

Above his sink is a medicine cabinet with mirrored doors. On impulse, I open it. Inside, I see the usual things—a jar of petroleum jelly, a package of Q-tips—and then on the bottom shelf, a row of amber pharmacy bottles. Eight of them. I don't recognize all the names, but my gaze catches on one word: *fluoxetine.* The generic form of Prozac.

I close the cabinets.

In the living room, I stretch out on the couch and pull a thin wool blanket over myself. After an hour of shifting around, I finally drift off.

CHAPTER THIRTEEN

Stanley lies on an operating table, unconscious. His ribs are splayed open, his lungs exposed, pink and damp and spongy. They inflate and deflate with each breath. Nestled between them, where his heart should be, there's a model plane with a painted smile. Veins and arteries run in and out of its little cockpit.

The wing is broken. If I don't fix it, he'll die. But I realize, with rising panic, that I have no idea what I'm doing. My latex-gloved hands tremble. I'm holding a bloodstained scalpel in one, a tube of superglue in the other. Stanley's breathing hisses softly through the mask over his mouth and nose. A heart monitor beeps in time with his pulse.

"Well? What the hell are you waiting for?" My head jerks up to see a nurse staring impatiently at me. It's Ms. Nell, her mouth and nose hidden by a surgical mask. "Patch him up!"

But I can't move.

The heart monitor lets out a loud, steady beep as he flatlines.

I wake with a start, pajama shirt clinging to sweaty skin. I kick off the covers, stumble over to the light switch, and turn it on. With light, reality reasserts itself. I exhale a shaky breath and flop back onto the couch. A vision of the broken plane flashes behind my closed eyelids.

I broke something precious to him. On my very first visit to his house.

I have to fix it. I have to at least *try*.

I creep down the hallway, toward his room. Outside his door, I pause. With luck, I can retrieve the plane and slip out without waking him.

I ease the door open a crack and peer in. Stanley has the covers pulled up over his head, so I can only see a bit of blond hair sticking out, and the plane is still sitting on his nightstand, in two pieces. Holding my breath, I tiptoe toward it.

I stop.

He's breathing oddly—small, hitching, shuddering gasps, not quite muffled by the covers. My eyes strain against the darkness. I can see him moving a little. A nightmare?

He utters a soft moan. His breaths rise and fall, rise and fall, getting faster.

"Stanley," I say loudly.

He lets out a startled cry. His head emerges from under the blankets. In the faint moonlight from the window, I can just make out his wide eyes, bed-mussed hair, and flushed cheeks. "Alvie! Wh-what the hell—?"

"You were breathing very fast," I say.

"I— What are you doing in here?"

"I want to fix your plane."

"Now?" His voice is oddly squeaky. He pulls the covers up to his neck, squirming. He won't look directly at me.

"What's wrong."

"Nothing!"

I stare. The intensity in his voice confirms that it's not, in fact, nothing.

"Please." He gulps. "I need a minute. Can you—can you go in the kitchen, or something?"

I think about the breathing, the movement, his flushed face. Something clicks into place inside my head. "You were masturbating."

He makes a sound like he's choking. "N-no! I just—"

"Go ahead." I step out of the room, close the door, and go into the kitchen. Getting back to sleep seems unlikely at this point, so I brew a pot of coffee, pour myself a cup, and sit at the table, waiting.

I hear the shower running, then creaking floorboards. Stanley steps into the kitchen, leaning on his cane, his skin still damp. He's wearing blue pajama pants, thick socks, and a rumpled, long-sleeved shirt with a *Tyrannosaurus rex* skeleton on the front. Slowly he lowers himself into a chair, not looking at me.

I sip my coffee. "Did you finish."

The flush in his cheeks brightens. He hunches over, curling in on himself, as if trying to disappear. "No. I took a cold shower."

I should have known he'd be embarrassed, but it still strikes me as peculiar. Animals don't attach any sense of humiliation to sexual pleasure; that would be counterproductive. Why are we the one species that does? "It's a common activity, you know. Over ninety percent of adult males do it, and the majority of females as well. Even fetuses do it."

"Really? Fetuses?"

"Ultrasounds have captured images of in-utero masturbation, yes."

"Huh." He rubs the back of his neck.

It occurs to me, suddenly, that he might have been fantasizing about me. I study my sock-clad feet.

"You came in because you wanted to fix my plane?" he asks.

"That's right."

"In the middle of the night?"

"I couldn't stop thinking about it."

"It's really not that big a deal, you know."

"Yes," I say. "It is. Your planes are important to you. And I won't feel good until it's in one piece again."

He looks at me for a few seconds. "I'll go get it."

A few minutes later, we're sitting at the kitchen table, the broken plane between us, along with a tube of glue, another of green paint, and a tiny paintbrush. Stanley sips coffee from a snowman mug as I apply a line of glue to the wing. He seems to have relaxed a little, now.

The plane, I notice, is not as well made as the others. Its wheels are a bit crooked, its paint job clumsy, its brush strokes visible in places. "When did you put this one together."

"With my dad, when I was eight years old. It was the first one we ever built."

Of course. It had to be this one that I broke.

My unhappiness must show on my face, because he adds hastily, "It's okay. Honestly, it is." He stares into space. "I mean, yeah, this plane is special, but . . . it's complicated. My dad got this for me as a sort of apology."

"For what."

"It doesn't matter now."

I attach the wing to the plane and blow on the glue to dry it. Stanley hasn't said much about his parents. "You said he isn't around anymore. What happened."

With one finger, he spins the little propeller on the end of the plane. "He and Mom separated when I was nine. It was pretty ugly." He fiddles with the tube of glue. His gaze remains fixed on the tabletop. "I wish she hadn't kicked him out. I mean . . . it's not like he meant to hurt me."

The words send a thin chill through me. "What do you mean."

Stanley's lips tighten. For almost a minute, he's silent. "Dad was always a very physical person. That's how he expressed affection. He liked to roughhouse. Just playing, you know? Sometimes, when he'd had a couple of drinks, he'd forget how strong he was and . . . well, he broke my arm."

I open my mouth, but nothing comes out.

"It was a bad break," Stanley said. "I needed surgery. Mom never forgave him. After he moved out, I only really saw him on holidays, and then even that stopped. Maybe he was afraid of hurting me again . . . or maybe he was just using that as an excuse because he didn't have the guts to stick around. God knows

I wasn't an easy kid to raise. But still, he didn't have to—" He stops. Takes a breath. "I still talk to him on the phone every once in a while, and he sends me money when I need it. He's paid for most of my classes and medical expenses. And I'm grateful for that . . . I am. Without it, I don't know where I'd be right now. But the last time I asked him if he wanted to meet for lunch sometime, he got really quiet. And then he said that it would be better if we didn't. Better for me." Stanley's hand curls slowly into a fist. "He didn't even show up for Mom's funeral. He called and apologized afterward—said it was just too painful for him. I had to stand there alone while they lowered her into the ground."

He picks up the model plane, gently blows on the glue, and puts a few dabs of paint on the wing. When he's done, he sets the plane on the table. "There. What did I tell you? Good as new."

A band of dark green paint covers the break. It's not quite the same shade; it's obvious that it's been repaired.

It takes me a few seconds to find my voice. "I'm sorry," I say. I don't know if I'm apologizing for the plane, or for everything else.

He smiles. There's a tightness around the edges, like it hurts. "It's okay. It could be a lot worse. I'm lucky, really—"

I touch the back of his hand, and he falls silent. For a few minutes, we don't speak. His eyes shine with unshed tears, and he blinks rapidly, never letting them slip out.

He wipes one sleeve across his eyes and smiles again. It looks a little more natural this time. "You want breakfast? I've got eggs."

CHAPTER FOURTEEN

When I leave Stanley's house later that morning, the world is wet with rain, the pavement shining, the sky nearly dark. The faint, pearl-gray light of dawn tinges the horizon.

There's a strange sensation in my chest. Hollowness—no, that's not quite right. Lightness. Everything feels heightened. As morning spreads over the world, it glows like an overexposed photograph, as if the air itself is charged with electric particles. So much has happened over the past few days, I don't know how to process it.

Overall, I decide, the experience was positive.

I'm not expecting to see Dr. Bernhardt for another week. But that afternoon, when I return from work, his car is parked in front of my building.

He's standing outside, wearing a tweed jacket and holding a black umbrella. I get out of the car and face him. His clothes are damp, his glasses misted with rain. A steady drizzle still falls from the sky, forming tiny ripples in the puddles on the pavement.

This is the second time he's shown up ahead of schedule. He *knows* how disconcerting that is to me. "It's not Wednesday," I say.

"I realize that. I apologize for visiting unannounced. But after that call the other day, I wanted to talk to you in person. To be honest, I was disturbed. You seemed . . . rattled. I don't think I'd ever heard so much emotion in your voice."

I study my shoes. "I shouldn't have called you. I know that. I was suffering from lack of sleep. My judgment was impaired—"

"No, no. I don't mean it like that. I just wanted to make sure you were all right."

"I'm fine now. I no longer want bupropion."

He frowns, studying my face through the small, round lenses of his spectacles. "Well, I'm glad, but I have to say . . . I'm concerned that *I* might have been responsible for that episode."

Rain plasters my shirt to my back. I'm starting to shiver. "What do you mean."

"*I* encouraged you to start meeting people. I thought that having more social contact might improve your stability, but it seems to have had the opposite effect."

The muscles in my back stiffen. "I *am* stable."

It's raining harder now. The droplets hammer down on us.

"Should we go inside?" he asks.

"I have things to do," I mutter.

He sighs. "All right. Let me just say this. Human connections are important. But becoming too attached too quickly can be just as detrimental as solitude. If your obsession with this boy has begun to disrupt your everyday life, you may be slipping into a codependent relationship."

I clutch my keys, the metal ridges digging into my fingers. "You want me to stop seeing Stanley."

"No. This is your choice. Just . . . be careful."

"Your advice is noted." I turn away from him, and walk toward the building.

"Alvie."

I freeze.

"Don't forget about the appointment with Judge Gray."

Cold rain trickles inside my shirt collar. What is Dr. Bernhardt trying to say?

He has no control over the judge's final decision. But his opinion as my caseworker will influence her. Will he speak poorly of my judgment if I keep seeing Stanley? It occurs to me that having to wait another year for legal independence is not the worst thing that could happen at that court appearance. Judge Gray might decide I need *more* state supervision. She might strip away some of the rights and freedoms I currently possess.

"I haven't forgotten," I say.

He nods, smiles an unreadable smile, and gets into the car. "I'll see you next Wednesday." The door closes, and he drives off, tires splashing through the puddles.

I grit my teeth. Dr. Bernhardt was the reason I started talking to Stanley online in the first place. He's the one who told me to open up to people. And now he seems to think I'm not ready for a relationship. *Codependent.* He's become another doctor, extracting my emotions and sticking medical labels on them. Or maybe he's like Toby's friend—maybe he believes that broken people like me shouldn't *have* relationships. At the thought, something inside my chest stiffens.

His words keep replaying in my head. *Becoming too attached too quickly can be just as detrimental as solitude.* For so long, I believed that getting close to another person would be dangerous for me. Dr. Bernhardt always told me that fear was unfounded—always insisted that I was capable of more than I thought—but now he seems to have changed his mind.

Maybe he's finally realized just how damaged I am.

The stairs creak beneath my feet as I make my way up to my floor. My fingers are still tightly curled around my keys.

In the hallway, an electric light sputters fitfully overhead. The smell of rancid Gouda invades my nostrils. A sneeze builds up, prickling, in my sinuses. My chest feels tight and hot; the air is thick and stale. It's like breathing flat, lukewarm soda. On impulse, I turn around and walk back out into the cool, rainy afternoon.

I need to see Stanley.

Westerly College is a collection of neutral beige buildings, grassy lawns, and trees. It resembles a corporate training camp. Stanley has told me before that he doesn't much like this school, but it's one of the few that's both affordable and close enough for an easy commute.

I know his class lets out at five o'clock today, so I park in the huge, nearly full lot in front of the science building, where he's presumably having his neurobiology class, and wait. I get out of my car, walk up to the building, and peer into the lobby. It's the first time I've actually seen his school up close. Inside, an anthropomorphic shark smiles from a pendant on the wall—a sports mascot of some type, I assume.

After a short while, students start to filter out of the building. The glass double doors swing open, and I glimpse Stanley's face. I start to relax—then every muscle in my body goes tense.

There's a girl his age walking next to him, arm hooked through his. She's wearing a glossy pink coat, and her blond hair drifts in gauzy puffs around her face, like cotton candy. They're smiling and talking together, though I can't make out the words. Stanley says something, and she laughs, her mouth opening wide to reveal rows of tiny white teeth.

They freeze in their tracks. Stanley blinks. "Alvie?"

The girl is small and pretty and has round blue eyes, like a doll's. She looks me up and down, taking in my oversized T-shirt, ragged-edged skirt, and rumpled stockings, then gives me a tight smile. There's a miniscule smear of pink lipstick on one of her incisors. "Oh, hello." Her arm is still linked with his.

He clears his throat and gently tugs the arm free. "This is Dorothy. Dorothy, this is my friend Alvie."

"Alvie, huh? Like that guy from the movie *Annie Hall*?"

"It's not spelled the same," I mutter. There's a heavy, sugary smell around her—perfume or shampoo, something artificial. It makes my nose itch.

"Do you like that movie?" she asks. I'm not sure which of us she's speaking to, but I haven't seen it, so I don't say anything.

Stanley takes it upon himself to fill the silence: "It's one of my favorites."

She beams. "Mine, too."

I want Dorothy to go away.

I inch closer to Stanley and grip his arm, so suddenly that he gives a start. Dorothy's gaze flicks toward my hand, clamped like talons around his biceps. I don't move. It's satisfying to watch her too-white smile fade.

She clears her throat. "So, um. I'll see you tomorrow?"

"Sure. See you."

Her gaze darts toward me, then back to Stanley. She lingers another few seconds, then turns and walks away, back toward the building.

"Alvie." Stanley's voice is strained.

I release his arm. "Sorry." Until that moment, I didn't realize quite how tightly I was gripping him.

"What's wrong?"

I cross my arms over my chest. A minute ago, I was eager to talk to him, but now I can't even remember what I wanted to say. "Are you— I mean, is she—" I swallow. There's a squeezing sensation in my chest, like strong fingers clamped around my heart.

"She's in my neurobiology class," he says, sounding puzzled.

"She was"—I point at his arm—"with you."

"Oh. That? That's just—you know." He gestures toward his cane. "She was being considerate. Ever since I broke my leg, she's insisted on walking me out. It's kind of annoying, actually, but I don't have the heart to tell her to stop."

The invisible hand stops squeezing my chest, but a strange sensation lingers in the pit of my stomach, an uncomfortable awareness of my own reactions.

"So what brings you here?" he asks. "I mean, I'm glad to see you. I just didn't expect it."

I study my shoes. Confusion swirls inside me. I need space to think, to process these feelings. "I just wanted to see you. But I—I can't stay."

"Oh." His brows bunch together. "Well, okay. I'll talk to you later, I guess."

I get into the car. As I drive away, my hands tighten on the steering wheel. She's just a fellow student; Stanley said so, and I believe him. But the hard knot lodged in my gut won't go away.

I managed to convince myself that Stanley and I were in the same situation—two outcasts on the fringes of society—but that isn't the case. He has plenty of options, even if he doesn't realize it. When he was with Dorothy, they both looked so relaxed, so at ease in that way that normal people take for granted.

This sick feeling in my stomach is not jealousy. Nothing so simple. It's the realization that I will never—can never give him that carefree feeling.

Nothing about me is easy.

CHAPTER FIFTEEN

I drive around for a while. I don't even know where I'm going. My mind drifts, and my body moves on autopilot. When I come back to myself, I'm sitting in the parking lot of my old grade school, a large, institutional-looking beige-brick building with narrow windows.

Why did I come *here*? I haven't set foot in this place for years.

Sometimes, in my dreams, I still see the hallways—the olive-green tiles and dull blue lockers. I remember the musty, papery smell, a blend of old carpet and laminated posters and sawdust.

Some of my memories are dim, because I spent much of my time here in a drugged haze. Dr. Evans, my psychiatrist, kept increasing the dosage of my antianxiety medication, but no matter how many pills I took, I could still feel the pressure building inside of me.

"I wish I didn't need the pills," I told her once, during our weekly meeting. "I wish I didn't have to control my feelings all the time."

"Symptoms," she replied. "The medication controls your *symptoms.*"

I left the office feeling as though she had eaten some invisible part of me.

Reflected sunlight strikes the school's windows, turning them molten gold. My vision goes fuzzy. And suddenly I am ten years old, a small, wiry girl with braided hair, pale skin, and a blank expression. I shuffle down the narrow hallway, watching my blurred reflection in the shiny tiles.

There's a burst of laughter. Ahead, I see a group of three boys clustered around a smaller, chubbier boy whose eyes are pink and puffy from tears. I recognize him. Last year, his father committed suicide. People talked about it.

"You know *why* he killed himself, right?" a voice says loudly. "It's because he couldn't stand having a fag for a son."

More laughter.

The blood pounds in my head, louder and louder. A red mist slips across my vision. Slowly I approach.

One of the bigger boys turns toward me, grinning. "Hey look, it's Robo-tard—"

My fist slams into his teeth, knocking him backward. His arms flail.

The fight itself is a blur. They pull my hair and grab me and try to push me down, but I just keep hitting and kicking them. Drops of blood spatter the tiles. A punch lands on my stomach, but I barely feel it. I bite down on a hand, and there's a scream.

I've lashed out at bullies before but never like this. I've snapped.

I don't know why it took the sight of them hurting someone else to make it happen, but it feels so good that I can't stop. When it's all over, the boys are scurrying down the hall, and I'm slumped against the lockers, panting and sweaty. There's blood on my knuckles.

Later, I sit in the principal's office, fidgeting in the hard plastic chair. My left cheek aches. A bruise is already forming.

The principal looks at me with his tiny, dark, shrewlike eyes.

He doesn't like me. I know this because, once, after a meltdown and a visit to his office, I pressed my ear to his closed door and overheard him talking to his secretary: *There's something unnatural about that girl. Sometimes she seems like a little adult, and sometimes she's like a wild animal. I never know how to handle her.*

"I'm not sure you really understand the seriousness of what you've done," he says. "You injured three other students. Several witnesses have said you attacked them unprovoked. I know you have unique challenges, and I've tried to be tolerant, but I can't have this kind of violence in my school. Do you understand?"

I glare. "What they said to that boy is worse than what I did to them."

He breathes in slowly through his nose, then exhales. "You should have found a teacher, or come straight to me and told me about it."

"I tried that before. I tried it when it was *me* being hurt, but nothing ever changed. If you think I'm going to keep taking it, you're an idiot."

His mouth is a small, flat line. He picks up the phone and dials.

Shortly after, Mama arrives in the principal's office. He tells her what happened. She listens in silence, her face getting paler and paler.

"I'm very sorry, Ms. Fitz. Your daughter needs more specialized care than we can give her. As I'm sure you're aware, there are schools for children like her, which will be better able to provide for her needs."

Mama clutches the strap of her purse. The skin around her fingernails turns white. "You can't do this to us." Her voice sounds small and shaky, like a little girl's. "Please. She—she was making so much progress—"

"This will be better for Alvie," the principal says. "For all of us, you included." His voice changes tone, going soft and syrupy. "You're under a lot of strain, aren't you? Working full-time, caring for your daughter alone. You need a rest. Perhaps if you had some extra support—"

Mama lurches to her feet. The principal tenses, grabs a thick binder and holds it up in front of him like a shield. I shift in my chair. Mama is breathing hard, glassy-eyed. "You don't know the first thing about me," she says. "You don't know what I've been through. Don't tell me what I *need.*"

"Of course." He fidgets. "I just mean—"

"What I *need* is for you to give my daughter another chance. She deserves to have a normal childhood. Do you understand?" Her voice is getting higher and higher. "If you expel her, I swear to God, I will sue you for everything you own. I'll bring down this entire school."

His face tightens. “Ms. Fitz, I’m going to have to ask you to leave. And take your child with you.”

Her fingers twitch and curl inward. She looks like she might lunge across the desk and grab his throat. “None of you understand.” The words are thick and choked. “You don’t know how hard she’s tried—how hard *I’ve* tried. You think you can just rip that away? Don’t you *see*—?”

“Mama,” I whisper. “It’s okay.”

She blinks a few times . . . then the tightness in her face loosens, and her shoulders sag. She turns away. “Let’s go, Alvie.”

When we leave the school, the air smells like rain, and clouds hang low in the sky. Little bits of gravel crunch under my shoes as we walk to the car. During the drive home, Mama doesn’t talk. She doesn’t even turn on the radio. I kick my feet. Outside, crows sit on the telephone wires, watching us.

“Mama,” I say, “do you know that a group of crows is called a murder.”

Silence.

“They can be called a flock, too. But sometimes people call it a murder of crows.”

Still nothing.

“Crows are really smart. They break off pieces of leaves or grass and use them as tools to get at food.”

“Alvie, please. Not now.”

When we get back home, she starts brewing a pot of coffee, then seems to forget about it. She wanders around in the kitchen, grabs a rag, and starts to wipe off the table, even though it’s already clean. She gets down on her knees, opens a drawer, and takes out a small piece of paper. I'm not close enough to see it, but I know what she keeps there. It's a picture of my father—the only one she has. He's standing in the sunlight, holding the handles of a bicycle, smiling. He's tall and lanky, with very short hair and thick, black-framed glasses. There's a date scratched onto the back in pencil; it's from a few months before I was born.

I grab an oversized, floppy plush rabbit from the couch and sit on the living room floor, the rabbit in my lap. After a few minutes, she puts the picture away, comes in, sits on the couch, and looks at me with tense lines around her eyes and mouth.

I wait for her to ask me questions about what happened, but she doesn't.

"You were so close, Alvie. You almost made it to the end of the school year." She rests her elbows on her knees, and her head falls into her hands. "Why *now*?"

I curl into a tighter ball and hide my face against the rabbit.

"Just tell me, please." Her voice breaks. "What is it you *want*? I'm trying, but I don't know how to help you. Tell me what you need. Tell me how I can make this stop. Should I send you to more doctors?"

"I don't want to go to doctors anymore," I say, my voice muffled against the rabbit's fur.

"What, then? Am I supposed to do what that man says and send you to a special school? To one of those places where half the children can't even talk?"

"I could just stay at home. You could teach me."

She pushes her fingers through her hair. "Honey, that's not . . . You need to learn social interaction. Keeping you isolated would be the *worst* thing. I want you to have a life. I want you to have friends. I want you to have the chance to go to college someday, and have children of your own. That will never happen if we don't fix this."

She puts her hands over her face. "I keep having this dream," she whispers through her hands, "where you're forty years old and everything is still the same. You're in your room all day, drawing those mazes over and over. I'm trying to do what's best for you, but it's so hard. It's so hard to know what's right."

My arms tighten around the plush rabbit. I curl into a tiny ball, the rabbit's head tucked under my chin, and begin to rock back and forth. I can't look directly at her, but I'm very aware of Mama's soft sniffling, her hitching breaths. Each one hurts.

"Sometimes," she whispers, "you seem so far away."

I don't know what she means. I'm sitting right in front of her.

"It's like this thing is getting worse," she says. "Like you're drifting away, and I can't save you."

Her words don't make any sense to me. But I know that she's sad right now, and I know it's my fault. My fingers dig into the rabbit's plush fur. I'm afraid of saying the wrong thing, of making her hurt even more, so I don't say anything.

She draws in a shaky breath. "I'm sorry." She wipes her eyes and gives me a wobbly smile. "Let's go out. We'll go to the lake. How does that sound?"

The tension eases out of me. I like the lake. "Okay."

As we drive, Mama says, "We'll get through this. You'll see. Things will change. I don't know how, yet, but I really believe they will. Do you want to listen to music?"

"Yes."

We play a cassette tape. I rest my cheek against the window. My breath fogs the glass as fields and houses roll past outside. There's a tightness around the base of my throat, like an invisible wire. "I'm sorry I'm so much trouble, Mama."

At first she doesn't say anything. "It's not your fault, honey. If anything, it's mine."

I shift in my seat. Outside, fields and strip malls roll past.

"You were such a happy baby." Her voice is very soft, like she's talking in her sleep. "You were perfectly normal. And then you started school, and suddenly there were all these . . . problems, and you couldn't seem to play with the other children. Sometimes you would come home and just sit on your bed rocking back and forth . . ." Her voice breaks. "The doctors all say that it's just something that happens, that the parents have nothing to do with it. But I keep thinking, what if they're wrong? What if it *is* something I did? Or what if I could have *changed* it, if I'd recognized it sooner and gotten you help before all the trouble started or . . . I don't know." She rubs at the corners of her eyes. "I feel like I—I failed you."

It's not like that. I *know* it's not. But I don't know how to make her understand. I don't have the words.

When she speaks again, her voice is barely audible: "I miss the real you."

A chill runs through me. *I* am *real, Mama,* I want to say, but suddenly my throat is locked.

"I know you're still in there, though," she adds quickly, as if realizing she's made a mistake. "Just . . . underneath . . . everything."

I can see the lake ahead, blue and peaceful, but the sick feeling in my stomach won't go away. *I'm not "in there," Mama. I'm right here. Don't you see me?*

When we get to the lake, Mama spreads a picnic blanket on the sand and puts out sandwiches. I sit next to her, holding a peanut butter and jelly sandwich and looking out at the glassy smooth water. It's part of Lake Michigan, Mama has told me, but just a little part; the lake is so big, it touches four different states, but this beach feels small and private. The sand is a little white crescent with a fringe of trees around the edge.

I take a bite. The sandwich feels dry and gluey in my mouth. I try to focus on the warmth of the sun, the cool breeze, and the soothing rush of the little waves lapping the shore.

Mama reaches out to stroke my hair. I'm not expecting it, so I flinch a little, and she pretends not to notice. "I love you so much. You're my world. You know that, don't you?"

A lump of sandwich sticks in my throat. I swallow it down.

I miss the real you.

I wonder which "me" Mama is talking to.

"You know that, don't you?" she says again.

I manage a tiny nod. Normally I would say, *I love you, too.* But I'm suddenly too afraid to speak at all.

A hermit crab crawls slowly across the sand. I shut out

everything else and observe the movement of its segmented legs, the wavering of its antennae, the gleam of its tiny bulbous eyes.

"Miss? Excuse me, miss?"

I look up, blinking. An overweight man with thin, graying hair stands outside my car, squinting at me. "May I ask what you're doing here?"

I don't know how long I've been sitting in the parking lot outside the school. But I'm surprised anyone is here this late. "Nothing." I shift the car into reverse.

"Do I know you?" the man asks in a strange voice.

I freeze and look up again. It's my old principal. He's heavier than I remember, and there are more lines etched into his face, but he has the same tiny, watery eyes. "No," I say. "We've never met." Before he has a chance to say anything else, I pull out of the lot.

The windshield wipers swish back and forth, cutting through the rain. The world is a gray haze.

My phone buzzes. There's a text message from Stanley. *Are you okay?* I stare at it until the words blur.

I pull over and text back: *Fine.*

You left so suddenly.

Sorry.

After a minute, he texts: *Are you free tonight?*

I reply: *Meet me at 8. Buster's.*

I glance in the rearview mirror. My complexion is pasty, making the dark circles under my eyes stand out. My lips are chapped and bitten.

If I am going to see Stanley, I have to at least try to make myself presentable. I don't own any makeup—I've always hated how it feels on my face—so I scrape together a few dollars from change buried under the seat cushions in my car and buy a small jar of foundation from the drugstore. I spread some over the dark flesh under my eyes and look in the rearview mirror. Not a big improvement, but it's something.

You're a beautiful, intelligent young woman, Stanley said last night at his house. It's absurd, but I don't want to give him any reason to stop thinking that.

CHAPTER SIXTEEN

"Alvie?"

I've been watching the cream swirl in my coffee. Now I look up, blinking. "What."

"I asked if you're thinking about anything," Stanley says.

We're sitting in a corner booth at Buster's. Stanley was already there, waiting, when I arrived.

I trace the rim of my coffee cup with one finger and reply, "I was thinking about rabbits. About how logical they are."

"Logical?"

"When a female rabbit is pregnant, but isn't ready to give birth—if she's under stress, or doesn't have enough food, or if there's something wrong with the embryo—she'll reabsorb the young into her body."

He frowns—uneasy, or maybe just puzzled.

A picture flashes through my head: the tranquil blue of the lake, and Mama sitting on the picnic blanket beside me, her bare, lightly freckled arms folded over her knees, her hair—the same red as mine—hanging around her face, her pale gray eyes fixed on a point in the far distance. Mama once told me that when she was a child, she was a lot like me. Very quiet, very shy. Maybe not to the same degree, but she was never the sort of woman who surrounded herself with friends. I suspect my father was the only man she ever slept with, and he didn't stay long.

She was nineteen when she had me. Only two years older than I am now.

"With rabbits," I continue, "no kits are born until the time is right." My gaze drifts toward the window. Outside, a truck rumbles by, salting the roads. "Logical. Isn't it."

"I guess so." His teeth catch on his lower lip, tugging. He always looks younger when he does that. "I mean, obviously it's better if these things are planned. But lots of kids aren't, and their parents still love them."

Love.

A shudder runs through my body, and something inside me clamps tightly shut. "Love doesn't magically fix a bad situation. It doesn't pay the bills or put food on the table."

"No. I guess not." His voice sounds very small and faraway.

I should have kept my mouth shut—I can tell he's uncomfortable—but I get tired of hearing people talk about love as if it's some magical medicine. Love can make people irrational, cause them to behave stupidly and recklessly. Or worse. I don't associate love with safety or warmth; I associate it with fear, with losing control. With drowning.

I finish my coffee, not tasting it. I didn't order anything to eat;

my appetite has shriveled up.

"Are you sure everything is okay?"

My shoulders stiffen. "I'm fine."

He looks away, his lips pressed together in a pale line. Outside the window, the rain has turned to wet, messy snow. It drifts down in fat flakes, piling up against the glass.

He takes a deep breath. "Alvie, I—"

The door swings open. Three teenage boys stomp in, wearing coats and knitted caps with poof balls on top, and slouch into a booth on the other side of the restaurant. They're talking loudly, voices overlapping and blending together. One of them, a blond with an assortment of piercings, pulls off his hat and props his feet on the table. Raucous laughter fills the restaurant.

Stanley glances at them, then turns back toward me. "Look . . . I'm not an idiot. I know something is wrong. I won't push you if you don't want to talk about it. But if I said or did something to upset you, I want to know. You—"

More laughter erupts from the table. One of the young men is holding two of the round, knitted hats over his chest like a pair of breasts while the other pretends to fondle them. Stanley grits his teeth.

"Ohhhh, baby!" one boy squawks in a piercing falsetto. The blond boy, meanwhile, is sucking the poof ball on the hat like a nipple.

"You suck dat titty, mista!" the other boy says in a phony accent. "You suck it good!"

More laughing.

"Hey," the blond says, "you heard this one? So a hot dog and a dick are talking, and the hot dog says—"

"Excuse me," Stanley calls, raising his voice and turning toward them, "could you keep it down? You're in a restaurant."

The young men fall silent, their gazes locking onto us. The blond narrows his eyes. He looks like Draco Malfoy from the Harry Potter movies, except for the silver studs in his ears and nose. "You want to say that again?" Draco says. "I didn't quite catch it."

"I said—"

I grip Stanley's arm. "Let's just go." Right now, the last thing I want to deal with is a pack of half-grown jackals eager to assert their dominance.

Stanley tenses and opens his mouth as if to argue. Then he drops his gaze, throws some money on the table, and stands, gripping his cane. He hobbles stiffly toward the door, and I trail behind him, positioning myself between him and the teenagers.

"Smart move," Draco calls. I ignore him.

Outside, in the parking lot, Stanley stumbles. I hook my arm around his, steadying him.

He tugs his arm free, gaze averted. "Where's your car?"

"I walked. What about yours."

"The lot was full." He gestures toward the row of cars in front of the restaurant. "I had to park down the street. It's another block or so."

I glance at one of the empty spots nearby.

"Those are handicapped spots," he says.

"But aren't you—" I stop, and close my mouth.

"Other people need those more than I do."

I look at him from the corner of my eye as we keep walking. His car stands at the end of the street, under a lone streetlight. It seems very far away.

His limp seems more pronounced than usual as our feet crunch in the thin, dirty layer of snow. The street is empty, and the silence is thick. Even my own heartbeat sounds oddly muted.

He stumbles again. I hook an arm through his. "Lean against me."

He pulls back. "I'm fine."

"Lean against me, or you'll fall."

He staggers away, topples against a streetlight, and clings to it for balance. "I'm fine!"

I stare.

He slides down the streetlight, to the pavement. His cane falls to his side. His breath hitches. "God damn it," he whispers hoarsely, and squeezes his eyes shut. He's breathing heavily, still clinging to the streetlight.

I take a small, hesitant step toward him. He doesn't look up. Then a steady *thump-thump* breaks the silence. Footsteps. Behind us.

A tingle of electricity runs through my nerves, and instantly, my body and mind are on high alert. When I turn, I see three forms walking down the street toward us, their faces lost in shadow.

I grab Stanley's hand and pull him to his feet.

He fumbles with his cane. "Alvie? What—"

I lean closer to him and whisper, "Keep moving." We begin to walk. I slip my hand into the pocket of my coat, where my keys are, and I hold them so they're sticking out between my fingers like brass knuckles.

Stanley glances over his shoulder, too. "They're probably just walking back to their car." But his tone is low and tense.

I don't say anything, just grip the keys harder. In my head I make a map of a human body with all the soft places marked in red: the eyes, the throat, the kidneys, the groin. I look around to see if there's anyone we can call out to for help, but the street is deserted.

The footsteps sound louder now. I look over my shoulder.

The guys behind us are walking faster, catching up. It's them—the ones from the restaurant, still wearing those stupid poof-ball hats. But they move with the swift, steady gait of predators.

"Alvie, run," Stanley whispers. He's breathing very fast. "Don't worry about me. Just get out of here."

"Forget it." My arm tightens on his. The young men behind us are ominously silent.

I grit my teeth.

One of them—the blond, the one I've been thinking of as Draco—breaks off from the group and circles around so that he's standing in front of us. He's smiling, showing a sliver of white teeth. The two others are still behind us, cutting off our path of retreat. They look so similar, they might as well be twins . . . and they're both huge, with letterman jackets, thick necks, and thin brown hair peeking out from under their hats. Somehow, they didn't seem nearly so big in the restaurant.

I press closer to Stanley's side. My heartbeat fills my whole body, down to my fingertips and toes. I recognize these people. I've never seen them before tonight, but I recognize them all the same.

They're the thousand enemies.

CHAPTER SEVENTEEN

"Relax," Draco says, still smiling. "We're not going to hurt you. We just want a polite, sincere apology." His accent and vocabulary have a whiff of college—upper middle class—but his shoulders are thrust forward in the aggressive stance of a thug. I wonder if he's armed.

Stanley's pulse jumps visibly in his throat. "We don't want any trouble."

"Great," Draco says. "Neither do we. So how about it? To show us you mean it, maybe you should get down on your knees first."

The twins snort laughter, lips pressed together to hide their smiles. They're trying to look menacing. They're big enough that they don't have to try very hard.

"What if we say no?" Stanley says.

Draco raises his eyebrows. "Well, then, we might have to express our disappointment."

My arm tightens on Stanley's. He moves in front of me, shielding me with his body.

Draco glances at me. "Who's the redhead? Does she talk?"

"Leave her alone," Stanley says, his voice forceful.

"Oh, suddenly he grows a dick," one of the twins says.

"This your girlfriend?" Draco is staring straight at me. I stare back. "Not bad."

"Stay away from her," Stanley says.

"Or what?"

My hand is still in my pocket, gripping my keys. My upper lip twitches and pulls back from my teeth. My head burns, and my brain seems to be swelling. I can feel it pulsing, pushing against the backs of my eyes.

"I mean it," Stanley says. "If you come any closer, I'll—"

"What? You're gonna fight me?" He gives Stanley a hard shove.

Stanley stumbles, then lunges forward. Draco pushes him again, and he reels backward, nearly falling. I catch him, stumbling under his weight. I can feel him shaking with fury as he gasps for breath.

The twins bark laughter. They sound like seals. Something is happening inside my head, like clouds churning, darkness seeping through my brain.

"What do you say?" Draco's gaze doesn't leave me. "Want to ditch this gimp loser and come with us?"

I open my mouth. But instead of words, a catlike hiss slides out of my throat.

The twins' laughter dies down to silence. Draco's smile fades.

When I was a small child, I would sometimes revert to animal behavior during stressful situations. I learned to control the tendency as I got older . . . but now the impulse wells up from some deep place inside me, and I give myself over to it. I clench my fists and stomp one foot on the ground, growling low in my throat, the way rabbits will do when they're warning off another animal.

The twins' mouths hang open.

I stomp harder, growling and hiss at them as loud as I can, spraying spittle into the air. "Enemy!" I shout. The blood roars in my skull like a waterfall. I snap my teeth together. "Enemy, enemy, enemy!"

Draco takes a step back. "Jesus," he mutters.

My heart beats faster. It's as if, suddenly, my strange, shameful tendencies have been transformed into a power.

I hiss and stomp some more. Draco's smirk slides back into place, but he's putting on a show now; I can sense his fear, almost smell it. He's not going to come another step closer. "Well, they say crazy girls are the best in bed," he says loudly.

On cue, the twins start laughing again. Stanley's back goes rigid. Without a sound, he charges at Draco and swings his cane, hard. It smacks against the side of Draco's head.

Draco staggers. "Fuck!" he yelps. Before he can regain his balance, Stanley swings the cane again, smacking him on the other side of the head. Draco's hand flies to his temple.

The twins are doubled over, howling, as if the whole thing is a show. "Nice job, TJ," one calls, "getting your ass kicked by a cripple."

"Shut up!"

I've fallen silent, caught off guard.

Stanley's breathing hard, brandishing the cane like a sword, teeth clenched. He and Draco—*TJ*—move in little jerks; TJ lurches at him, and Stanley jabs him in the stomach with the cane. "I'm going to shove that thing up your ass!" TJ growls. He glares at the twins. "Help me, you dumb fucks!"

"Nah," one says, leaning against the other, "this is funny."

TJ is panting, eyes bugging out with rage. He lunges at Stanley again, and Stanley swings his cane. It whistles through the air, but this time TJ ducks, avoiding it. He catches the cane and yanks, and Stanley staggers. With a sweep of one arm, TJ knocks the cane from his grasp. Stanley swings a fist, and TJ's head snaps to one side. For a second, they're both a blur of movement, then TJ kicks him in the stomach, hard.

Stanley goes down, lands on his arm, and cries out. His forehead bounces off the pavement. In the next instant, TJ kicks Stanley's ribs and stomps on his arm. I hear a *crack*, and Stanley cries out.

I go cold inside.

The twins aren't laughing anymore. "Hey, c'mon, TJ. You don't have to—"

"Fuck you!" TJ brays. "You want to stand there and watch? Watch *this*." He raises his boot again, about to bring it down on Stanley's face, and Stanley curls up, covering his head with both arms.

I lunge. White noise fills my head. Beneath the roar of static, someone is screaming.

When the red curtain lifts, TJ is on the pavement, on his back, gasping and choking. I'm on top of him, my hands locked around his throat, thumbs pressing into his trachea. Crimson stains his pale neck, and I taste blood on my tongue, bright and coppery. His ear is bleeding.

Hands grab me from above, and I snap at them. The twins seize my arms and drag me away.

TJ lurches to his feet and runs away, making sobbing, panting sounds, one hand pressed to his ear. The twins throw me to the ground, then stand there a minute, as if they're not sure what to do next. One of them looks at me, with my blood-smeared mouth and bloodstained fingertips, and mutters, "Christ. Let's just get out of here."

They turn and run after TJ. Their pounding footsteps fade as their forms melt into the shadows.

I climb to my feet, breathing hard. My hoodie is torn. Blood stains my shirt and my chin and my lips, but I don't know how much of it is mine and how much is TJ's. I wipe one sleeve across my face.

The road is dark and quiet, painted in moonlight and shadows. Stanley is curled on the pavement, cradling his arm.

Slowly I approach and crouch beside him. He looks up at me. His breathing is labored, his face ashen. "My arm is broken." His voice sounds oddly calm. Blood soaks through the sleeve of his coat. There's a rip in the fabric, and something is sticking out through the blood-drenched shirt beneath. Something white and sharp.

Dizziness rolls over me. I close my eyes for a moment, regaining control. "I'm going to call an ambulance."

He shakes his head. "Just drive me to the hospital." His voice is very soft, his eyes drowsy and heavy lidded. Everything about this seems wrong. There's a bone sticking out through his skin. He should be screaming, but instead he looks like he's about to drift off to sleep.

"Stanley . . ."

"Ambulances are expensive." He smiles—an eerie, distant smile. "It's not as bad as it looks."

He's not losing consciousness. He's not bleeding to death; he hasn't lost that much. It's just endorphins, flooding his system, numbing him to the pain and putting him into a drug-like trance. But it's still terrifying. It feels like he's floating away to a place where I can't reach him.

"I'll get the car," I say.

I sit in the waiting room, shoulders hunched, arms crossed tightly over my chest. Hours have gone by. As soon as we arrived, the nurses rushed Stanley to the surgical unit to reset the bone. As far as I know, he's still there.

Someone touches my shoulder, and I jerk upright. A young, bespectacled Asian man, probably a nurse, hovers over me. "It'll be a while," he says. "Even after he gets out of surgery, they won't release him for another day or two."

"I want to see him."

The nurse hesitates. "What's your relationship to him?"

What do I say? How can I sum it up in a few words? My mind is a mass of fog; I try to think, but it's like trying to hold water in my fingers. "I'm his friend." As the word leaves my mouth, I feel that I've failed Stanley.

"You can come back tomorrow during visiting hours," the man says. "He won't be up to receiving visitors until then, anyway."

I shake my head. "I'll stay."

"There's nothing you can do right now, and he's in good hands. Go home. Get some sleep."

I glance down at the red smear on my shirt. If anyone noticed, they probably assumed it was from Stanley's injury, but the taste of TJ's blood still lingers faintly in my mouth, despite the countless times I rinsed it out in the sink of the hospital bathroom.

A feeling like that hasn't come over me since . . .

Will Stanley even *want* to see me, after what he witnessed?

I leave the hospital, but I don't go home. I curl up in the backseat of Stanley's car and fall into a numb, empty sleep. I wake a few hours later, shivering, and turn the heat on.

The hospital windows glow, tiny yellow squares in the darkness. I imagine Stanley helpless and unconscious on a surgical table. White-masked faces. Gloves, fingers stained with his blood.

I stay in the car, drifting in and out of darkness, until morning.

CHAPTER EIGHTEEN

When I see Stanley the next day, he's sitting up in his hospital bed, propped on a stack of pillows, his arm in a fiberglass cast and a sling. He's pale, the flesh beneath his eyes dark and bruised.

"Hey." His voice sounds different. It's like hearing a song slightly off-key. He won't meet my gaze.

I hang in the doorway, uncertain. "How is your arm."

"Hurts, but I'll live. They're releasing me today. They wanted me to stay longer, but I said no. This is nothing I haven't been through before. I just want to go home." He gives me a hazy smile. "Think you could drive me?"

During the drive, he remains silent and withdrawn. Maybe he's still groggy from the pain medication.

I wonder if he's going to report the attack to the police. I don't deal with the authorities if I can help it, but as far as I know, he has no such inhibitions. "What did you tell the people at the hospital. About what happened."

"I told them I slipped on a patch of ice."

I clutch my bloodied shirt with one hand, wondering—was it for my sake that he lied? So I wouldn't have to deal with the repercussions?

"I owe you one," he remarks. "If you hadn't done what you did, I'd probably be in a full body cast instead of a sling." But still, he doesn't look at me. He's disturbed. Of course he is. He just saw me go full primate. He watched me almost bite off a man's ear.

When we arrive at his house, I help him into his bed and prop up a stack of pillows. I notice him shivering and pull the covers up to his chest.

"Thanks." The lamp is on, but the room is full of shadows. The model planes stand in rows on his shelf, their colors muted in the dim glow.

I sit on the edge of the bed.

His eyes slip shut, the lids thin and bruised-looking. "I'm sorry," he whispers.

I blink. "For what."

"He said those awful things to you. I was so . . . so *angry.* But I couldn't do anything. It wasn't even a fight, it was a beating."

That's what's bothering him? "It's over now. It doesn't matter."

"Of course it matters." His hand curls into a fist. "The world is full of those people. What good am I if I can't even protect you from them?"

My shoulders stiffen. "I never said I needed to be protected."

"I know. But I *want* to. Just for once, I want to make someone's life easier instead of more difficult. I want to *not* be a burden. Is that wrong?"

"You aren't a burden. Stop saying ridiculous things." The words come out harsher than I intend.

His unsteady breathing fills the room. "Sorry." He smiles without teeth, gaze averted. "Just groggy, I guess."

I push myself to my feet. "You should take your pain meds."

I give him his pills we got from the pharmacy earlier, along with a glass of water, and he swallows them down. "You can go, if you want," he murmurs. "I'm just going to sleep for a while."

I don't move. Something is wrong, something that goes beyond what happened with those thugs. "Talk to me."

His lips press into a thin line. He looks away.

"Stanley."

He closes his eyes. Several minutes pass, and I start to think he's fallen asleep. Then he begins to speak, his voice quiet and strangely calm. "You've noticed, right? I mean . . . my eyes."

"What about them."

"I thought for sure you'd have figured it out by now," he says. "You know so much about so many things. But then, it's a pretty rare condition."

"What is."

"Osteogenesis imperfecta. Which is a fancy way of saying my bones break easily. I can do most things without trouble, but . . . let's just say I didn't play a whole lot of sports as a kid."

I remember him talking about breaking his fibula, about how much he hated hospitals. *I'm a klutz*, he had said. "How many did you break."

"Over my whole life? I don't know. I lost count around fifty."

"Fifty breaks." My voice sounds odd. Distant.

"Most of those happened when I was a kid. Bones are more fragile when they're growing. I missed a lot of school. Lots of surgeries. Sometimes I feel like Frankenstein's monster, I've been cut apart and sewn back together so many times." He chuckles. Like it's a joke. "I set off metal detectors now, because I've got surgically implanted rods in both my femurs. Otherwise I wouldn't be able to walk without crutches. But I get around pretty well, all things considered. And I haven't lost my hearing, which happens to a lot of people with OI. I'm lucky." A brief pause. "Anyway, that's my long-winded explanation for why I have these weird-looking eyeballs. Something to do with the collagen not forming correctly."

There's a pressure and tightness in my chest. It takes me a moment to identify it as guilt—though guilt about *what*, I'm not entirely sure. "I'm sorry."

"It's all right. I'm okay with how I am. Sort of. But I know what it's like, walking around with a diagnostic label hung around your neck, being told by the world that you have limitations, that there are certain things you'll never be able to do."

I sit motionless, arms crossed over my chest, knees locked together. Looking back, it seems so obvious—his cane, his eyes, the way he talked about breaking bones as if it was more or less routine. How did I not see? Did I not want to?

"My parents were always fighting," he says. "Mostly about money, because there was never enough. It all went toward my medical bills. I was in the hospital so often, I got to know all the doctors and nurses by name. They liked me, because I smiled for them, and when they asked me how I was, I always said I was fine. I told them how lucky I felt to have so many people taking such good care of me. They all thought I was this brave little soldier. But it wasn't like that. I mean, they were the ones cutting me open and filling me with pins and pushing the button that gave me my pain meds. I *needed* them to like me. It wasn't bravery, it was survival."

My hand drifts toward one braid and starts tugging.

"I was thinking about that last night," he continues. "And I remembered that thing you said. About rabbit moms, how they reabsorb the baby if there's something wrong with it."

I draw in my breath sharply.

"It's like you said. Love doesn't pay the bills."

No, no, no. I want to jump back in space-time and erase those words. "I wasn't talking about you," I whisper.

"I know. But this is going to be my life, Alvie. More breaking bones and more trips to the hospital and being stuck in a sling or on crutches for months on end and needing help with everything. And maybe someday I *will* go deaf, or end up in a wheelchair, or both. Am I supposed to pretend like that doesn't matter? Like it's not a big deal? How can I ask anyone—" His voice cracks.

I clutch my arm, fingers pressing into my own flesh with bruising force. "I'm broken, too."

"No, you're not. You should have seen yourself." He smiles, his expression tight with pain. "You don't need some white knight rushing in to save you. And even if you did, I can't—" His voice splinters again. "I'm just a useless—"

I kiss him. I don't even think about it; my body moves on its own.

I come in too fast. Our teeth knock together, and he gasps against my mouth. I pull back a little, then come in again, gentler, softer. His lips are warm, slightly rough and chapped against mine. I can't tell if I'm doing this right. Maybe it doesn't matter.

I pull back, and he looks up at me, eyes wide and dazed. "Why did you—?"

"Because I wanted to."

He blinks a few times. His expression has gone blank, as if a tiny nuclear bomb has gone off in his cortex, obliterating his thoughts.

"You are someone who should exist, Stanley. I shouldn't have said those things at Buster's. I wasn't thinking. I was upset because—" The words stop as if they've hit a wall in my throat. Somehow, this is very hard to admit. "—because I didn't like seeing you with her."

"I. Wait. Who?"

My face burns. "That girl. Dorothy."

His jaw drops. "*That's* what was bothering you?"

I want to crawl under the bed and hide.

"Alvie . . . I told you, Dorothy and I just sit next to each other in class. We're not even friends."

"She likes you," I mutter.

"She likes to mother me. Girls tend to treat me that way,

because I'm the quiet, nerdy guy with the cane. I've never been on their radar, not like that. That's why I was so surprised when you asked me to . . ." A light flush rises into his cheeks. "You know."

Of course—Stanley doesn't see himself as attractive. He wouldn't realize that woman was flirting with him if she flipped her skirt up and presented her rump like a bonobo in heat.

"Alvie. Look at me."

I force myself to meet his gaze.

"I don't want her. I want—I would like to be with—you."

My insides are a confused muddle. If I were a better person, I would push Stanley right into Dorothy's arms, because she can give him so many things that I can't. But I can't deny the stab of fierce animal joy I feel at those words. *I want you.*

He reaches up, cupping the back of my neck, and leans up, toward me.

The kiss is slower this time. Softer. He tastes faintly of cherries; he must have eaten some Jell-O in the hospital.

Before now, I never understood the appeal of this. I always thought it would be disgusting, sharing saliva with another person, but somehow it's not. Maybe because it's Stanley.

I pull back and lick my lips. "It's very wet," I say. "Kissing."

"That's kind of the idea." His eyes search my face. "Do you want to keep going?"

"Keep going."

His lips move against mine. His eyes open a crack, and he peeks out at me through his eyelashes. "Close your eyes," he whispers.

I do, and I see immediately why. It's more intense without the distraction of sight. The room suddenly feels a lot warmer; I'm dizzy, off-balance. Everything about this is dangerous. I am walking a tightrope over a bottomless abyss, and one wrong step will drag us both down into oblivion. But I don't want to stop. I can't.

When I finally pull back, he breathes a small, shivery sigh. His eyes slowly open, soft and unfocused.

He squirms, and I wonder if his arm is hurting him.

Then I notice something hard pressing against my thigh. "Oh," I say.

He scoots his hips away from mine. His blush is visible even in the dim light. "Sorry."

I remember that night in the motel room. The way his breathing quickened when he looked at me. His gentle, tentative caresses. The warmth of his hands.

Under the blanket, I lightly touch his thigh, and his muscles tense. I don't plan the words, my next words; they just come out. "We could try again, if you want."

"Are you serious?"

"Yes." My hand rests on his thigh.

He's silent, unmoving, not even breathing.

"Stanley?" The end of his name curves up a little in a question.

He takes a slow, deep breath and lets it out through his nose. "You remember, before, I told you I felt like Frankenstein's monster? It wasn't really a joke."

After more than fifty breaks, it would be surprising if he *didn't* have a collection of scars. "So."

"You haven't seen me. Whatever you're imagining, it's worse."

"They're just scars."

He swallows; I hear the *click* in his throat. Lightly he touches my shoulder. His hand slowly slides down my side, along the curve of my waist, to rest on my hip, a gentle, steady weight. I can feel the outline of his fingers, even through the thin denim of my jeans. I wait, holding my breath. A part of me wants to pull away, because even now, that simple contact is almost overwhelming. Waves of sensation pulse through my whole body, as if I were nothing but a collection of raw nerves. The instinctive fear of human touch is still there, pressing against the base of my throat. But there's pleasure, too—a slowly undulating heat.

Then his hand slides away, leaving a cold spot on my hip. "I don't know if this is the best time." He gives me a small, apologetic smile.

I nod. I don't leave the bed, though; I don't want to.

Gradually his breathing slows. "Alvie?" His voice is drowsy, faraway.

"Yes."

"Earlier, when we fought those guys, you were hissing and growling. And stomping your foot."

"Rabbits will do that sometimes, when they're threatened."

"Oh."

I expect him to ask more questions, but he just dozes off, as if that's all the explanation he needs.

For a few minutes, I lie still, listening to him breathe. He's very close and very warm. Though I'm feeling the physical symptoms of exhaustion—dry eyes, headache, a heaviness in my limbs—my mind is wide-awake. Maybe it's the discomfort of being in a strange bed, the unfamiliar texture of the sheets, the scent of him clinging to the pillow. I turn my face and breathe it in deeply, holding it in my lungs. Particles of his, mingling with mine.

After a while, my bladder starts to ache. Carefully I slide out of the bed. Stanley stirs and murmurs something incoherent under his breath, but he doesn't wake. Moonlight filters through the curtains, lighting the way as I tiptoe out of the room and down the hall.

On the way back from the bathroom, I pass a closed door and pause. Just a guest room, Stanley said.

I try the door. It creaks open, and I peek in.

The walls, the curtains, and the bedspread are patterned with bunches of pink roses. There are a few necklaces strewn on the dresser. A hairbrush. A stick of deodorant. A floral-patterned blouse hanging inside a half-open closet. And rows upon rows of porcelain figurines inside a huge glass cabinet—children, puppies, kittens, birds, all staring at me with their disproportionately large, inanimate eyes.

I take a few steps inside and touch the pillow. There's a thin layer of dust that comes off on my hand. On the table next to the bed stands a picture—a blond woman and a tiny blond boy in a blue polo shirt, maybe five or six years old, smiling up at the camera. Stanley and his mother.

Her room. Her things. Left untouched all this time.

Outside the window, a cloud passes over the moon, and the shadows shift. For a moment, the covers on the bed seem to ripple, as if a breeze were blowing through the room, and the hairs on my neck stiffen. I retreat, easing the door shut behind me, then quietly slip back into bed with Stanley and curl against his side.

CHAPTER NINETEEN

"You seem to be in good spirits today," Dr. Bernhardt remarks.

I sit across from him in my living room. Today he has a clipboard and a thick folder. "I'm in a good mood."

His eyebrows climb toward his receding hairline. "I can't remember the last time you've said that."

I shrug. It's true. Over a week has passed since that night with Stanley, and the whole time, I've felt strangely light—euphoric, almost. But I've avoided mentioning that to Dr. Bernhardt. After our conversation outside the apartment—after he warned me that I was becoming *codependent*—Stanley is the last thing I want to discuss with him. "What's in the folder?" I ask instead.

"Ah." He consults his clipboard, then pulls out a stack of papers. "I just wanted to go over a few things. When you meet with Judge Gray, obviously, you'll want to present yourself as professional and mature. She'll probably ask a lot of questions about your job, your living situation, that sort of thing. Let's do a practice run—I'll pretend to be the judge, and you answer my questions. So, Alvie.

How do you like living on your own?"

"Fine."

"It says here that you work at a zoo. . . . Do you enjoy the work?"

"It's fine."

"You can't answer every question with 'fine.' Elaborate a little. You like the animals, don't you? Talk about that. It's important to be professional, but you also want to come across as . . . warm. Human."

"That I'm human should be obvious. Do you think she'll assume that I'm an android. Or an alien."

"You know what I mean. Make her sympathize with you. Make her like you."

"She's there to decide whether I'm fit to live on my own. It shouldn't matter if she likes me or not."

"You're right. It shouldn't. But it does." He smiles, lips thin and tight. His gaze shifts away. "You know, a lot of people don't like social workers. It's a necessary job, but we're seen as fussy, moral busybodies, telling others how to live their lives. And when people don't like you, it makes things harder. It isn't fair, but that's how the world works."

I shift in my chair, not sure how to respond. He doesn't usually talk about himself like this. I don't exactly like Dr. Bernhardt, myself. But then, I don't like very many people. And I must admit—with the exception of our last encounter, he has generally been one of the more tolerable adults in my life. "I don't *dis*like you," I say.

"Well, I'm pleased to hear that," he says. "It's hard to tell, sometimes."

It never occurred to me that Dr. Bernhardt might care about whether I liked him.

"How are things going with your friend?" he asks. "Stanley, was it?"

I freeze. Now that he's asked me directly, I can't avoid the subject—not without lying. So I give him my usual response: "Fine."

"You're still seeing him, then?"

When I'm silent, he averts his gaze. "I realize that I expressed some reservations about your friendship with him. But I might have spoken out of turn. I meant what I said—it's your decision. I won't try to interfere."

Is it possible? Did I misunderstand him, before? Maybe he wasn't threatening me—maybe my state of mind affected my perceptions. I want to believe him, but I've been betrayed in the past.

I decide, on impulse, to take him at his word. "Good. Because Stanley is my friend, and that's not going to change, regardless of what you think about it."

He looks me in the eye. "Maybe it's none of my business, but . . . *is* he just a friend?"

Even if I wanted to answer that question, I wouldn't know how. The truth is, I'm still not sure what kind of relationship Stanley and I have. We haven't kissed since the night he broke his arm. We haven't talked about it, and he hasn't tried to do it again. Maybe he's waiting for me to take the initiative. Given my boundary issues, that makes sense. I keep thinking about it, replaying the moment in my head. A part of me wants to try it again. But a vague anxiety always stops me, a whisper of warning from inside the Vault.

"We're friends. That's all." It's starting to feel like a mantra. "I would prefer not to discuss him."

He lets out a small sigh and glances down at the clipboard. "All right. Let's continue."

As we go over the questions, his words echo in my head: *When people don't like you, it makes things harder.* Judge Gray, based on my limited memories of her, is a severe, no-nonsense woman. A bit like Ms. Nell, but without the eye-abrading fashion sense. And I am not the sort of person who easily inspires sympathy in others.

If Dr. Bernhardt is correct—if the judge's decision will be based on whether she finds me likable—I'm in big trouble.

"So this is Chance," Stanley remarks.

I nod.

Chance preens his wing and shifts his weight, claws flexing and clenching on the branch.

"He's beautiful," Stanley says. "You said you feed him by hand?"

"Yes. He's grown more comfortable around me. I still have to be careful, though."

"Is he dangerous?"

"Only to those who don't respect him. I'm the only one he'll tolerate inside his cage, but I don't have any special secret. It's just a matter of moving slowly and being patient." Common sense. But many people don't seem to have that kind of patience.

Stanley glances at me, blue sclerae flashing. They're especially striking in the sunlight, as if the vivid azure of his irises has seeped into the whites. I wait for him to ask what happened to Chance's amputated wing—everyone seems to ask that—but he doesn't.

I start to walk. "This way. I'll show you the other animals."

We follow the curving path past the hyenas, the river otters, and the pair of gibbons. Buttercup, the lone cougar, is curled in the sun, her head resting on paws the size of dinner plates.

I glance over at Stanley, my gaze focusing briefly on his lips. With an effort, I look away.

Since the night we kissed, it feels as if we've stalled; as though neither one of us is quite sure where to go or what to do next. It has occurred to me that maybe I should invite him to my apartment—but I haven't, and he hasn't brought it up. Perhaps he senses my reluctance.

It's not that I don't trust him. True, the idea of allowing someone else into my space is uncomfortably intimate, but the larger reason is more straightforward: my apartment is objectively disgusting. I've grown accustomed to it out of necessity, but I don't see any reason to subject him to the oppressive cheesy smell or the earwigs lurking in the bathroom.

"You said your lunch break is at one thirty?" he asks.

"Yes. I just need to clock out, then we can meet somewhere and eat together."

"How about the dolphin exhibit? The map says there's an underwater viewing area. It could be a nice place to sit."

I stop walking.

I avoid the dolphin exhibit when I can. It's a very large pool, almost fifteen feet deep, and being near any deep body of water tends to trigger feelings of unease and anxiety. If I suggest a different meeting place, however, I'll have to explain why, and I really don't want to explain this. I'm not even sure how I could.

"Alvie?"

I close my eyes briefly, collecting myself. My lunch break is only a half hour. I should be able to endure it for that long. "I'll meet you there."

I clock out, grab my lunch from my car, and walk to the dolphin enclosure. A long, curving cement path leads into the underwater viewing area. It's dark, with rough pebble-textured walls, like a cave. Stanley is already sitting on the low stone bench, bathed in blue luminescence. He looks up at the sound of my footsteps.

I sit next to him, clutching my paper lunch sack.

"What've you got?"

"Bologna on white bread." My usual. Affordable and filling enough, if not terribly nutritious.

Beyond a sheet of clear Plexiglas lies the expanse of the dolphin pool. With its smooth, curved white walls, it looks like the inside of a giant egg. The two dolphins, Charlie and Silver, glide smoothly through the blue. They're Ms. Nell's favorite animals, probably because they bring in the most guests.

He watches them. "Dolphins always look so happy, don't they? Like there's not a thing in the world that bothers them or makes them angry."

I swallow a mouthful of sandwich. "Bottlenose dolphins can be very aggressive, actually. Males will band together to attack and kill porpoises. No one knows why. Porpoises don't share their diet, so they aren't competitors for their food supply. Killing them doesn't give the dolphins any obvious evolutionary advantage. Apparently they just don't like them."

His brows knit together.

Charlie glides close to the glass, one dark eye staring out. His smiling mouth opens, showing rows of tiny, sharp teeth. Faintly I can see my reflection sitting next to Stanley's in the Plexiglas. Just an inch of solid material between us and all that . . . water.

A lump of sandwich sits in my mouth, dry and tasteless as paper. I force it down my throat.

Stanley rests his forearm across the top of his cane. "You don't idealize them, do you? Animals, I mean."

I lick a drop of mustard from my finger. "They're no more inherently good or evil than humans. They're a lot like us, actually. We all eat, we all mate, we all struggle to survive. We all kill, though we humans try to hide that fact from ourselves. This bologna was a living creature, once. Well, probably several."

"I guess so. But killing for food is different."

The dolphins swim past again, followed by a flurry of bubbles. It's my imagination, I know, but it seems that I can *hear* the water—a dull rumble in the center of my head, a vibration in my marrow.

Silver lets out a high-pitched call—*eh-eh-eh-eh-ee*! Like mocking laughter. The water makes rippling patterns on the concrete floor. I move my foot away from the dancing spots of light.

"Alvie?"

The rumble in my head grows louder, drowning out my thoughts. The pressure builds and builds inside me, and suddenly it's too much. When I close my eyes, a vision explodes in my head: I see the Plexiglas cracking, then shattering. Water pours out, flooding the viewing area. Water sweeps over my head. The world is blurry, and when I gasp, water rushes in. It presses in around me, cold and dark. My head breaks the surface, but a wave bears down on me, roaring, and drags me under again, into blackness—

Stanley touches my arm, and I give a start. My eyes snap open. The Plexiglas is intact, the water blue and placid behind it.

"Hey," he says. "What's wrong?"

My own ragged breathing fills my ears. The half-eaten sandwich slips from my hands and lands in several pieces on the floor. "I have to go." I stumble up the curving cement path, into the sunlight. I huddle in a ball on the ground and rock back and forth on my heels, cradling my head in both hands.

When the brain haze clears, I hear Stanley calling my name over and over. I hear his slow, unsteady footsteps coming closer and closer. His shadow falls over me. I don't want him to see me like this. Panting, trembling, I lurch to my feet and turn away.

His hand comes down on my shoulder. I'm not expecting it, and a sickening jolt of pain goes through me, like an electric shock. My body reacts automatically: in an instant, I'm on my feet. In another instant, I spin toward Stanley, and my fist sails toward him, independent of my volition. Time slows, stretching.

I see his eyes grow huge. I see him flinch back and duck his head, squeezing his eyes shut.

I'm going to hit him. I'm going to hit him, and I can't stop myself.

No!

The signals from my brain finally reach my arm. I freeze, my fist an inch from his face. He stands, hunched, breathing hard. Slowly his eyes open. There's a flat, glassy sheen on them; the word *dissociation* floats through my mind. "Alvie?" he whispers.

I back away and slump against the nearby wall of the reptile house. The world blurs and tilts. When it comes back into focus, Stanley's expression is dazed, but that weird glassy look is gone. I swallow. "Stanley . . . are you . . ."

"I'm fine."

I hug myself, fingers digging into my biceps, and bow my head. "I'm sorry."

He hesitates. I can feel his gaze on me. "What happened?"

I take a deep breath. "Meltdown," I mutter.

As a child, whenever I lost control of myself at school—whenever I kicked over desks or hit bullies or hid in the janitor's closet—that's what teachers and doctors always called it. A meltdown. Like I wasn't just an angry and frightened girl but a nuclear power plant spewing radioactive waste. Maybe it's not an inaccurate metaphor.

"But why?" Stanley's voice is low and calming, but the question still makes me flinch.

I hate telling people this. But I don't see any alternative. "I don't like water." My face burns.

"*All* water?"

"Not all." My gaze remains fixed on my shoes. "I'm not bothered by water from the sink, or in toilets, or anything like that. The duck pond in the park isn't bad, because it's shallow. But I don't like being submerged in water, and I don't like being near so much of it. It—it makes me feel like I'm drowning."

"Why didn't you tell me?"

My ears burn. "Because being afraid of water is stupid."

"It's not. Not at all."

I give him a skeptical look.

He shrugs. "I saw this talk show once about a guy who was scared of pickles, and a woman who was scared of buttons. You know, like buttons on people's clothes. As a little kid, I was terrified of carousels."

"Carousels."

"I mean, I'm fine with them now. But when I was five years old, my dad took me to a carnival and tried to get me on the carousel. It was this huge thing, and it was spinning really fast—or at least, it seemed fast to me—and something about the combination of the movement and the weird calliope music and those horses going up and down just freaked me out. He had to buy me some cotton candy to calm me down. Compared to that, being afraid of water isn't so weird."

There's a knot in my throat. I swallow, but it won't go down. "I almost hit you."

"But you didn't. You stopped yourself."

"Barely." And if I hadn't . . .

In my head, I see my fist crash into his jaw. Bones crack and crunch. He's on the ground, contorted in pain. He's back in the hospital, having surgical pins inserted into his jaw to hold the bone fragments in place. Months of agony, because I didn't stop myself in time.

I shudder. "I could have hurt you."

"In the future, I'll be more careful. This won't happen again. Okay?"

I look into his blue-within-blue eyes. "I don't understand why you're not afraid of me," I whisper.

"I've spent most of my life being afraid, Alvie. I'm tired of it. I'm not going to avoid you because of one little mistake." He smiles and rubs the back of his neck. "Though if you don't like water, I guess my plans for tonight won't work out."

"What plans."

"Oh. It's nothing. It was going to be a surprise."

"But it involves water."

"Well, sort of. Frozen water."

I consider this for a moment, trying to remember if ice has ever negatively affected me. "Frozen is all right."

"Well, in that case . . . you want to meet in the park?"

I'm tempted to ask him exactly what he's planning—but then, he said he wanted it to be a surprise. I wonder if I'm being reckless. Lately I've been taking a lot more chances. But I know what Stanley means when he says he's tired of being afraid. Maybe surprises aren't always a bad thing.

"Yes," I say.

CHAPTER TWENTY

At five o'clock, I pick Stanley up from the park. Since his arm is in a sling, I drive, and he gives me directions. I can't begin to guess where he's taking us. When we finally pull into the parking lot, my confusion only increases.

Ahead is a large, open lawn surrounded by trees and illuminated by stadium lights. In the center, there's a smooth, glassy surface encircled by a low fence. As we approach, I realize what I'm looking at, and I wonder if this is his peculiar idea of a joke. "This is an ice-skating rink."

"Yep."

"We don't have skates."

He points to a little wooden building with a peaked roof. "We can rent some in there. They sell hot chocolate, too."

I stare at his cane, then at his broken arm. He just stands there, smiling. Apparently he's not going to address the obvious—that for someone in his condition, ice-skating is about the most risky activity imaginable, outside of throwing himself repeatedly down the stairs.

"I don't know how," I say.

"That's okay. I barely remember, either."

He told me he used to skate as a child, until he broke his scapula. Does this have something to do with that? Probably. Even so, this seems like a foolish way of confronting his demons. Like a burn victim deciding to overcome his fear by setting his house on fire.

His smile fades. "I haven't gone crazy, honest. I just want to go out and stand on the ice for a few minutes. I don't really know how to explain this. It's just something I need. And I thought . . ." A light flush rises into his cheeks. "I thought it would be easier, if you were with me." He looks away. "I'm being kind of selfish, I guess. If you don't want to do this, we don't have to."

My gaze wanders back to the rink, which is currently deserted. The ice looks solid, though the weather doesn't seem cold enough for that. It's probably not even real ice, I tell myself. Lots of rinks use a chemical substitute like high-density polyethylene. That would explain why it's so hard, even though the temperature is above freezing. And even if it *is* water, there's absolutely no risk of drowning; I just have to keep reminding myself of that.

"Let's do it," I say.

We rent two pairs of skates and sit on a bench.

The light of sunset has mostly faded, and colors are muted. The ring of stadium lights is on, but not at full power; they glow with a soft white radiance. All around us, snow falls in fat flakes, piling up on the bench and on our clothes and hair. I lace up my skates, then lean down to tie his, knotting them securely and looping the slack around his ankles for extra support. "Do they fit okay."

"Yeah. Thanks."

For a few minutes, he just stares out at the ice, his expression distant and closed off. I notice the fingers of one hand digging into his thigh. "Stanley . . ."

"Sorry." He exhales a tense breath. "Having second thoughts."

Awkwardly I fold my arms around him. I'm still not good at hugging—my arms are stiff and wooden, like a store mannequin's—but his trembling gradually subsides. It's a new feeling, being able to ease someone else's fear. A powerful feeling. "I won't let you fall," I say.

He laughs weakly. "I should be the one saying that to you, shouldn't I? I mean, it's your first time."

I release him and cross my arms. "Well, don't let *me* fall, either."

"I won't." He places a hand on my shoulder, pushing himself to his feet. Facing me, he extends a glove. "Ready?"

I take his hand, and he leads me out onto the ice, leaving his cane where it is, propped against the bench. He moves in small, careful shuffles, leaning against my shoulder.

My legs feel wobbly. I stay close to the edge, inching my way along the low wall surrounding the rink. Stanley grips my hand. "Let's go out a little farther."

I grit my teeth, every limb rigid with tension, as we shuffle away from the wall. How did I let him talk me into this? "I think I've changed my mind." I squeeze the words through my clenched jaws.

"We won't fall. I promise."

I move clumsily, sliding one skate forward, then the other. My body tilts back and forth; my arms are stiff at my sides. And still, he clings to my hand. "I mean it," I growl. "I don't think I can do this."

"Just hold on."

I glare at him, but he looks utterly sincere. Now that he's actually on the ice, he seems to have gotten over his anxiety. I, on the other hand, was relatively calm until I actually felt how unstable these skates are. How does anyone stand up on these?

But this is important to Stanley. I take a deep breath and nod.

He starts to move, and I let him guide me. I begin to relax, almost against my will. His foot slips, and I catch him with an arm around his waist. He grips my coat. My heart beats rapidly against his.

"You okay?" he asks.

I nod but don't move, afraid that if I do, we'll both spill onto the ice. I feel clumsy and unsteady, like a foal taking its first steps.

"See?" he whispers against my ear. "Nothing to it."

He rests his chin briefly atop my hair. For a minute or two, we just stand there. It's strange, touching someone and not feeling the urge to pull away.

He guides me back to the wall. A tiny smile grows from one corner of his mouth. "Hey, watch this."

I don't like the sound of that. "Watch what."

He breaks away and moves in small, shuffling movements toward the center of the rink, leaving me leaning against the edge, helpless. "Just watch!" he calls.

And all at once, he's gliding across the ice, so suddenly and gracefully it's surreal. He starts to loop around and manages to do one half of a figure eight before his legs wobble and give out. He doesn't fall so much as crumple.

I try to run to him. The ice flies out from under me, and I land on my knees with a painful jolt. Panting, I crawl toward him. He's lying on his back, splayed on the ice. "Stanley!"

To my astonishment, he's laughing, though the sound is strained and breathless—more like gasping.

"You're a lunatic." I help him to his feet, and he curls an arm around my waist. He's limping a bit more than usual as we make our way toward the edge of the rink. We sit together on the bench, breathless and flushed. He smiles at me, eyes crinkling at the corners.

I look down at his legs. "Are you sure nothing's broken."

"Don't worry about me. I've got metal rods in my femurs, remember?" He knocks a fist against one leg. "I'm the bionic man. Indestructible."

"Well, you've certainly got an indestructible head. It's solid rock all the way through."

He blinks. For a moment, he looks baffled. "Wait—was that a joke?" A broad smile breaks across his face. "I don't believe it. You made a *joke*."

"I *can* do that, you know."

He takes his hat off and rubs his head, grinning. The flush in his cheeks is bright, his nose pink from the cold, and his hair is mussed up, flattened in places and sticking up in others. There's a string of Christmas lights on the nearby tree—though it's not even December yet—and I can see them reflected in his eyes. I wish I had a camera. Instead, I close one eye and think *click*, which is something I do when I don't ever want to forget a particular image. I reach out and stroke his coat sleeve. It's soft against my fingertips.

Then I notice how labored his breathing has become. "How much pain," I ask. "One to ten."

He hesitates, then mumbles, "Four."

I look at his pulse, hammering in his throat—135 beats per minute—and mentally adjust that to a six. He overexerted himself today, but I know better than to say anything about it. This was something he needed to do.

Stanley fidgets, opens his mouth, and then closes it. Finally he takes a deep breath, reaches into his coat, and pulls something out. It's a carnation. The bloom is bloodred, with lots of delicate crinkly petals, and half-flattened from being stuck inside his coat for so long.

He holds it out to me. His Adam's apple moves up and down. "Here."

I stare.

"I said I wanted to court you. Remember?"

Slowly I take it from him. I feel off-balance. Dizzy. A red carnation means something, in the language of flowers. But when I try to remember, something inside me flinches shut.

Stanley sits, shoulders tense, hands tightly interlaced in his laps. The flush in his cheeks grows brighter, creeping into his ears.

"Stanley . . . I . . ." My fingers tighten on the carnation's stem. "I—"

"I just wanted to give it to you. That's all. You don't have to say anything."

I clutch the carnation. I'm not sure what to do with it, so I stuff it into my coat pocket.

His hands tighten on his knees. He pulls his hat back over his ears, picks up his cane and pushes himself to his feet. "Want to head back?"

I stand, and we walk toward the car.

Back at my apartment, alone, I take the carnation out of my coat pocket and study it. The petals are flattened, the leaves bent, the stem broken, oozing clear sap like blood. I've already crushed the life out of it with my clumsy paws.

Still, I can't just throw it away. I get a bit of clear tape and wrap it around the broken stem like a bandage. Then I fill a glass with water, put the carnation inside it, and set it on my coffee table.

A flower is a morbid gift, if you think about it—the severed reproductive organ of a plant, preserved and kept alive through the equivalent of a feeding tube. What sense is there in prolonging its inevitable death?

But maybe that's the point. Everything dies. All that we do in the meantime is just delay the inevitable . . . and yet there's still beauty and softness. Is it worth it?

With a fingertip, I stroke one bloodred petal. I think about Stanley's smile.

Then I remember what he said to me after he broke his arm, about how people like him sometimes lose their hearing. If that happens, how will I communicate with him?

I pull on my coat, walk to the library, and check out three books. I sit at one of the long tables and open the largest book, titled simply *American Sign Language*. I find the sign for "friend" and practice it, interlocking my index fingers once, then twice.

I turn the page—and freeze. There's an illustration of a hand with the forefinger, thumb, and pinkie finger extended. *Love.*

A dull rumble emanates from within the Vault, and the massive doors shudder. From the basement of my brain, a voice whispers, *Whatever happens, it's because I love you.*

I slam the book shut. It takes me a few minutes to get my breathing under control.

CHAPTER TWENTY-ONE

My appointment with the judge is approaching fast; I cross off the days on my calendar, and the collection of red *x*'s grows until they fill the page.

On Wednesday, Dr. Bernhardt arrives at the usual time, his thinning hair neatly combed. "Well," he says. "This is it. Our final meeting." He takes a seat and folds his hands. "How do you feel?"

"I feel . . ." I start to say *fine*, then stop. "I don't know."

"Is there anything in particular you want to talk about?"

I fidget in my chair. *Our final meeting.* The thought is strange. Unsettling. "I don't think I'm ready," I blurt out.

"It's not too late to change your mind."

I can't turn back now, when I'm so close. "I haven't changed my mind. I'm just . . ."

"Scared?"

I don't answer. It's obvious. Of course I'm scared. I breathe in slowly through my nose. "I'm going through with this. I'll do whatever it takes. I want to be independent."

The muscles of his face tighten. After a moment, he takes off his glasses and polishes them on his sleeve. Without the lenses to magnify them, his eyes look small and watery and defenseless. "Are my visits really that unpleasant for you?"

The question catches me off guard. I shift my weight in the chair. "It isn't that."

"What, then? Why are you so desperate to be emancipated? You're already very independent. The only difference is that I won't be visiting anymore. And you'll lose certain legal protections."

I give my left braid two sharp tugs. Part of it is the fear of being sent back to the group home. But there's more to it. I don't know how to explain it in a way he'll understand. "When I was younger, some of the doctors said that I would never be able to live on my own. That I couldn't have a normal life. I want to prove them wrong."

"Having a normal life doesn't mean never needing help. Besides . . . you're still very young. You're a seventeen-year-old girl, already working full-time and paying rent. That's not unheard-of, but it's not typical, either. Most children your age are still receiving support, in some form or another. It has nothing to do with your condition."

It has everything to do with my condition. If not for my condition, I wouldn't be in this situation in the first place. "I made up my mind to be emancipated. So I will be. That's all."

He smiles, gaze downcast. "I thought you would say that.

Well . . . if it means that much to you, I'll do everything I can to help you achieve that goal."

My shoulders relax. I nod once.

He glances at the carnation, still sitting on my coffee table. It's already dried-out, petals stiffening and crinkling into a brittle sculpture. "I believe this is the first time I've ever seen a flower in your apartment."

I ought to throw it away. But somehow, I can't bring myself to do it. I touch the piece of tape holding the stem together. Without thinking, I tell the truth: "It's from Stanley."

He raises his eyebrows, crinkling his forehead. "Well." A tiny smile tugs at his lips. "That's wonderful."

I hadn't expected him to be pleased.

"You know," he says, "you still haven't told me very much about this boy."

I tug my braid. "Are you going to put this in the report."

"No. I'm just curious."

Where do I even start? There are so many random details I've absorbed through my conversations with Stanley, it's hard to choose. "He likes cats. But he's allergic to them, so he can't have one. He owns a pet gerbil named Matilda. His favorite smell is fresh-cut cucumbers."

"It sounds as though you're getting closer to each other."

"We are. But . . ." There's a quiver in my throat, as if words are bubbling up inside me, trying to escape. I clamp my lips shut, out of habit . . . but somehow, holding everything in doesn't seem worth the effort. I need to talk to *someone* to make sense of the confusing mess of my feelings. This is Dr. Bernhardt's last visit. It might as well be now. "I don't—" I stop, gripping my knees. My throat stiffens; I swallow until it loosens enough to let my voice through. "I don't know how to do this. Be someone's friend. I feel like I'm making so many mistakes. And there are . . . certain things . . . he doesn't know. About . . . my past."

He sits, studying me in silence for a moment. "How much have you told him?" he asks quietly.

"Almost nothing."

He breathes in slowly through his nose, then out. "I don't want to overstep my bounds. And I don't know how serious you are with him. But even if you *are* just friends, if you want this boy to be a part of your life, sooner or later you'll have to tell him."

"And if I don't. What then."

"The truth has a way of coming out, sooner or later. The best you can do is choose the time and place. I'm not speaking as your social worker. Consider it a piece of advice from one adult to another. Keeping secrets from the people closest to you will only cause you pain."

I open my mouth to respond, but nothing comes out. I'm shaking.

"It doesn't have to be everything at once," he says. "Start with the easier things, and then . . ." He leaves the rest of the sentence unspoken.

He's right. Stanley has told me so much about himself, and I've revealed so little. I can't keep hiding behind walls.

I know what I need to do.

***

"Where are we going?" Stanley asks.

The two-lane highway stretches out before us, fading into the horizon. Winter-brown cornfields glide past on either side. "It's a surprise," I say.

"Is it a new restaurant?"

"No."

"Secret gateway to a parallel universe?"

"You're getting warmer."

He laughs.

We've been driving for almost two hours. We're far out in the country now. The fields are vast, dotted with small houses and silos. Pale clouds blanket the sky in a uniform layer, so solid and thick it looks like a person could walk on it. We pass a dilapidated fence with a line of crows perched atop it. Their heads turn, following us as we drive past.

As I turn down Oak Lane, my heartbeat quickens.

I am about to reveal something to him that I haven't revealed to anyone for a long, long time. It's not the thing in the Vault—God, no. But even so, this won't be easy.

"I have to admit," he says. "I'm completely stumped. We're in the middle of nowhere. What could you possibly want to show me out here?"

I pull into a gravel driveway and park. "This."

The yard is overgrown with weeds and wild bushes. The house itself stands a ways back from the road, smothered in shadow. There's no car in the driveway. The windows are dark, and a yellow sign is tacked to the door—probably a foreclosure notice. Who knows how long that's been there.

I open the car door and get out.

Stanley's brow furrows. "Whose house is this?"

"It's mine," I reply. "Or rather, it used to be." I lead him around to the backyard, where an old, rusted swing set stands next to a wooden horse on a spring. I sit in one of the swings.

Stanley gingerly sits in the other. The structure creaks in protest, but it holds us both.

The tips of my black sneakers are stained with mud. I kick the damp earth beneath me. "I lived here with my mother until I was eleven years old. After that, I lived in several different foster homes, but that didn't work out. I was a difficult child. Eventually I was transferred to a group home for teenagers with emotional and behavioral issues. That didn't work out, either. I didn't get along with the other girls. There were several who were accustomed to being in charge and getting their way. I refused to submit to them, so they did everything possible to break me. They hid tacks in my shoes and dead insects in my bed. Once, a dead mouse. And, of course, once they found out I was afraid of water—" I break off, unable to continue, but the memory looms large in my head—two laughing older girls shoving me into a shower stall and turning it on full blast, icy cold, holding me down while I screamed. "It was pretty bad," I continued. My voice remains flat and neutral, but a tremor has crept into my hands. "I kept running away and getting in trouble with the law, until finally Dr. Bernhardt helped me get my own place."

"Who?"

I realize I've never mentioned Dr. Bernhardt to Stanley. "A social worker. If not for him, I would probably be dead or in prison by now." In retrospect, I probably should have shown him more gratitude for that. Soon, if all goes well, his visits will be over. I'll never again hear him fussing over the lack of fruit in my kitchen. My feelings about that are a bit more complicated and ambiguous than I anticipated.

I take my Rubik's Cube from my pocket and fiddle with it as I stare at my house, the familiar back porch made of yellow pine. Even the birdbath is still there, though now cracked and empty.

I haven't been back here since the incident. I was sure that by now, I'd be panicking, but somehow I'm not. Maybe because Stanley's here, too.

A few tiny raindrops strike my face like icy pinpricks. Dark clouds mass in the sky, and more drops fall. "When I was little," I say, "whenever something was bothering me, I used to come out here and swing as hard as I could. I would imagine that if I swung far and high enough, the momentum would carry me straight into the sky, and I could fly away."

"Fly away from what?"

"Everything."

Wind whistles through the trees, and they creak like the timbers of an old ship.

"I drove you all the way out here just to stare at an abandoned house," I say. "This probably isn't the sort of surprise you were expecting."

"No," he says quietly. "But I'm glad you brought me here."

The muscles in my back relax a little. I swing lightly back and forth, back and forth. The rocking movement is calming. But a dull ache has spread across the inside of my ribs. There's a brief flash of memory—I am very small, maybe three or four years old, and Mama is pushing me on the swing. I close my eyes. In my memory, the world feels clean and bright and new. Sunlight dapples the green grass. When I open my eyes, the yard is empty and gray again. "'My heart has joined the Thousand,'" I murmur, "'for my friend stopped running today.'"

"What's that?"

"It's from *Watership Down*."

"Oh . . . right. That's what the rabbits say when one of them dies?"

I nod.

His brows knit together. "Did someone . . ."

"Not recently."

I always thought those words were the most accurate expression of grief I had ever encountered. When you lose someone, the heart itself becomes one of the thousand enemies—a force of destruction, ripping you apart from the inside, like a knot of shining razor wire. Sometimes, the only way to survive is to kill your heart. Or lock it in a cage.

Thunder rumbles.

"Do you want to head back?" he asks.

Maybe he expects me to be bothered by the rain and thunder. It would be a reasonable assumption, considering how the sound of water affects me. But I shake my head. It's strange. I can't stand fireworks or explosions. Or silverware clattering, or glasses clinking together. Sometimes, even ticking clocks make me want to crawl out of my skin. But I don't mind thunder. I find it calming.

A gust of wind makes the rocking horse sway back and forth. Its spring squeaks.

"Alvie . . ." He bites his lower lip, and I know he wants to ask me something.

I wait.

"What happened to your mother?"

I look down at the Rubik's Cube in my hands, and my fingers tighten on the smooth plastic. I knew this was coming, of course. Stanley's aware that I never met my father, but I haven't said anything to him about my mother. It's only natural for him to be curious. And I surmised that bringing him here, to this place, would trigger certain questions about my past. I mentally prepared myself. Still, my hands start to shake. "She—" My voice stops as if it's hit a wall inside me. I force myself to finish: "She died."

"How?"

I look at him. My mouth opens, and for an instant, words tremble in my throat. Then they retreat, and all that comes out is a small, choked sound. I lower my head.

"It's okay," Stanley says, very softly. "You don't have to answer that."

I don't say anything else. I don't dare. I close my eyes and breathe. In and out. The tightness in my chest loosens.

Rain falls thicker and faster from the sky, the drops stinging my skin, but it feels good. It calms my nerves. I slip the Rubik's Cube into my pocket. "What happens if you get your cast wet," I ask.

"It's fiberglass, so it's no big deal. I could even go swimming with it, if I wanted. Not that I ever go swimming."

I start to ask why not, then I realize—of course. The scars.

I watch the rain running in rivulets from the swing set and dripping from the wooden horse.

"Years ago," I say, "whenever there was a storm, I would sneak out of the house. I would lie on my back in these woods, and I would let the rain pound down on me and listen to the thunder. And I'd forget about everything."

He looks at me. In the dim light, the blue of his eyes is bright, almost electric.

He rises from the swing and stretches out on the grass. For a moment, I can only stare in surprise . . . then, slowly I stretch out next to him. He reaches for my hand. I slip my fingers between his, and we watch the sky darken as the storm sweeps in. I shiver in the cold, teeth chattering, rain soaking through my coat and plastering my shirt against my body. His hand is warm against mine.

Lightning darts across the sky, filling the woods with pale blue light. Goose bumps ripple across my flesh, and a thrill darts through my body, licking my insides like a flame.

We lie on our backs, clutching each other's hands, as the storm rages all around us and the trees lash back and forth and the wind howls, high and sharp. I know this is dangerous—we could be struck by lightning, we could get hypothermia from being drenched with cold water. But maybe that's why it's exciting. Maybe it's like Stanley going to the ice rink. We have to do risky things sometimes, to remind ourselves that we're still alive.

At last the wind dies down, and the driving rain tapers off into a light patter. I sit up, my clothes plastered to my body with water and mud. "Are you all right."

For a few seconds, he doesn't answer. He's still lying on his back, smiling up at the sky. "That was . . ." He lets out a breathless laugh. "Wow." He sits up, rakes a hand through his wet hair, and smiles—a dizzying, beautiful smile. He's panting, flushed and soaked. "I'm fine. What about you?"

I examine my own inner state. I feel . . . calmer, somehow, and lighter, as if a weight I'd been carrying around is gone. "I'm good," I say.

I help him to his feet. His teeth are chattering.

"We should go back to the car," I say.

We trudge out of the forest and across the muddy field, drenched and shivering. When we get into the car, I turn the heat on full blast. Rain taps against the windshield.

We don't talk during the drive home. But it's a comfortable silence.

When we pull up in front of Stanley's house, it's very late. He clears his throat. "You want to come in? I could make some coffee. And we could change." He glances down at his wet, muddy clothes.

I nod.

Inside, he starts a pot of coffee and changes into fresh clothes. He lends me a T-shirt and sweatpants, and I have to roll up the sleeves and pant legs. We sit together on the couch, sipping our coffee, its heat chasing away the chill of the rain. The smell of hazelnut and chicory fills my nose, and something else; a pleasant, bookish smell that permeates Stanley's home, like a natural extension of his own scent. The room is bright and warm, a sharp contrast to the darkness outside.

"Thank you," he says.

"For what."

"Today. I know it took a lot of courage."

"I didn't do much."

"Alvie? Give yourself some credit."

Our eyes meet. Strange feelings well up in me, sudden and powerful, and after a moment, I have to look away. A faint alarm bell clangs somewhere in my brain, letting me know that I'm approaching a danger point; my emotions are starting to overload. I need to withdraw, to reassess and process everything I've experienced today. I set down my coffee cup and say, "I should go."

"Wait." He sets down his cup, too, and wets his lips.

A branch taps against the window like a skeletal finger. A flash of lightning momentarily lights the sky, and the branch's shadow stretches across the wall, long and black. I grip the edge of the couch.

"I've been doing a lot of thinking lately," he says.

The alarm bells in my brain *clang* louder. *Pull back.* "About what."

"Us."

At the word, I twitch, fingers digging into the upholstery.

The air has shifted. Though my eyes are open, I can see the doors of the Vault in front of me. They're dull gray, flecked with rust, so close and real I could touch them. I blink rapidly. "Can we talk about it later."

"I really need to get this out." He runs a hand over his hair and rubs the back of his neck. Then he picks up his coffee cup and sips it, as if taking time to collect his thoughts. His hands are shaking. As he sets the cup down, it rattles against the coffee table. "I've wanted to say this for a while, but I waited. Because what we have now is really important to me, and I don't want to lose it."

There's a tiny crack on the wall, near the floor; my mind latches on to it.

"I wanted to take things slow. But I feel like I need to know where we stand. I need to know what this is. What *we* are. And I . . ."

"Stanley," I blurt out.

He stops.

I'm having trouble breathing. The wall crack is jagged and dark, and it seems to grow, opening into a void. "I need to go." I start to stand.

"Alvie, *please.*"

The words freeze me.

"Don't run away. Please."

I'm sliding backward, falling deeper and deeper into myself. My body's gone numb. I'm floating somewhere outside it, above it.

"Just let me say it, and then you can go, if you still want to. I—"

"Stanley." My voice is faint and hoarse.

"I love you."

The words hang in the air between us, and for the space of a breath, there is nothing. No reaction, no movement—as if we've plunged off the edge of a cliff and we're hanging suspended in midair, the world frozen in that single breath before the plummet.

"Alvie?"

"You can't," I whisper.

Something has shifted in his expression. His brows draw together. "But I do. I . . . I know you might not feel the same, but—"

"Stop." My hand drifts to my chest and clutches, fingers clenching and twisting on my shirt, over the ripping pain beneath. "Just—just stop talking."

Stanley reaches across the space between us, and I flinch away.

Static fills my head, growing louder. No—not static. Water, rushing and swelling, pressing in around me, swallowing me in icy blackness. My vision blurs, and the room tilts. I lurch to my feet and back away until my back hits the wall.

"Alvie? What's going on? Talk to me."

I shake my head, braids swinging. "No." The word escapes on a breath, faint and panicked. "No. No." My knees buckle, and I crumple to the floor, hands pressed to my temples. Stanley is still frantically calling my name. I hear him dimly, his voice muffled and distorted, and when I look up I can only see a blurred shadow coming toward me. He stretches out a hand.

I hit him. I don't decide to do it; it just happens. I watch my fist flying out, watch it connect with his jaw.

He cries out and stumbles backward, almost falling to his knees. At the last instant he grabs the arm of the couch, steadying himself, and he stares at me, eyes huge, face white as a skull. There's a red mark on his face. His hand drifts slowly up to touch it. We stare at each other across the room.

There's a sensation of falling, as if the floor has vanished.

I have to get out of here. Now.

I run out into the night, panting, and get into my car. My hands are shaking as I start the engine, and I drive away without looking back, windshield wipers slicing through the rain. A dull roar drowns out my thoughts, and I can't tell if it's thunder or if the sound is coming from within me.

In my mind, the image of Stanley falling to the floor replays over and over. I don't think I broke any bones. But the impact was hard enough for me to feel all the way down my arm.

He's not safe around me. I need to get far, far away.

I drive and drive. When I finally stop, I'm staring out at a dark expanse of water. A lake. *The* lake. The one where I went with Mama so many times.

Moving like a sleepwalker, I get out of the car. Cold rain hammers my head and back, drenching my shirt. The sky is dark. The water froths and churns like the storm clouds above; when lightning flashes, the waves reflect it, so there's no boundary between sea and sky, and the whole world—except for the thin line of shore beneath my feet—is a dark, roiling mass. My feet carry me forward. The water pulls me to itself as if there's a fishing line hooked into my navel, running into the cold depths of the lake, trying to drag me down. Lightning cuts the sky in half, blinding me for a few seconds.

It's calling me. The lake is calling. *I love you, Alvie.*

No, no. Clutching my head, I run back to my car.

Once I arrive back at my apartment, I collapse onto my mattress. I'm still wearing Stanley's clothes. They smell like him, that mild, warm smell, like cinnamon and old books. I rip them off, ball them up, and shove them into the deepest corner of the closet, and I stretch out naked on the sheets, gasping, but it's not enough. I still feel like I'm suffocating. My apartment's heater rattles; it's old and only half works, and the air is frigid, but despite that I'm bathed in sweat. If I could peel off my skin like a wet suit, I would.

My hands shake as I pick up my cell phone and turn it on. There's one missed call from Stanley. He's left a voice mail. My thumb hovers, trembling, over the button. I raise the phone to my ear and play the message.

"Alvie, I . . . when you get this, call me. We can talk about this. Whatever's going on, however I hurt you—"

I stab the button with my thumb, deleting the message.

I can't go back. If I stay with Stanley, I could seriously injure him. Any stupid little thing could set me off, trigger a meltdown; I could put him in the hospital without even trying. But even then, he would smile through the pain and forgive, because he doesn't understand that I'm a monster. He'll keep feeding the monster and giving it shelter and loving it even as it eats him, piece by piece.

Just like Mama.

I shut my eyes and breathe in slowly. A strange, cold calm descends, and in that space, I know what I have to do. I have to let him go. For his sake. If I leave him now, it will hurt him, but he will recover. If I stay . . .

A memory flares, sharp and clear—a cold hand slipping from mine.

I always knew, deep down, that it couldn't possibly work between Stanley and me. I was living in a fantasy, but I was too selfish and deluded to admit it. I wanted to experience—if just for a little while—what *normal* felt like. It was a dream, and now it's over, and he's suffering for my stupidity. I can't take back what I've done, but I can keep things from getting any worse. Sever the cord, quick and clean.

I send a text message. *It would be better if we didn't see each other again.*

CHAPTER TWENTY-TWO

Over the next few days, Stanley leaves more voice mails. I delete them without listening.

At first, the pain is constant, like a weight sitting on my chest. It's hard to breathe through it. But I keep going through the motions—showing up at work, reading books, taking walks—though I avoid the park now. Little by little, my old routines reestablish themselves, and the ache begins to fade.

As long as I can be with the animals, I'll survive. They are my purpose. I should have known that all along. I don't belong in the human world. But I've learned from my mistakes; I won't repeat them.

My phone rings, and I give a start. I start to reach for it, to shut it off—then freeze. The number isn't Stanley's; it's Dr. Bernhardt's. With a shaking hand, I raise the phone to my ear. "Hello."

"Hello, Alvie. Just checking in. I wanted to make sure you're ready for your appointment with Judge Gray tomorrow morning."

At the words, I feel a sharp jolt. I've been so preoccupied, so focused on just surviving each day, I almost forgot about the meeting with the judge. My mouth is dry. I hear myself say the words, "I'm ready."

"Good. I'll meet you at the courthouse at seven thirty." A pause.

"Remember everything we talked about."

"Okay."

I hang up.

I lied to him—I don't feel ready at all. But it's too late to back out now. This is what I wanted.

I imagine taking all my pain and confusion, folding it up, and tucking it into a drawer in the back of my mind, close to the Vault. When I meet Judge Gray tomorrow, I have to put on a mask of normality. I can't be distracted.

I lock the drawer, putting Stanley firmly in the past.

The courthouse is on the other side of town, a fifteen-minute drive away. It looks the same as I remember: a huge, square building made of dark stone blocks polished to a reflective sheen, with wide steps leading up to a pair of heavy gray double doors.

Dr. Bernhardt is waiting at the top of the stairs, his cheeks flushed in the cold, a knitted scarf wrapped around his neck. He's holding a store bag, which he pushes into my hands. "Here. Wear this."

I remove a cardboard box, which contains a dark gray pantsuit with thin white stripes. "Why."

"Because you want to look professional and mature."

I glance down at my skirt, black-and-white-striped stockings, and T-shirt. The words HEAVY METAL gleam, shiny and metallic, above a faded graphic of a woman in armor riding a pterodactyl-like creature. "What's wrong with the clothes I'm wearing."

He laughs and shakes his head. I tense. "Sorry," he says. "I'm not making fun of you. Just trust me on this one, all right?"

We go in. A security guard asks us to empty our pockets into a plastic bin, then waves us through a metal detector—I hold my breath, wondering if someone will try to give me a pat-down, but thankfully, no one tries to touch me. I change in the bathroom, putting my old clothes in the paper bag. The pantsuit is polyester; the material feels stiff and unpleasant against my skin, but I'll only have to wear it for a few hours.

When I exit the bathroom, Dr. Bernhardt is waiting. "Better." He gives me a smile. "Just remember—be honest, but not *too* honest. And stay calm."

"I'll try." My stomach hurts. What happens if this goes wrong? No—I can't allow myself to think that way, or I'll start to panic.

"You can handle this," he says.

I hesitate. "If the judge grants our request, does that mean you won't be visiting me in the future."

"Yes. You won't have to put up with my nagging anymore." He smiles.

I try to respond and find that, for some reason, there's a lump blocking my throat. *This is what you wanted*, I remind myself.

He extends a hand. "Good luck, Alvie."

I brace myself, grip his hand, and shake once. His skin is soft and dry; the physical contact doesn't bother me as much as I thought it might. "Thank you," I say.

I release him, and he turns and walks away.

I stare at the hallway ahead of me. The courtroom is at the end. I feel very small and very alone, and I'm filled with a sudden conviction that this is going to be a disaster. My legs don't want to move, but I force them to walk forward . . . slowly, because my knees keep wobbling.

The courtroom isn't large; it feels private and enclosed, like an interrogation chamber. Dingy blue carpet covers the floor, and the walls are wood paneled. Judge Gray—a fiftyish woman with a small, pinched mouth—is already there, sitting in a chair behind a massive desk. She's the same woman who presided over my case when I first asked for emancipation. Only one other person is there, a younger woman sitting behind another desk, who I assume is a transcriptionist or notetaker.

I sit in the smaller chair facing Judge Gray, folding my hands in my lap. She studies me for a moment in silence, then examines a sheet of paper in her hand. I fidget. Already, I want my Rubik's Cube, but I left it outside in the paper bag with my clothes; it wouldn't fit in the pocket of my pantsuit. I try to remember the questions and answers I rehearsed with Dr. Bernhardt over the past few weeks, but my mind is a blank.

"Alvie Fitz," she says. "You're seventeen years old now. Is that correct?"

Hot fluorescents beat down on the top of my head. "Yes."

"And you've been living in your own apartment and working at the Hickory Park Zoo as a full-time employee for eighteen months."

"That's correct."

"Mr. Bernhardt has stated—"

"Doctor."

She frowns. "Excuse me?"

"Dr. Bernhardt," I correct, and immediately realize I should have kept my mouth shut. But because I've already said it, I feel inclined to clarify. "He has a PhD in sociology."

"I see. Well." She clears her throat. "*Dr.* Bernhardt says your condition has improved." She folds her hands and clicks her long thumbnails together. The sound makes me squirm. "As I recall, when we last met, you were living in the Safe Rest Home for girls. You ran away on three separate occasions, and on one of those occasions, there was a police report filed. Prior to your stay at Safe Rest Home, you spent several years in a psychiatric ward. Is that right?"

My nails dig into my palms. I struggle to control my breathing. "That is correct."

"Are you currently seeing a counselor?"

"No."

"And why is that?"

I speak slowly, choosing my words with care. "My emotional issues are under control. I'm much more stable now than I was a year and a half ago. I don't see a need for therapy."

Her pale blue eyes narrow slightly. "Do you believe your earlier diagnosis was inaccurate, then?"

Sweat pools at the small of my back. My fingers itch to start pulling my braids, but I resist. I know that any twitch, any display of emotion, of anger or fear, could be interpreted as a sign of instability. What am I supposed to say? What's the right answer? My eyes dart back and forth. The urge to start rocking and tugging my braids grows stronger and stronger, until it feels like trying not to blink.

"Ms. Fitz? Do you understand the question?"

"Which diagnosis do you mean," I ask, stalling for time. "There have been several."

"I'm referring to the diagnosis of Asperger's syndrome. If you have a mental disability, I'm sure you understand why that would influence my decision."

I think about pointing out that Asperger's isn't a mental disability, it's a *social* disability, or perhaps just a natural variation on the standard neurological configuration. But I have the sense that arguing with her would not impact her views, and might make her angry. "You mean, if I'm mentally disabled, you won't hold me accountable for the things I did."

"No. I mean, it might necessitate placing you under permanent guardianship. The state would appoint someone to help you manage your affairs."

Permanent guardianship. I start to shake. Is this really happening? Is she going to hand over control of my life to a total stranger? I struggle to hold my tone steady. "Not everyone with autism is under guardianship. Many people with an Asperger's diagnosis have gone on to have successful careers, even get married and have children."

"If that's the case, they were obviously not diagnosed accurately in the first place." She sniffs. "Doctors love to throw around diagnostic labels. Perhaps I'm old-fashioned, but I believe there's such a thing as simple bad decision making, and that sometimes, a case of immaturity and teenaged rebelliousness can be cured by a dose of cold, hard reality."

I want to tell her that it's not that simple. Being able to hold down a job doesn't mean I'm not *different.* My brain hasn't changed just because my situation has. But what I say next will determine the course of my entire future. I have to be extremely careful. "What are you asking, exactly."

"I'm asking you if you consider yourself autistic," she says.

A flash of panic goes off in my head like a bomb, and my vision goes fuzzy and white. No matter what I say, I feel, it will be wrong. But I have to say *something.* In a split second, I make a decision. "No. I believe my diagnosis was a mistake."

"So, you're perfectly normal, then?"

I try to swallow the burning at the back of my throat. I wish I could read voices; I can't tell if she's being sarcastic or asking a serious question. But it's too late to backtrack now. "Yes."

She presses the tips of her index fingers together. Her expression is blank. "Well," she says at last, "it seems you've grown up quite a bit in the past year and a half. And I believe in giving second chances to those who are willing to work for them. Seeing as how you've successfully lived on your own for this long and become a contributing member of society, I see no reason why I shouldn't grant your request for emancipation." She stamps the paper in front of her. "You're free to go."

I'm in a daze as I walk out of the courtroom, clutching my certificate of adulthood in one hand. I'm still waiting for it to sink in. My whole body feels uncomfortably hot and prickly, and the back of my throat burns dully. Acid reflux, perhaps, from the stress.

I suspect the pantsuit had something to do with my unexpected success . . . though it seems absurd that something as trivial as clothing should have an impact on the judgment of a person whose entire purpose is to impartially and objectively mete out the law. The idea of buying new clothes for the hearing did not even cross my mind. In retrospect, I should have done more to prepare. Without Dr. Bernhardt's help, I might still be a ward of the state.

I never even thanked him—not properly. My short, cursory expression of gratitude feels inadequate. I scan my surroundings, but he's nowhere to be seen.

Maybe he left already. There's a faint ache in my chest that I recognize, after a moment, as disappointment. But then, he has no more responsibility toward me, and he probably has other things he needs to do, other disturbed teenagers to visit.

For a few minutes, I just stand there in the middle of the broad hallway with its glossy, black-marble-tiled floor. After all those months of struggling to prove myself, the decision was made in less than ten minutes, and all I had to do was lie. I look at the document with the judge's official stamp of approval declaring me a functional member of society, and I feel strangely empty.

Back home, I stick the certificate in a desk drawer.

A glance at the clock tells me it's almost nine thirty. I push aside my misgivings, strip off the pantsuit, and grab my khaki-colored uniform.

Time for work.

CHAPTER TWENTY-THREE

The sun is bright, the day clear and cold. When I arrive at Hickory Park's main office building to clock in, I see a cluster of zoo employees huddled in the hallway. Ms. Nell's flamingo-pink jacket stands out in the crowd. Toby is slumped against a wall, his face pale as cottage cheese. When I walk closer, I see that he's holding a towel against his arm. Blood soaks through, red against white.

"Didn't I warn you?" Ms. Nell shouts.

"I just wanted to feed him," Toby whines. "I see that Alvie chick doing it all the time. But when I opened the cage door he went psycho!"

My stomach turns hollow. *Chance.* He's talking about Chance.

"Never mind." Ms. Nell sighs. "I'll call your parents. You keep pressure on that cut until the ambulance gets here."

He sniffles. "Hey, I get workmen's comp for this, right?"

"We'll talk about that later." She glares at the crowd. "All of you, get lost! You got work to do!"

The crowd disperses. Ms. Nell ushers Toby into the break room, then bustles back through the hall, muttering to herself.

Before I have a chance to ask her any questions, she retreats into her office and slams the door. I wait a few minutes, then press my ear against the wood, listening.

"Yes? No, he's fine. . . . Your boy is fine." A pause. "Let's not start talking about lawyers. This was a simple accident. I'm sure we can come to some kind of agreement." Another pause. "Now, listen here. We can't be held accountable for employees breaking the rules. Toby was repeatedly warned about going into that enclosure."

A sneeze builds in my nose, tickling. I muffle it against one arm, but Ms. Nell falls silent, and I know she's heard me. I slip away and hurry down the path toward Chance.

I find him sitting on his perch, unharmed. Traces of blood gleam on his long, curved black claws. As I approach, he croaks low in his throat. *Guh-ruk.*

I sit down on the ground next to the enclosure. I don't move for a long time.

The next day, when I arrive, there's a white truck parked in my usual spot. I try to remember what it's for. The food delivery truck is yellow; the veterinary supplies truck is green. I've never seen this one.

I clock in at the main office building, then follow the cobblestone path between the rows of birch trees. When I get to Chance's cage, my chest seizes up. The cage is empty.

I run straight to the main building, to Ms. Nell's office. Her door is unlocked, and she's hunched over her desk, reading a paperback romance. When the door bangs open, she jerks upright. "Alvie? What the hell?"

I stride forward and stop when my knees bump against her desk. Her shoulders tense.

"Listen here. You can't just barge into my office and—"

"Where is Chance."

She grimaces, then sighs. "I couldn't keep that bird around, not after what happened. It was too aggressive, too unpredictable."

"What happened wasn't Chance's fault," I say, speaking as calmly as I can. "He just panicked. I *know* him. He didn't mean to hurt Toby."

She rubs the bridge of her nose. "That's not the issue. The kid's parents were foaming at the mouth. His mother's a rich-as-piss lawyer, his dad's a doctor, and their precious baby-poo had come home with five stitches in his arm. They wanted blood. I had to do *something*."

As she speaks, the coldness in my stomach deepens and spreads. "Where is Chance."

She looks away. "It's too late, Alvie. He's gone."

I lean forward and plant my hands on the desk. "Where. Is. He."

Her red-painted lips are pressed into a thin, almost invisible line, her fingers clenched tight on the paperback. A shirtless man in a cowboy hat stares out of the cover. "Do I need to call security?"

My breathing comes shallow and fast. As realization sinks in, light-headedness passes over me. "You killed him," I whisper.

She freezes. A muscle twitches in her cheek. When she speaks again, her voice is dangerously soft. "I did the responsible thing. Chance was sick—"

"No, he wasn't."

"He was sick in the head," she snaps. "And he wasn't getting any better. Putting him down was a mercy."

I want to scream. "You killed him because he was inconvenient to you."

The blood drains from her face. Then she flushes, and her eyes narrow. "You think I *wanted* to do this? I had no choice. Those rich assholes could shut this place down. One crazy-ass bird ain't worth my livelihood . . . not to mention my employees! What the hell would you do without this place, anyway? What the hell do you know?"

"I know that you had a responsibility to Chance." I'm making things worse, but I can't stop myself.

A vein pulses in her temple. "Well, this isn't your zoo, and it's not your call to make. It's mine. This is going to happen, and there's nothing you can do about it."

Going to happen. That means it hasn't happened yet. There's still a chance to stop it. Breathing hard, I turn to walk out of the office, and Ms. Nell's voice stops me: "I'm not through with you. Sit down."

I stand, feet rooted to the spot. My heart knocks against my sternum.

"If you walk out now, don't bother coming back. Ever. I gave you so many chances, Alvie. I forgave every blunder, every stupid remark you made to the customers, because I felt sorry for you. But I'm done giving you second chances. If you don't sit down right now, you can kiss this job good-bye."

My nails dig into my palms, hard enough to send twinges of pain shooting up my arms.

I walk out.

The sunlight glares at me, blinding white, as I stride through the zoo and into the parking lot. The truck is still there, idling. Two men stand beside it, smoking and talking.

I get into my car and watch, heart thudding, as the men get into the truck. Slowly it pulls out of the parking lot. I wait a moment or two, then follow.

The time slips by, dreamy and unreal, as I tail the truck past strip malls and fields, down long, lonely highways, always staying far enough back that my presence isn't too obvious. I don't have a plan. I don't even know where they're going; all I can do is keep following.

At last, the truck pulls into a lot in front of a small, gray windowless building. The sky above is smudged with dark clouds.

I park in front of a doughnut shop across the street and watch in the rearview mirror as the men park, get out, and open the back of the truck. Because of the angle, I can't see what's inside. The men circle around and disappear behind the building, probably going through a back entrance to get a pushcart for the truck's cargo. I get out of my car and dash across the street toward the building. Behind it, I see a fenced-in area covered with stubbly yellow grass. In the center stands a small structure, a rectangle of brick. It might be a storage shed.

As I move closer, a peculiar smell invades my nostrils: a cold, dead, ashy smell. I take another look at the shed. There's a small metal door, too small for a person to go through without stooping. The bricks are blackened around the edges with soot. Down near the base of the door, on one rounded brick, is a smear of something rust-colored. The hairs on the back of my neck rise. It's not a shed at all. It's an incinerator.

Angry buzzing fills my ears. Black flecks race across my vision.

Death itself is just part of the order of things; I know that. Every day, I fed dead mice to Chance. I've seen gazelles ripped apart on nature shows. But this—this is different. This isn't about killing to eat, killing to live. This is a place where animals deemed worthless are erased from existence, burned away until there's nothing left, not even bones. The rust-colored smear on the stone seems to swell, filling my vision, then dissolves into a swirl of red and gray. The colors melt into black. I shut my eyes tightly and back away, hands against my temples.

I want Stanley. I want his warmth, his calming scent. But Stanley isn't here now, and that's my own doing. I have to deal with this myself.

The men are nowhere in sight. I circle toward the back of the truck.

Inside, pairs of small, reflective eyes stare at me through cage bars—more unwanted animals. I see a few scrawny, mangy cats, a quivering brown dog with one eye, and an obese guinea pig. And there, in the back, almost obscured by the other cages, is Chance. It *must* be him. The mass of brown feathers inside the carrier cage is motionless, and for a sickening moment, I think I'm too late—then I discern the slight rise and fall of his chest. He's alive. Sedated, most likely.

I climb into the truck, grab the carrier, hop out, and start to run—then freeze. The other animals stare at me, glassy-eyed with fear.

If I set them free, where will they go? I can't care for them myself; I don't have the room or the resources. They'll be alone, probably frightened. There will be no guarantee of survival. But if I leave them here, they'll definitely be killed.

The dog whimpers.

The cages have simple latch locks. I flip them all open. Sometimes, an animal that has been caged for a long time will choose to ignore an open door, preferring the comfort of captivity. I can't force them to escape. All I can do is give them the option.

But I won't leave Chance. I've destroyed nearly everything that matters to me, but I can save *him*, at least. I can do this much.

I seize his carrier from the truck and make a dash for my car. My body feels oddly weightless, yet I seem to be moving in slow motion, as if I were running on the moon. I open the door, shove the carrier onto the passenger seat, and fumble with my keys.

As I drive, the world floats past, and my mind seems to be suspended somewhere outside my body, like a balloon. Beneath the thin layer of calm, there's a rising tide of panic.

For now, I'll take Chance back to my apartment. There, I'll have a minute to calm myself and analyze the best possible course of action. Somehow, I'll make this work.

He'll need food, so I make a stop at an exotic pet store, home to snakes, iguanas, and a few large birds. I buy a box of frozen feeder mice sealed in individual bags, stiff and cold under the clear plastic, like white furry Popsicles.

I arrive home, elbow my door shut, and set the carrier cage on the coffee table.

Scrape, scrape. Chance's carrier wobbles. He's waking up.

When I unlatch the door, he lunges out and tumbles onto the couch in a feathered heap. His beak is open, his copper-gold eyes pinning with agitation, pupils dilating and contracting rapidly.

I reach out. He leaps off the couch, flapping his wing hard, and slams against the window; his claws snag on the curtain and rip it down. Tangled in cloth, he falls and flops around on the carpet. I grab the curtain and tug it off, freeing him. He promptly tries to launch himself into the air again and instead crashes into a pile of books and magazines, scattering them. His talons splay across the glossy cover of a science fiction paperback as his wing and tail feathers fan out, seeking balance.

For a minute, he paces the room, his movements rapid and jerky. His tail feathers lift, and a dropping falls to the floor.

Well, the carpet is already filthy. The excrement practically blends in with its dirty off-white color.

Breathe in, breathe out. *Focus.* One problem at a time.

I spread some newspapers across the floor. I tape some more on the window to replace the torn curtain.

Next: food for my new houseguest.

In my kitchen, I boil some water on the stove, then turn off the flame and submerge the frozen mice in the kettle. They bob up and down, beady black eyes staring up at me.

Keeping a bird of prey is illegal unless you have a license, which I do not. I have to be careful, but as long as no one finds out about Chance, he should be safe here. For a while. The bigger issue is my newfound unemployment.

For eighteen months, my job at Hickory Park Zoo was my anchor. It was proof that I was a functioning adult, that I could make it on my own, that I wasn't the useless, helpless burden that so many people assumed I was. And now it's gone.

I can't afford to waste time moping. Rent is due in five days, and I have sixty-two dollars in my checking account. I need a new job.

I squeeze one of the bagged mice, making sure it's soft and squishy. Then I unbag it and deposit it on the floor near Chance's feet. "Dinner," I say.

Chance cocks his head and blinks with his inner eyelids, filmy membranes flicking across the bright orbs. He punctures the mouse's belly with his beak and pulls out a long string of guts, like pink spaghetti.

Sitting on the couch, I power up my laptop and do a search for jobs in the area. Burrito Mania, the Mexican takeout place a few blocks from my house, is hiring.

I bring up an online application. On the screen, a cartoon

burrito in a sombrero smiles at me as I read the first question: *So, why are YOU passionate about working at Burrito Mania?*

I don't know how to answer this. I don't understand why anyone would be passionate about working at Burrito Mania. I've been told before that "I need money" is not an acceptable answer, even though that's why most people are looking for work. I finally write *I like burritos*, which is both true and relevant. It's possible that I'll get a discount on the food if I work there. In the interest of full disclosure, I add that Mexican food makes me gassy, so I try not to consume it more than once or twice a week.

The next question asks, *Are you a "people person"?*

I don't see any way to answer that honestly without making myself look bad, so I leave it blank.

As I glance through more applications for restaurants and stores, I find myself leaving lots of lines blank.

Do you consider yourself a team player?

Are you outgoing?

What makes you fun to be around?

How would your friends describe you?

The words start to blur and dance around on the screen like malevolent ants.

On a coffee shop website, I click on a link, bringing up another application. *What are your core values, and how do you think working at Jitters would help you express those values?*

I believe that it's important to be honest, and I believe that the feelings of all beings should be respected, and I believe that it's wrong to hurt people or animals, unless it's in self-defense.

But I don't understand how working at a coffee shop will help me express any of these values, except that I'm not planning to murder any customers.

What do you consider to be your greatest flaw?

I don't understand why I can't just show up and do the job. I don't understand why simple competence isn't enough, why they have to dig around in my psyche and examine every filthy secret.

Describe a problem at your last job and explain how you resolved that problem.

I resolved it by getting fired.

My stomach clenches in a spasm. I can't do this. I can't—I can't—

I jerk to my feet and kick over the coffee table. The laptop tumbles to the floor, and Chance's head swivels toward me. A string of mouse guts dangles from his beak.

All the strength runs out of me, and I slump against the wall as if all my bones have turned liquid. My chest heaves.

I need to get a grip on myself.

I sit down, pick up my laptop. One by one, I go through the applications and fill out the parts that I know I can do: my name, my address and phone number, my education and previous experience. I leave everything else blank. I'll just have to send them in like this and hope that it's enough.

Once I'm finished, I collapse on the couch, exhausted, and drift in and out of a troubled sleep. Outside the window, wind howls, and sleet hammers the glass. It's begun to storm. My vision blurs, then goes dark as I sink inside myself.

CHAPTER TWENTY-FOUR

It's July, and the world outside is velvety dark green. The air is hot and sticky and filled with the syrupy hum of cicadas. Our air conditioner is broken, and damp clothes cling to my sweaty skin.

"You know, you can't just stay at home all the time," Mama says. "You're not making any progress like this."

I kick my legs against the chair, looking at her across the breakfast table. Since I was expelled a few months ago, I've spent most of my time reading. I swallow a mouthful of pancakes and say, "I'm learning about rabbit behavior."

She smiles a tight, closed-lipped smile and says, "That's not what I mean, honey."

I poke at the pancakes with my fork. Her shirt, I notice, is inside out and backward. The tag juts out from the collar.

"I think we should take you to see another doctor," Mama says. "A specialist."

There was a time when Mama and I were friends, when we used to laugh together, when she didn't care so much about the fact that I wasn't like other children. I was just her little girl. Now, everything is about counselors and treatments and therapies. I know it's my own fault for causing so much trouble, but I wish things could go back to the way they used to be. "Doctors cost too much money," I point out. "You're always saying so."

"That doesn't matter." She grips her fork like a weapon. "I'll spend whatever it takes. I'll find a way. I want you to get better."

I tug on my braid.

"I know it's difficult, but please try not to do that," she says. "You remember what Dr. Evans said? It's better if you learn to control that now, while you're young."

I sit on my hands. My breathing comes short and shallow.

"I've already made an appointment," she says. "We're going to see Dr. Ash this afternoon."

There's no point in arguing, no point in saying anything. The decision has been made. Once, a while back, I tried hiding under my bed when I didn't want to go to an appointment. Mama forcibly dragged me out, ignoring my cries of protest.

At four, we arrive at Dr. Ash's office, and he asks Mama to wait in the room outside while he talks to me. I sit in the chair, tense and fidgeting. Dr. Ash has thinning blond hair, a lot of diplomas on his walls, and a plastic multicolored brain on his desk. He notices me studying the brain, smiles, and says, "You want to pick that up?"

I nod.

"Go ahead."

I turn it over in my hands. It's like a puzzle, with different pieces that snap together. I take it apart, feel the hippocampus—which is small and curled up, like a shrimp—and explore the whorls and convolutions of the cortex.

"Your mother tells me you read a lot."

"Yes."

He takes out a notepad. "What else do you enjoy doing?"

"Drawing. Mazes mostly. And I like animals."

He writes something down. "Now, I'm just going to ask a few more questions. You were diagnosed with PDD-NOS a few years ago, and you received some counseling and treatment for it, but you've continued to struggle at school. Is that correct?"

I nod, clutching the plastic hippocampus against my chest. Something about its shape is comforting.

"And recently you were expelled. Can you tell me what happened?"

"I hit some boys," I mutter.

He folds his hands, and his thin sandy eyebrows wrinkle together. "And why did you do that?"

I think about those bullies, laughing and saying their ugly, cruel words. My nails dig into my palms. "Because they deserved it."

He hums in his throat, taps his thumbs together, and studies me in silence for a few seconds. Then he asks a question I don't expect: "Do you ever have the feeling that everyone is against you? The teachers or other students, for instance?"

I think about the other children, whispering about me behind my back. I think about the girls on the playground who laughed when I barked like a dog, about the teacher who put me in a box. I think about the principal staring at me with his dark beady eyes, his words to the secretary, when he thought I wasn't listening: *There's something unnatural about that girl.* I gulp, my heartbeat quickening. "Yes."

He writes something else down on his pad of paper. "Can you talk about that more?"

I bow my head. "No one cares about me. They all say they want to help, but they don't."

"Mmm. Do you feel that way about your mother, too?"

I hesitate. "No. Mama isn't like that." After a few seconds, I add, "But sometimes I think she only likes the other me."

He raises his eyebrows. "The *other* you?"

"Yes." My body rocks slowly in the chair as I grip the plastic hippocampus in one hand, groping for the words to explain. *I miss the real you.* "Mama says there's another 'me' inside me. Sometimes I think Mama is talking to her."

"Well, that's . . . interesting." He clears his throat and writes something else down. "Alvie, do you ever see or hear anything strange? Do you ever notice things, for instance, that the people around you don't seem aware of?"

I think about the way that clinking glass scrapes along my nerves, the way ticking clocks echo inside my head and loud voices make me want to curl up into a ball and hide. No one else ever seems to notice these things. "Yes."

"Are they voices, or noises, or something else?"

"Both."

"Do these things bother you or cause you stress?"

"Yes."

Dr. Ash nods and writes down a few more things. "That must have made school very difficult for you."

My heart is beating fast. Maybe this, at last, is the doctor who will actually *listen* to me. Maybe he'll be the one who takes me seriously and helps me instead of thinking that it's all my fault. "Yes."

Then he leans forward and speaks in a low, serious voice. "Now, I need you to answer this question very truthfully, even if you think I won't like the answer."

I nod.

"Have you ever heard voices telling you to hurt someone?"

The hairs on my neck tingle and stand on end. Something has shifted. He's looking at me too intently. There's something frightening behind his mild expression, like a panther crouched and ready to spring. I don't know what's changed or why he's asking me a question like that, but somehow I feel like whatever I say, it will be the wrong answer.

I look at the wall. "I don't want to talk about this anymore."

"Why not?"

I don't say anything.

He keeps asking questions, but I don't respond. Finally Dr. Ash brings Mama into the room. She sits, clutching her purse strap. She's wearing makeup today, which she almost never does. Her lips look like they've been drawn on in bright red crayon, and her moist eyes stare out from messy blue-black circles, like bruises.

"Ms. Fitz . . . this might seem like an odd question, but can you tell me anything about Alvie's father? You mentioned you haven't been in contact with him for a while. What was he like? Did he ever exhibit any unusual behavior?"

"Unusual?" She presses her lips together, smudging her lipstick. "He was . . . a little eccentric, I suppose. He had all kinds of ideas about conspiracies and the government and chemical trails in the sky. I never really understood the things he talked about. I never even graduated high school." She gives a weak chuckle.

"Tell me more," Dr. Ash says. "Was he ever violent?"

Her smile fades. "He never raised a hand against me or anyone else. He wasn't that sort of person."

Dr. Ash simply waits, looking at her.

"He had terrible mood swings," Mama says. "When it got very bad, he would start shouting—railing against everyone and everything. He knocked over tables and chairs. It was . . . frightening. But he *never* hit me. And afterward, he would apologize over and over. He told me that I was the brightest thing in his world."

"I see."

"He left when she was only a baby. He told me that he wasn't fit to be a father." Her eyes drift off to the side. "It was very hard."

"Hm," the doctor says. "And was he ever evaluated by a psychologist?"

"No. Why are you asking these questions?"

"I'm wondering if Alvie has any history of schizophrenia in her family."

"What? No. You don't think she's . . . oh God." The blood drains from her face, and she clutches the chair's arm as if she thinks she might fall off. "No. That can't be it. None of the other doctors said anything about that."

I squirm in my chair.

"It's rare for this condition to occur in children her age," Dr. Ash says, "but it's not unheard-of. And it does run in families."

Mama presses a hand to her mouth and closes her eyes.

"We might have caught it in the early stages," he says. "I can't be sure, since she seems reticent about answering questions. But based on some of the things she's been telling me, and her history of violent outbursts, I think we're better off erring on the side of caution."

"What should I do?" Mama whispers.

Dr. Ash glances at me, then away. "I can write you a prescription for a new medication. In addition to curbing any delusions or psychotic breaks, the drug should cause an emotional flattening—a desirable effect, in this case. It'll level her out, so to speak."

I stare at my feet. "There's nothing wrong with me."

"We're trying to help you," Dr. Ash says.

I feel sick. I thought he was different, but I was wrong. "I don't need your help. I never asked for help. I just want people to leave me alone."

"Please, Alvie," Mama says in a small voice. "Just do what he says?"

I bow my head.

"If you have any problems," Dr. Ash says, scribbling something on a little piece of paper, "give me a call."

I take the pills. I don't want to, but Mama begs me.

Over the next few weeks, a black haze swallows me. I've taken medications before, but it was nothing like this. These drugs dull my thoughts as well as my feelings. I feel like I'm living and walking inside a bubble of water that muffles people's voices and makes everything blurry and wobbly. I watch my own body from outside as I dress myself, eat breakfast, and sleepwalk through day after day. Nothing bothers me anymore, because nothing matters anymore.

Somewhere deep beneath the haze, in the part of me that can still feel, I hate it.

Every morning, Mama makes me take a pill with breakfast, and she makes me open my mouth to be sure I've swallowed it. I start to hide the pills under my tongue, then spit them out into the sink later, but soon Mama figures out this trick and starts checking under my tongue. So I start swallowing the pills, then sticking my fingers down my throat and vomiting them up in the bathroom. Then Mama overhears me, and after that she won't let me go to the bathroom until two hours after I take the pill.

It's hard to think with the drugs swimming in my head, but I know I have to find some way out, or I'll feel this way forever.

When I finally stumble on a solution, it's almost absurdly simple. I find some vitamins at the local drugstore that look just like my pills, and I buy several bottles with my allowance. While Mama is asleep one night, I dump all the pills down the toilet and replace them with the vitamins.

It works. Mama thinks I'm taking the medication, and the haze slowly dissipates.

Thank God.

Once my head is clear again, I go to the library and do some reading on the drug that Dr. Ash prescribed me, and I'm shocked at the long list of side effects, some of them serious and life-threatening. These grown-ups are trying to kill me.

No, I think, not Mama. Mama just believes everything the doctors tell her. But I have to be more careful in the future. Telling things to grown-ups isn't safe.

A few weeks later, Mama takes me back to Dr. Ash. I make sure to tell him that everything is fine, that I'm feeling better, that I'm not angry or scared anymore, and that I've been taking my medicine. All lies. He says that my behavior has improved dramatically and that I can return to school in the fall. Obviously I can't go back to my old school, but Mama picks out another one—a normal public school with normal children.

"You see?" Mama says, beaming. "You just needed the right medication."

When we get a refill at the pharmacy, I sneak out of my bedroom at night after Mama goes to bed, take the bottle from the medicine cabinet, dump the pills down the toilet, and replace them with vitamins again.

For a while, everything is okay.

Then things start to change. I notice Mama sitting at the desk in her bedroom more and more, looking through papers and writing things down, muttering to herself the whole time. The phone starts ringing more and more often. And whenever I go to pick it up, she says, "Don't answer." We start getting envelopes with big red letters saying FINAL NOTICE on the front. I know something is happening, but whenever I ask Mama, she just shakes her head and smiles and says, "It's nothing you need to worry about."

One day, near the end of August, Mama comes home from her job with a strange look on her face. Her eyes are wide and glazed, her mouth open slightly, like she's not quite awake. "Mama," I say, "what's wrong."

"Nothing." She locks herself in the bedroom.

I call to her. I knock on the door. At first, she doesn't respond. Then I hear her feet shuffling across the carpet, and she whispers in a weak, hoarse voice, "I'm not feeling well, honey. I need some time alone."

For the rest of the night, she doesn't come out, not even to eat. She doesn't come out the next morning, either. I start to get scared. I knock on the door. "Mama. Are you okay." After a few minutes, I knock again. "Mama."

I hear her voice at last, scratchy and almost inaudible through the door: "I have the flu. I just need to rest."

Another day goes by, and Mama is still locked in her bedroom. I don't know how to cook, so I eat cereal out of the box.

Just a little longer, I think. She'll be better soon.

Except I know it's not the flu.

The phone calls keep coming, shrill rings echoing through the house, until finally she comes out. Her expression is blank, her eyes puffy, her hair in a disarray. She shuffles over to the phone, unplugs it from the wall, then goes back into her bedroom and shuts the door again.

When Mama finally comes out of her room, I find her sitting at the kitchen table, head cradled in her hands.

"Mama . . ."

Very slowly she raises her head. "How long has it been?"

I hesitate. "Three days."

"God." She closes her eyes and presses the heels of her hands against them. I wait. "I'm sorry. It's just . . . I don't know what to do anymore." There's a long pause. "I lost my job."

I approach cautiously, as if she were a wounded animal, and I sit down in the chair next to hers. "It's okay. You can get another job."

"It's not that easy."

I place my hand over hers, because I don't know what else to do.

"I left you alone," she whispers. Her hand trembles beneath mine. "I left my baby alone."

"It's all right. I'm fine." My stomach is a hard, tight ball.

A tear drips to the table. "I'm so sorry, Alvie."

I tug my braid over and over.

Her eyes focus on my hand, and she watches me. Then her head drops into her hands again.

When she finally speaks, her voice is soft and hoarse. "I'm a failure as a mother. I can't take care of you the way you need. I've never been able to do it. And now, I can't even pay for your medication. Things were just starting to get better, and now it's all over." She hangs her head, long red hair swinging like a curtain in front of her face. Her thin shoulders hunch. "There's nothing left. I don't even know how I'm going to pay the electric bill this month. The air conditioner is broken. Everything is broken."

I tug harder on my braid, rocking back and forth in my chair.

"Please don't," she whispers.

I catch my wrist and force myself to stop.

Then she shakes her head. "No, no. You can't help it. I'm sorry. It's just . . . I don't know what to do. Without that job, we have no health insurance, and I don't know what you're going to do without those pills."

But, Mama, I haven't taken them for weeks and I'm fine, see?

I don't say this out loud, because I don't know what will happen if I tell her what I've been doing. It might make things worse. "I don't think there's anything wrong with me," I say instead, cautiously.

She smiles bleakly. "Your father always said the same thing."

I don't know how to respond to this. So I start to fill a teapot with water for chamomile tea. Sometimes tea makes Mama feel better, but it doesn't always work. I have a feeling it won't work this time.

"I don't know what to do," she whispers.

I put the teapot on the stove. "I'm making tea," I say.

Mama stares straight ahead. Her face is limp, mouth slightly open, like she's forgotten how to move the muscles. "I can't keep going like this. I just can't. But I can't leave you alone."

I stop. A chill runs down my back. "Are you going away."

She's silent.

"Please don't leave me," I say.

She looks up, a strange expression on her face. Her eyes lose focus. Then she smiles. "Don't worry, honey. I'm not going anywhere."

CHAPTER TWENTY-FIVE

A twitch has developed at the corner of my left eye. I note the involuntary fluttering of the muscle beneath my skin. It happens in fits, twitching for several minutes at a time, then subsiding for a half hour or so before it starts up again. I wonder if this is an early sign of an approaching mental breakdown.

Chance is perched atop the back of my armchair; the upholstery is now peppered with talon punctures. I sit on my couch, eating dry Cocoa Puffs from the box with one hand and watching an old episode of *Cosmos*. Usually the show is effective at reducing anxiety—remembering the vastness of the universe helps me put my own problems in perspective—but today, it's not working.

A week has passed since I lost my job. I've turned in over a hundred applications, and so far, no one has called me. I'm down to my last few boxes of cereal, my checking account is empty, and despite my cleaning efforts, my apartment is always covered in mouse blood, feathers, and bird shit. By now, it's probably not an exaggeration to say that I'm living in the midst of a biohazard. I douse the apartment with pine-scented aerosol spray to mask the smell.

I reach into the box again, and my hand comes out empty. I upend the box, collecting the last bit of chocolate-flavored sugar dust from the bottom, then lick my palm clean. I feel disgusting. I *am* disgusting. But I'm not about to waste precious calories. My ribs are already showing.

There's a sudden, loud knocking. I give a start, and Chance's head swivels toward the door.

"Miss Fitz?" It's Mrs. Schultz, the landlady. Her full, booming voice cuts through the silence. "Miss Fitz, may I speak with you?"

I swallow the half-chewed lump of cereal in my mouth. It sticks in my throat. Of course I know what she wants to talk about. She's already left three voice mails about rent, which I've ignored, because I have nothing to tell her—or at least, nothing that would help my situation. *I got fired for vigilante animal rights activity* would probably not make her more sympathetic to my plight.

More knocking. "I know you're in there. Do I need to keep shouting at you, or are you going to open this door?"

I look at Chance. If she sees him, I'll be instantly evicted. "No."

There's a brief silence. When she speaks again, her voice is sharper, almost shrill. "You think this is some kinda *joke*?"

"No. I just don't want to open the door right now. I'm—" I pause, fumbling for an excuse. "I'm in a robe." It's true, anyway.

She breathes a low, heavy sigh and mutters something incoherent under her breath, then raises her voice again. "You know that your rent's overdue, right?"

"Yes."

Chance shifts his weight, talons flexing and clenching. I grip the armrest. *Please don't start shrieking.*

"Well, have you got the money?"

"No." I swallow. I need to offer her some kind of explanation; she won't let up, otherwise. "I lost my job at the zoo. But I'm going to get another one soon. I've been sending in job applications every day." Even if I leave parts blank, it still counts. "I'll get you the money. I just need a little more time."

There's a long pause. "I'll give you till the end of the month. After that, you're gonna be looking for a new apartment. You understand?"

My throat cinches shut. I swallow a few times, trying to loosen it. "I understand."

"Good. 'Cause I'm not playing around." There's a pause, then: "What's that smell?"

I look at the white-spattered newspapers and the small, compact clump of glistening rat intestines near the foot of my coffee table. I'm normally not good at lying on the spot, but there happens to be a commercial for Burrito Mania on TV. The cartoon burrito dances around, grinning as the camera floats over a plate of enchiladas smothered in something orange. In a burst of inspiration, I say, "I had Mexican takeout last night. It affects my digestion."

This is also true, though if my gas actually smelled *this* potent, it would be a sign that I needed urgent medical attention. I can only hope she'll believe the excuse.

"Christ on a cracker," she mutters. The floorboards creak under her receding footsteps.

I exhale slowly. Whether she believes me or not, it seems I've been granted a temporary reprieve . . . but I now have a deadline. The end of the month. Fifteen days.

Chance watches me. His inner eyelids flick back and forth.

More than once, I've gotten so low that I've thought about calling Dr. Bernhardt and asking for help. But he's no longer my guardian; he has no obligation to help me. What could he do, anyway?

I grab my coat and decide that I'm not going to come back to my apartment until I've found a job. If I'm evicted, there's no telling what will happen to Chance. It's not just my own home at stake; it's his, too.

If I could just set him free, this would be much simpler. But of course, that's not an option. Chance might survive a few weeks in the wild, if he was lucky. But eventually he'd die of starvation, if another predator didn't grab him first.

I wonder if there is any place in the world for a creature so fierce, yet so in need of care.

As I'm walking, my phone rings.

"Hello?" It's a man's voice. I don't recognize it. "Miss, uh, Alvie Fitz?"

"Y-yes."

"This is Maxon's Burgers. We received your application. Looks like you've got some experience working with customers, and we need a position filled ASAP, so—are you available for an interview later today?"

So soon. The world seems to be turning slowly around me. "Yes, I'm available," I say, trying to keep my voice from shaking.

"Great. How's three o'clock?"

I agree and hang up. For a moment, I can't remember how to breathe, then I suck air into my lungs with a whoosh.

I can do this.

I arrive at the restaurant at exactly three o'clock. The walls are covered with old Coca-Cola advertisements and Japanese movie posters for *Godzilla* and *Mothra* and a replica of the *Mona Lisa* with a mustache. There's a carousel horse in the lobby and a bicycle hanging from the ceiling and a string of green Christmas lights. Trying to make sense of it hurts my brain, so I just focus on the space directly in front of me and avoid looking at the walls. My palms are slick with sweat, so I dry them on my pants.

The manager sits across from me at a small table in the mostly empty restaurant, looking over my answers. He has a little goatee and a pair of black-framed glasses that catch the light. "This is only part-time, you know," he says, "and only for the holiday season. We need cashiers. You'll have to work weekends, evenings."

"My schedule is open."

"Good. Aside from that, you know, just be fun, engage with the customers."

Being fun is not my strong suit, but I nod anyway.

"I'll just ask you a few questions. Pretty routine stuff," he says, folding his pudgy, soft hands in front of him. "What does good customer service mean to you?"

To *me*? What a strange question. The definition of words is not up for negotiation. I roll my eyes toward the ceiling, thinking. "Customer service," I say, "is a series of actions intended to enhance customer satisfaction before, during, and after a purchase. Good customer service would mean that these actions are completed successfully."

"Uh-huh." He clears his throat. "So what does that mean to *you*?"

I start to tug on my braid, then lower my hand. "I don't understand."

"How do you see yourself making customers happy? Giving them the Maxon's experience?"

I blink a few times. A bead of cold sweat trickles down the center of my back. Already, I sense, I'm not doing very well.

"Uh . . . Miss?"

I close my eyes. "Wait." *Visualize a successful encounter.*

About twenty seconds later, I open my eyes. "They come in and eat. They get precisely what they ordered. The steak fries are not soggy. The burger is cooked medium well, as they specified. They consider the prices reasonable. There are no surprises. They come to the register to pay. I ask them how their meal was. They say it was fine. I give them their change, and it's correct. I say, 'Have a nice day.' They leave the restaurant."

He stares at me for a moment, his mouth slightly open. "Okay. That was . . . very specific." He clears his throat. "And, uh, what are some things you enjoy doing, in your free time?"

What does that have to do with being a cashier? "I like reading about quantum theory, playing Go, doing puzzles, and watching nature shows."

"Uh-huh."

"I like animals. Especially rabbits." I know this isn't what he wants to hear about, but I'm nervous now; it's harder for me to think of appropriate things to say, so words just rush out of my mouth, like air rushing to fill a void. "One of the rarest species is the Sumatran striped rabbit. It's nocturnal and very timid. The local people don't have a name for it because they don't even know it exists."

"Okay. I think that's all we need. We'll keep your application on file."

There's a little twinge of panic in my chest. When people say that, what they mean is: *We're never going to call you.* "Did I do something wrong."

"Well . . ."

"I know I'm not good at interviews, but I can do the job, I promise. I can work any shifts you need. Give me a chance. Just one day."

He shakes his head. "I'm sorry. It's nothing personal. You're just not what we're looking for."

I leave the restaurant.

This is nothing new, of course. All I want is a chance to work and be paid for that work, like the rest of the population. But I rarely get past the interview process.

As I drive back home, I play a Mozart CD.

It's been speculated that Mozart had Asperger's. Maybe he, too, had trouble expressing his thoughts, and music was the only way he could translate them into something the world could understand. Of course, there were times when he was quite clear. There's a lesser-known canon called "Leck mich im Arsch" (translated, "Lick me in the ass") whose lyrics consist of that phrase repeated over and over.

Once, in detention at my old grade school, I asked the teacher if I could play some Mozart while I did my homework. She said yes, and I played that canon on my CD player. And I didn't get in trouble, because the teacher didn't speak German.

Sometimes when I'm angry at the world, I play that song, and I feel a little bit better.

The sun sinks low in the sky, a tiny white circle burning through the clouds as I walk down the street, hands shoved deep into my pockets. A thin layer of sleet coats the pavement.

I pass a small red-and-yellow building with a fiberglass sculpture of a smiling rooster on the sign outside. CLUCKY'S CHICKEN, reads the sign. There's a piece of poster board in the window, with the words NOW HIRING written in red marker.

I go in.

A few minutes later, I'm sitting at one of the crumb-covered tables in the lobby, filling out a simple one-page application. The manager, Linda—who has dark circles under her eyes and threads of gray in her hair—offers me an interview on the spot. She sits across from me at a table and looks over my experience. "A zoo, huh? Well, you'll feel right at home here." She laughs. I don't understand the joke. "You got a car?"

"Yes."

"Good. Can you start tonight? The cashier I had on schedule just quit, and no one's available to take his shift, so I need someone to handle the dinner rush."

My heartbeat quickens. This can't be real. It seems too easy.

"That—that sounds good."

She slides a package across the table; a yellow uniform wrapped in transparent crinkly plastic. "Welcome to the crew."

I change in the bathroom. The uniform feels stiff and starchy against my skin, and the hat is bright yellow with a red chicken's comb on top. When I come in, Linda walks me through a door marked EMPLOYEES ONLY, into a steam-filled kitchen. There are apron-clad men and women working in back, frying chicken in vats of bubbling orange grease. One of the men grins at me, showing a flash of very white teeth, and says something in rapid Spanish. The others laugh.

A schedule hangs on the wall. Someone has scrawled the words FUCK CLUCKY's across it in black marker.

Linda glances at it and laughs again. "That's probably from Rob."

I assume Rob is the one who quit today. I'm not sure how to respond.

She gives me a quick tour and shows me how to operate the register. "I'll try to train you as we go, but we're understaffed right now, so it's going to be a little hectic. You take the orders, I tray them up. Just remember, after you repeat back the order, ask them if they want potato fingers with that."

"What are those."

"Fries. But don't call them fries."

Customers start filtering in. For the first hour or so, things go reasonably well. All I have to do is repeat their orders and hand them their change. Then more and more people crowd into the lobby, and it becomes harder to keep up. A long line forms. The clatter of dishes fills the kitchen, distracting me. Every sound is magnified.

"Do you want potato fingers with that," I ask.

A man in a business suit scrunches up his forehead, and his toupee slides back. "I just ordered some."

"I have to ask that every time. It's a rule."

"So . . . are you asking me if I want another order of them, or what?"

I freeze.

"Just give me the damn fries," he says.

Linda, who's been traying up food, has to go take care of an angry customer on the phone. I'm left alone. Each time I take an order, I have to turn around and scoop pieces of fried chicken, thin wedges of potato, and dollops of macaroni and cheese onto Styrofoam plates.

"Hey, hurry up!" someone shouts. "I've been waiting for fifteen minutes back here!"

I give a start and drop a piece of chicken on the floor.

The phone in the office is ringing again. I don't know where Linda is. The oven keeps beeping, which means whatever's inside it is done, but there's no time to go back and get it. The smell of burning biscuits fills the air. My hands start to shake, making it difficult to scoop the right change out of the register.

At Hickory Park, whenever I got overwhelmed by crowds or noise, it was easy to find a secluded spot where I could get myself under control. Here, there's nowhere to hide, no space to breathe.

Things start to blur together as my body moves on autopilot. Clucky, the chicken mascot, grins at me from a poster on the wall. His face starts to melt, eyeballs dripping from their sockets like runny paint. Or maybe it's my brain that's melting. The people in front of me wiggle and warp, as if I'm looking at them in a funhouse mirror, and the walls bleed into a swirl of red and yellow. My skull has become an echo chamber, distorting every sound. Someone is shouting. Then lots of people are shouting. I'm falling, collapsing into myself.

My body moves of its own accord as I climb over the counter and push my way through the crowd, toward the doors. My own rapid breathing echoes in my ears, drowning out the noise. When my head finally clears, I'm huddled in a ball behind the Dumpsters out back, surrounded by soggy, crumpled balls of wax paper.

A few hours later, I give back my uniform, and Linda pays me in cash for my single night of work. Thirty-five dollars.

When I get home, there's a note on the door: *Several other tenants have told me there are strange noises coming from your apartment. They said it sounds like an animal. As you know, pets are NOT allowed. Please deal with this IMMEDIATELY. If I receive one more complaint, I'm shortening the rent deadline to NOW.*

Lots of capital letters. That's usually not a good sign.

When I open the door, Chance is sitting in his usual place on the back of the couch. He tilts his head, and for a moment, he looks almost concerned. His beak opens, like he's about to ask me a question, but he just croaks. *Gah-ruk.* I have the sudden urge to clutch him tight and bury my face against his feathers, but I'd probably just get scratched.

I collapse into the chair.

I know what I should do. I should take him to a wildlife rehabilitation center, somewhere he'll be truly safe. Expecting Chance to fill the void in my life isn't fair to him.

"I have to let you go," I whisper.

He yawns and preens his breast feathers. Hawks are immune to sentimentality.

Slowly I reach out. Stop. Then keep going. He fixes one brilliant copper eye on me as I hold out an arm. A current of recognition passes between us. Casually—as if he's done it a thousand times—he hops onto my arm and grips it with strong talons. When I lower him into the carrier cage, he doesn't struggle.

Chance's thoughts and feelings may be different from mine, but I have no doubt that his inner world is as rich and complex as any human's. In some way that I don't have the words for, we are the same.

During the drive, he's surprisingly calm and quiet.

My destination is Elmbrooke Wildlife Center—close enough to visit, and its staff has an excellent reputation. None of that stops me from feeling like I'm abandoning my friend.

If I were living in one of those animal movies, like *Free Willy* or *Duma*, Chance would have both wings, and I could just pull over into one of the nearby fields and let him out. He would fly away into the woods while inspiring music played in the background. The reality is far less satisfying.

I pull into the parking lot in front of Elmbrooke Wildlife Center—a small, yellow-brick building, surrounded by woods. I write Chance's name on a slip of paper and stick it between the bars of the carrier door, then carry it across the lot, to the building's entrance. On the other side of the window, the receptionist sits behind a desk, staring at her computer. I set the carrier down near the door and knock a few times. The woman starts to raise her head, but before she can get a good look at me, I turn and run back to the car. By the time she walks out and picks up the carrier, I'm already driving away.

My chest hurts.

This is better for Chance. I should be happy, but I'm not. I lost Stanley, I lost my job, and now . . . I want to break something.

An image flashes through my head—that stupid sign at Hickory Park Zoo, the one that advises visitors not to "anthropomorphize" animals by attributing feelings to them. I always fantasized about ripping it out and destroying it.

What's to stop me now?

Night falls. Streetlights glow through the misty darkness, spots of yellow. Cars glide past like ghosts.

I park several blocks away and walk to Hickory Park Zoo. It's deserted and locked up, of course. There's only one security camera—the zoo can't afford an elaborate system—and it's easy to avoid. I climb the wire fence surrounding the property.

I wander the dark paths. The cougar looks up as I pass, her eyes yellow coins of reflected light. The hyenas stir in their enclosure and flick their ears toward me.

The sign stands in its usual place.

Happy? Sad? Mad? Attributing human feelings to animals is called—

I kick the sign post until the wood breaks.

I creep toward the fence, the sign tucked under one arm. The fence isn't high. I can probably hurl the sign over the top, then climb.

Pale light touches the sky. Headlights. My heart pounds, and I quicken my pace, weaving through the maze of cobblestone paths. I round a corner—and freeze.

Two men in khaki-colored uniforms stand in the path, staring at me. I recognize their faces. Maintenance workers. Maybe Ms. Nell finally called someone to fix that clogged toilet in the bathroom.

I turn and start to run, but the taller man grabs my arm. The sign clatters to the ground. I twist, trying to free myself from his grip.

"What the hell are you doing here?" he asks.

I thrash and flail blindly.

"Jesus, what's your problem?"

"Hey, I've seen her before," the shorter man says. "She used to work here."

He's still gripping my arm. It hurts. "Let me go!"

"Tell us what you're doing here, *then* I'll let you go."

But I can't think, I can't breathe while he's touching me. I stomp on his foot.

"Ow! Shit!"

He releases me, and I bolt for the fence, but he runs after me and seizes me in a bear hug, pinning my arms to my sides. I struggle, kicking and screaming.

The shorter man stares at me and shakes his head. "How did this nutjob ever get hired in the first place?"

"Beats me." His arms clamp tighter around me. "Hold still," he growls. "You're just making this worse for yourself."

I scream.

The shorter man fishes a cell phone out of his pocket and dials. "Hey, Mrs. Nell? Sorry, *Ms.* Nell. We've got a trespasser. Yeah, it's the chick with red hair and braids. What should we do with her?"

After kicking and struggling a while longer, I go limp with exhaustion. My vision blurs, and I seem to be sliding backward, down a long tunnel. The men are talking, but their voices sound muffled and distant, and I can't make out the words.

They drag me to the office building in the center of the zoo. I'm no longer fighting or trying to run, but they push me into a closet and slam the door shut.

"Does it lock?" the taller man grunts.

"No."

"Well, what are we supposed to do then?"

"Just wedge a chair under the knob."

There's a scrape of wood against tile. I ram my shoulder against the door, trying to force it open. It rattles but doesn't budge. I try the knob, jiggling it, but it refuses to turn. No way out. I slump against the back wall. It's dark, and the lemony smell of cleaning supplies hangs thick in the air. It makes me gag. I pound on the door.

"Keep it down, you. Nell says you've gotta stay here till the police show up."

"Hey, when did they say they'd get here?"

"An hour or so."

"An *hour*? Are you serious? This is an emergency!"

"Not according to them."

I stop pounding and sink to the floor. A heavy numbness creeps over me.

"Hey," the taller man calls through the door, "what were you planning to do with that sign, anyway?"

I don't answer. My mouth opens, but all that comes out is a faint croak. The words won't line up, won't form proper sentences. "Lies," I manage to whisper.

"What?"

"Don't bother trying to talk to her," the other says. "I don't think anyone's home upstairs."

The blood pounds in my head, making me dizzy. A thin, reedy sound fills my ears, like an animal in distress, and I realize it's coming from my own throat. I huddle in a tiny ball on the floor and begin to rock back and forth. I can't stop myself. I rock harder and harder until my head is banging against the back of the closet.

"What's she *doing* in there?" one man mutters.

"Just ignore her."

The rocking speeds up. My head knocks against the wall again and again. *Bang, bang, bang.*

I'm glad they don't open the door, glad they can't see me like this, because I know what I look like. I look like what I am: an autistic girl having a meltdown.

My body won't stop, so I let it go, rocking over and over until the pain numbs me and my movements slow, like a toy winding down. When it's over, I am squeezed into a corner of the closet, fists bunched up and pressed against my temples, and the world is dark and still. The overpowering lemon smell still snarls inside my nostrils. A dull ache pounds in my forehead. When I touch the ache, my fingers come away wet with blood.

I do a few algebra problems in my head to make sure I don't have a concussion. Breathing shallowly through my mouth, I press my ear against the door, but I can't hear any voices or movement. I don't know if the men are still there or if they left the office. For a few minutes I just sit, listening. The shuddering little gulps of my own breathing fill the silence.

I try the doorknob, but it won't open. My hand falls, limp, to my side.

Soon the police will arrive. I've never been arrested, so I don't know what will happen after that. Will they handcuff me? Will I have to spend the night in jail?

I try the knob again. I jiggle it. I kick the door and then kick it a few more times, and something jars loose and clatters to the floor. The chair? For a few minutes I stand motionless, holding my breath, but I still don't hear anything from outside. I try the knob again. This time, it turns smoothly.

When I open the door, the office is empty, dimly lit by the faint sunlight spilling in through the window, and the chair is lying on the floor. I creep out of the closet, hunker down, and peek over the windowsill. Outside, I can see the men standing and smoking.

"How long has it been, anyway?" one says.

The other snorts. "Bet they don't even show up. The cops in this city are a joke."

Holding my breath, I duck back into the office. If I go out through the door, they'll see me. I open the window on the opposite wall and squeeze through, then run and run until I reach the wire fence. I scramble over it and keep running until I find my car, parked on a narrow residential street.

I sag against the car, my body weighted with exhaustion, and close my eyes.

Will anyone come looking for me? I don't think hunting down some crazy girl who broke into a zoo will be a big priority for the police. I try to remember where I dropped the sign, but it doesn't matter. They'll probably just put it back up tomorrow.

It's started to snow. Fat, heavy flakes drift down from the sky and settle onto my hair and clothes. I watch them for a few minutes, then get into my car.

When I return to my apartment, there's a bright yellow eviction notice on the door.

CHAPTER TWENTY-SIX

I stare numbly.

I thought I had a little more time. But it doesn't matter. Either way, I don't have the money, and Mrs. Schwartz has been looking for a chance to get rid of me. I decide to leave now and spare myself the indignity of being removed by force.

There's not a lot to take. The TV is ancient and the furniture is mostly junk. I stuff my clothes, toiletries, Rubik's Cube, laptop, my last bit of cash, and as many books as I can fit into a duffel bag. I pause, looking at the single carnation, still in its glass on the coffee table, now brittle and dead. I take it from the glass and place it in my duffel bag, atop the pile of clothes.

I sling the bag over my shoulder, then pause again, looking back at the living room where I spent so many nights watching TV on the couch, eating cereal or Cool Whip and washing it down with orange soda. Bare walls and mangy, threadbare carpeting stare back at me. Not much, but it is—*was* mine. The first place that was ever mine.

I toss all my possessions into the backseat of my car.

My cell phone buzzes in my pocket. I flip it open, and my heartbeat speeds. A text from Stanley: *I know what we had was real. I didn't imagine it.*

He's still trying. Even after all this time.

I think about calling him back and trying to explain things to him. But I'm not that strong. I know that I'll end up telling him everything, and then he'll feel obligated to help me. If I don't walk away now, it won't ever happen. But it *needs* to happen. The kindest thing I can do is to break his heart.

A cramp seizes my stomach. I double over, gasping, one hand pressed to my abdomen.

Stanley is sitting next to me on the park bench, holding out his hand to me.

He's in the motel room with me, touching me, whispering that I'm beautiful.

He's guiding me across the ice. He steadies me when I slip and holds me close as snow drifts down around us.

We're in his bed, our bodies pressed together, so warm and close that we could melt into each other like two puddles of candle wax.

We're lying side by side in the grass, holding hands as cold rain pounds down on us and lightning flashes, and through the roaring frenzy of the storm I hear the most unexpected sound—his laughter, high and young and beautiful.

Slowly I straighten. I stare at the screen of my phone, and I send a text: *Good-bye.* I delete his name from my contact list, leaving my phone totally empty. Then I toss it into the Dumpster behind my apartment.

And just like that, he is out of my world. There's no number he can call, no address where he can find me. I'm on my own.

I drive across town and park in a deserted lot where I won't be bothered. I curl up in the backseat, head pillowed on my duffel bag, and sink into a foggy half sleep. I have a strange, chaotic dream about a Buddhist fable I once read.

There's a monkey, an otter, a jackal, and a rabbit. They all decide to do an act of charity, believing that great virtue will bring a great reward. So they find an old beggar man sitting next to a fire. He's starving. The monkey gathers fruits, and the otter gathers fish, and the jackal steals a pot of milk, but the rabbit can only gather grass.

They all bring their offerings to the old man and lay them next to the fire. But the old man can't eat the grass, of course, and the rabbit feels a great sense of shame and worthlessness for the inadequacy of his gift. So he throws himself onto the fire, offering his flesh.

In the fable, the old man turns out to be a saint with mystical powers who brings the rabbit back to life and offers him a great reward for his selflessness. But in the dream, this doesn't happen. The rabbit just burns and burns.

CHAPTER TWENTY-SEVEN

Christmas lights glimmer around the windows of stores as I walk past. Wet, dirty slush piles up along the edges of the street. More slush sprays out from the wheels of cars zooming past. A cold breeze stirs the limp ribbons of wreaths hung from streetlights and store windows.

I walk into a hot dog restaurant and push a few crumpled singles across the counter. "One chili cheese dog with everything."

The cashier hands me a sopping, paper-wrapped hot dog, along with a quarter and a penny, which is now—literally—my last bit of money.

I sit in one of the hard plastic booths, soaking up the heat and brightness of the restaurant, and bite into the chili dog. It tastes incredible. When you're homeless, it's amazing how you learn to appreciate the simple pleasures: warmth, a full meal, a clean bathroom.

I've been living and sleeping in my car for over a week, now. I've worn the same shirt for three days in a row, and my hair is matted and filthy. I look like any other street person—which is exactly what I am. In a way, it's a relief.

Oh, it's horrible, of course. I wake up every morning with the knife of hunger in my belly and I go to sleep cold and still hungry. I'm always itchy because I hardly ever have a chance to wash. And I am aware that, statistically, I'm now at a much greater risk for being raped or murdered. Yet beneath the skin-crawling misery of it all, I feel more relaxed and free than I have in a long, long time. This is it—the bottom. There's nowhere left to fall. I can finally stop trying so damn hard. And if I start muttering to myself or rocking back and forth, no one notices or cares, because street people are expected to be crazy.

I eat the chili dog messily, not bothering to wipe up the meaty juice that dribbles down my chin and onto my shirt. After I finish, I lick my fingers clean and wipe them on the paper place mat. The other customers are frowning at me. A woman shakes her head and mutters something to the man next to her. At another time, their stares might have bothered me, but I find that I no longer care. Distantly I wonder what Stanley would think if he saw me now. I push the thought away.

After a while, a manager walks up to me and quietly asks me to leave. I walk out without saying anything to him.

There's an old man sitting by the sidewalk, jingling a Styrofoam cup full of change and dollar bills. A pair of sunglasses perch on his long nose, and there's a small, scruffy brown dog curled up next to him. The man is singing "Have Yourself a Merry Little Christmas" in a deep, resonant voice.

The dog yawns, showing a tiny pink tongue, and licks a small wound on his paw.

I listen for a few minutes, then toss my last twenty-six cents into the cup. The man stops singing and arches an eyebrow. "That really all you can spare?"

I glance at the dog, who looks like some sort of terrier mix. He wags his stubby tail, wriggles, and licks his wound again. "His paw is injured. You should buy some ointment for it."

The man chuckles. "Pretty bossy for someone who only gave me two coins."

There's nothing I can do. So I walk on.

The man's voice rises behind me, rich and sonorous, in a rendition of "O Come, All Ye Faithful."

My head itches, and I scratch it, wondering if I have lice. Does that even happen to people in the winter?

My car is parked in the lot outside a Dunkin' Donuts. I've been driving from place to place so I won't get ticketed or arrested for loitering. Every once in a while I'll fill out another job application, but I don't know why I bother. I don't have a phone, so there's no way anyone could contact me, even if they wanted to. I've taken to being completely honest; I take a perverse pleasure in writing answers that I know will get my application chucked in the trash. When they ask me why I want the job, I write, *Homeless. Need food.* When they ask me why I left my last position of employment, I write, *Boss tried to kill my friend.* When they ask me my greatest flaw, I write, *I destroy everything I care about.*

I sit in my car for a few minutes, staring into space. All my cash is gone, including the emergency twenty I kept hidden in the glove compartment. Pretty soon I'll be like that man, asking for change on the sidewalk. I hate the idea of begging, but the knife-like hunger pains in my stomach are getting worse all the time. I could sell my car, but then I'd have nowhere to sleep. I already pawned off my laptop.

A glance at my fuel gauge tells me I have less than a quarter tank left, and after this, I won't be able to fill it up again unless I somehow, miraculously acquire more money.

I climb into the backseat and unzip the duffel bag. The dried-out carnation still rests atop a rumpled pile of shirts.

It's the only thing I have left of Stanley's. Even now, I can't let go of it.

He won't be in the park, of course. But I drive there anyway and park in the lot across the street. Snow floats down from the sky as I walk across the expanse of grass, toward the bench where I first saw him. With one gloved hand, I brush snow from the wood and sit.

A heavy exhaustion steals over me. I sink to the bench and curl up, tucking my knees against my chest. The cold seeps into my bones, numbing me, but there's something comforting about the numbness. I feel like I could float away, and it wouldn't matter. Is this peace? Is this freedom?

My eyelids slip shut as I drift into the murky space between sleep and waking.

After Mama's death, I spent some time in an institution. I don't recall much of it. For a while, I just drifted, surrounded by a gray haze. Words like *catatonic* and *unresponsive* floated at the periphery of my awareness.

Little by little, I realize that I'm in a room with pale lime-green tiles on the floor. I start to notice things like the pattern on my sheets, the grain of the fake wood paneling on my wall, the taste of the stringy green beans the white-coated woman pushes into my mouth with a spoon, and the number of pills in the little paper cup they give me every morning and every night. There are nine.

One evening, the white-coated woman comes into my room wheeling the tray of green beans and chicken, with the paper cup full of pills next to it. She picks up the cup. "Time for dinner and medication, Alvie. Can you say 'ahhh?'"

Slowly I sit up and run a dry tongue over drier lips. In my head, it makes a sound like sandpaper. With a sweep of my arm, I knock the cup and plate of mushy food off the tray, and it scatters across the floor. The nurse lets out a little shriek.

Later, I learn that this is the first time I've moved on my own in four weeks.

Over the next few months, I improve, which is to say I start to walk around, go to the bathroom without help, and eat on my own. But I'm hard and empty inside, like a nutshell. I can't even cry. Every morning I stare into the mirror and wait for the tears to come, but it never happens. I don't say a word to the nurses or doctors. They think that I've "regressed," that I've lost whatever verbal abilities I possessed due to trauma. But it's not that I *can't* speak; I just don't particularly want to.

Because there's not much else to do in the institution, I read a lot, mostly books about science and animal behavior. The doctors don't seem to realize that I can understand the books; they think I'm just looking at the pictures, or counting the words. I don't care, as long as they don't try to stop me.

One day, I find a big book of European folklore on the shelf of the rec room. It has a thick leather cover with a border of shiny, raised gold leaves and detailed pictures of dragons and knights and forests. I'm not usually interested in fairy tales or history, but there's something hypnotic about the images.

Inside, there's a chapter called "The Changeling," with an illustration of a horned troll—its wrinkly face creased in a smile—lifting a baby out of its crib.

Hundreds of years ago (the book says), some people believed that trolls and elves were real, that they lived in the forest, and that once in a while, these supernatural beings would sneak into a village to steal a human baby and replace it with one of their own offspring—a creature that looks human but isn't. This child is called a changeling.

If a child started acting strangely, parents would get scared and think he was a changeling. The legend held that tormenting the imposter—by beating it or putting it in a hot oven—would make the kidnappers return the real child to its human parents.

I wonder how many children were burned in ovens or beaten to death by their parents because of this quaint little myth.

I go to the window and crack it open. The windows in the rec room only open a little, because they don't want us jumping out, but there's enough of a gap that I can slide the book through. I push it out and watch it turn over and over as it falls and lands on the pavement with a distant, muffled *thud.*

When I turn around, there's a nurse standing in the room. "Oh, honey," she says, "did the pictures in that book scare you? I can bring you some nicer books, if you like."

I tilt my head. She doesn't really expect a response. I haven't spoken to anyone since I first came to the institution, almost six months ago. "Can you bring me some books on quantum mechanics," I say. "I've been wanting to learn more about that."

Her jaw drops.

She tells everyone, of course, and the doctors start bombarding me with questions, which makes me wish I'd never opened my mouth.

But I realize that, for the first time in months, I do feel something: restlessness. I want to get out of this place. I don't know what I'll do once I get out. I don't care. I'm just sick of it—sick of the smell, the pea-colored tiles, the mushy green beans with every meal. I want to see animals again. Real ones, not the stupid cartoon cutouts pinned to the bulletin board.

So I keep talking. I answer the doctors' questions. I read more and more; the nurses start to call me Little Einstein, and bring me books as presents. One of them gives me a copy of *Watership Down.*

After a while, a doctor says, "Good news, Alvie. You've improved so much, you're going to be released into the foster care system. You'll have a family. Isn't that wonderful?"

I wait to feel something. Anything, even a flicker of relief. But there's no response from inside me.

What they called improvement was simply a slow process of locking everything away, deep in the recesses of my mind, until I was numb enough to function. Over the past few months I have been building the Vault, stone by stone. Now I walk and talk, but a part of me is still far away, and I don't know how to reach it.

Mama is dead because of me. I should be with her, rotting at the bottom of the lake.

Maybe I am, and that's why I can't feel anything. Maybe I'm like Schrödinger's cat, alive and dead at the same time.

CHAPTER TWENTY-EIGHT

The screech of rubber on pavement yanks me awake. My body jerks upright on the bench, and I open my eyes just in time to see a car swerve, narrowly avoiding a squirrel in the road. The squirrel freezes, then darts away in a blur of brown fur and vanishes.

If things had happened in a slightly different way—if a quantum particle spun in one direction instead of another—maybe the driver wouldn't have braked in time, and the squirrel would have been hit. Maybe in another universe, that *did* happen. Or maybe in yet another reality, the car hit a person instead. It could have been me. Or anyone.

Snow falls thick and fast, covering the world in a blanket that muffles all sound. My breath steams in the air.

I climb into my car and huddle in the backseat, though it's not much warmer here. Shivering, I rummage inside my duffel bag until I find my tattered, dog-eared copy of *Watership Down*, the same copy the nurse gave me over six years ago. I read it for the first time that very night, in a single sitting.

Before that point, I'd never had much interest in fiction—I preferred nature and science books, even as a child. Novels were always about feelings and relationships, things that confused and intimidated me. But somehow, *Watership Down* was different. I couldn't stop turning the pages. Hazel and Fiver and Bigwig became every bit as real as the flesh-and-blood people around me. I was there with them in the pages. I felt it all—their hunger and fear and desperate yearning for a place they could call home.

I touch the pages, my gaze lingering on a familiar phrase: *My heart has joined the Thousand, for my friend stopped running today.*

For some reason, the words send a chill through me.

I close the book and gently tuck it back into my duffel bag. My fingers are numb inside my gloves; I flex them, trying to restore circulation.

I don't want to waste my last bit of gas by running the heat, but if I stay here, I'm going to get frostbite. There's a convenience store across the street, the windows bright, glowing with inviting warmth. Maybe I can spend twenty minutes or so there before getting kicked out.

A bell jingles overhead as I walk in. I realize that this is the same store I used to shop at back when I had my apartment. The clerk glances at me, then away. Does he even recognize me, with my ragged, filthy clothes and matted hair?

I pretend to browse through the newspapers. My gaze skims over the text, not really absorbing it . . . and then I freeze.

The headline reads SCHAUMBURG TEEN CHARGED

WITH ASSAULT AND BATTERY. I recognize the photo. It's TJ.

Beneath that: *18-year-old Timothy J. Hawke was arrested following an altercation in a public park with 19-year-old Stanley Finkel, during which Finkel was allegedly beaten with his own cane. Hawke claimed that Finkel initiated the confrontation between them, provoked him verbally, and struck the first blow, but only Finkel sustained injuries, the extent of which are unknown. Hawke awaits a court appearance on Monday, while Finkel remains hospitalized.*

The words blur. My hand begins to tremble, and my fingers tighten on the paper, crumpling it.

I drop the newspaper and run out of the store.

CHAPTER TWENTY-NINE

When I arrive at Saint Matthew's Hospital, they don't want to let me past the lobby. Maybe because I'm not part of Stanley's immediate family, maybe because I look like a crazy person, with my grimy clothes and matted hair. But I won't leave. I park myself in one of the seating areas. Whenever anyone says anything to me, I just repeat in a monotone that I want to see Stanley Finkel.

I'm exhausted and dizzy with hunger, but I don't care. I'll stay here as long as it takes.

Finally a nurse arrives in the lobby and says, "We informed him that you're here. He says you can come up."

I follow her into an elevator, and we get out on the third floor. She leads me down a long, sterile white hall and stops in front of a door. "He's been in and out of surgery," she says. "I'd advise you to keep your visit short."

She opens the door. I step forward—then stop. There's only one bed in the room, and there's a sort of curtain tent around it.

I take a deep breath and enter the room. The nurse closes the door behind me.

"Stanley," I say. There's no response.

Slowly I approach and tug the curtains aside.

The sight hits me with a jolt, and my vision momentarily blurs. There's barely a single part of him that's not covered by casts or bandages. Tubes run from his wrist, more from his chest, as if he were part machine, sprouting wires. Thick plaster casts swath his body up to the waist; his legs are suspended in place with wires attached to the canopy of his bed. A cervical collar rings his neck, and there's a bandage taped to his forehead, with a small rust-colored spot of dried blood soaking through.

His eyelids open a crack. Ragged breathing echoes through the silence. He moistens his chapped lips with the tip of his tongue. "Hey." His voice is faint and hoarse. He stares at me for a moment, his expression unreadable. Then his eyes close again, as if he's too tired to keep them open.

I can't stop looking at him. It hurts to breathe. "How do you feel." It's a stupid question, but I have to say something.

"Sleepy. They're keeping me pretty doped up."

He doesn't sound angry, or even particularly upset. Feeling unsure of myself, I pull up a chair and sit. "I saw the article."

"They wrote an article about it?"

"Yes."

His eyes roll toward me. There's a little starburst of red in one sclera, where a blood vessel has ruptured, but the irises are still clear and brilliant blue. "Slow news day, I guess."

"He's lying to the police. He's saying you started it. That you provoked him."

"I did," Stanley says.

My mouth falls open.

His eyes slip shut again. "We ran into each other in the park. Pure chance. It was just him, without his goons. He was going to walk away, but I started shouting at him, calling him an asshole. He kept telling me to shut up, but I wouldn't. Not even when he knocked me down. And then, when it was over . . . he stopped and we just looked at each other and . . ." His breath hitches. "He was just a kid. Just some stupid kid with a few piercings and a leather jacket. And he looked so scared. Not of me. Of himself . . . of what he'd done."

The light outside the window begins to deepen in color, turning honey amber, and his eyelids look thin and fragile. They're almost translucent.

"How many breaks," I ask.

"Seventeen. Mostly in my legs, but I fractured my collarbone and bruised some ribs, too." His eyes remain closed. His breathing rasps softly. When he speaks, his voice is oddly calm: "You don't have to be here, you know. Knowing you're hanging around out of guilt just makes it hurt more."

A sharp pain jabs through my chest. "That's not why I'm here."

"Then why?"

I open my mouth, but nothing comes out.

"Just go." Still, there's no anger in his voice; it would almost be easier if there were. "You don't have to worry about me. I've been through this a million times. Go home."

"I can't go home."

He blinks and looks at me as if seeing me for the first time—the disheveled hair, the dirty clothes. His forehead wrinkles. "What do you mean?"

"I've been living out of my car."

His eyes widen. "When were you planning to tell me about this?"

I look down and self-consciously tug one braid. "I wasn't."

There's a long pause. His breathing sounds strange; I can't tell what he's thinking or feeling. "You can sleep in my house. My keys are over there, next to my wallet, on the table by the window. Eat whatever you want in the kitchen, and if you need to buy more food or anything else, just use whatever cash is in there."

There's a lump in my throat. "It—it's getting cold. So thank you," I manage to whisper. But I don't move. We look at each other.

"I'm sorry," I say. "I shouldn't have left the way I did."

He stares at the ceiling. "It doesn't matter now." His voice is flat. Empty.

For a few minutes, I sit, hands balled into fists in my lap. Finally I stand, walk into the adjoining bathroom, and wet a cloth in the sink. I lean over him and wipe his sweat-damp brow.

"Don't," he whispers, voice cracking. "Don't do this."

"Is it too cold."

A tear leaks out from the corner of his eye. "Don't you understand? I'd already given up." He squeezes his eyes shut. "Just leave me alone."

I lower my gaze. Of course he's not happy to see me. I broke his heart. I don't understand human emotions very well, but I know that once you've hurt someone, you can't just come back and have everything be okay again.

But I can't leave him. Not now, not like this.

After a moment, I resume wiping his forehead. He doesn't protest; he doesn't say anything. The pink glow of sunlight illuminates the plane of his left cheek. As the last bit of daylight fades, the light turns a soft blue, then purple, then disappears. His eyes stare through me, as if he's lost somewhere inside himself.

CHAPTER THIRTY

Over the next week, I visit Stanley in the hospital every day. I help him eat when he's not feeling well enough to sit up. I keep the damp cloth on his brow moistened, and when his pain medication is getting low, I badger the nurses to refill it. I sit with him through blood draws and CAT scans.

The nurses no longer object to my presence. I have been to Stanley's house and washed up and cleaned what clothes I have.

Through it all, he remains withdrawn. He answers questions with monosyllables, always in that mechanical voice. I'm not sure if it's because he's still angry at me or because he's medicated most of the time. Or maybe it's depression. He's stuck in this place he hates, enduring a barrage of uncomfortable and invasive tests, and it will be months before his injuries heal. Of course he's depressed.

He feels so far away. But he's not, I remind myself. He's right here. And he needs me.

Things can never go back to the way they were; I'm aware of that. But right now, neither of us has anyone else to rely on.

***

By the time they release Stanley, the bulky casts on his legs have been replaced with wrappings and braces, but he still can't walk, not even with crutches.

I drive him home. As soon as we're away from the hospital, there's a noticeable shift in his demeanor. Though still quiet, he seems more awake, more alert.

Back at Stanley's house, I retrieve a wheelchair from the garage and park it in the living room. As I help him into it, he sighs. "I was hoping to never need this stupid thing again."

"It's just temporary."

"Yeah, I know. Mostly I'm just glad to be out of the hospital. I can't wait to take a real bath."

In his current condition, that will be difficult. Still, I hesitate a few seconds before asking, "Do you want help."

His shoulders tense. A flush rises into his cheeks, and the muscles of his throat constrict as he swallows. "Just get me into the tub and bring me a washcloth. I'll take it from there."

Lowering him into the tub takes a lot of maneuvering, even with the metal rails already in place. He has some mobility in his left arm now, at least; the sling from his first encounter with TJ is gone. Still, he winces when he tries to pull his shirt off.

"I'll help with your clothes," I say.

"That's okay."

"The doctor said you shouldn't move around too much yet." I reach out.

He catches my wrist. "I can handle it."

"I want to help." I start to tug his shirt up, and his whole body goes rigid.

"Alvie, *stop*!"

I freeze.

His gaze is downcast, his cheeks burning, his breathing rapid. "Please," he whispers. "Let me do this on my own."

A burning, prickling lump fills my throat. I swallow. "I know you're angry at me. But there's no sense in injuring yourself just because—"

"It's not *about* that."

In a flash, I remember the motel room, the way he seemed so reluctant to take off his clothes. Even now, he doesn't want me to see him. I want to tell him that his scars don't matter, but I know that words won't make a difference. "What if I kept my eyes closed while I washed you."

A pause. "You could do that?"

"Yes. I won't look. I promise."

"And you'll stop if I ask you to?"

"I will." I'm surprised he even needs to ask.

Slowly, he nods.

I close my eyes and reach down to unbutton his shirt. Without sight, it's tricky; my hand comes down on his face. I pat my way down his neck until I find the first button and undo it. After that, it's easier. My fingertips graze something rough and puckered on his chest, and his breath hisses between his teeth, as if the touch burns.

"Sorry," I say.

"It's okay."

I start to tug the shirt off, being careful to touch only cloth, not skin. It takes a few minutes.

"Hang on," Stanley says. "Let me—okay, now."

The shirt comes off. My hands move down to unbutton his slacks, and he twitches. His breathing quickens as I tug the pants down a little, then a little more. This would be much easier if he were standing, but he's not in any condition to stand. The process takes a few minutes, but I manage to remove the slacks. I set them carefully aside, then pull off his socks. My palm brushes against his leg; I feel the cool metal and smooth leather of the brace, the rough linen of the bandage beneath.

Soft, shuddering breaths echo through the silence. Aside from the bandages and braces on his legs, he's naked, every inch of him exposed.

I dunk the cloth in a bucket of warm, soapy water, wring it out, and lay it against his chest. A small sigh escapes his throat.

"Let me know if the water is too cold."

"It's fine."

Taking care not to touch his skin directly, I wash him. His breathing sounds very loud in the quiet as I run the cloth over his chest, his shoulders, and abdomen.

My fingers brush against his cheek, and I feel the heat in his skin. "Are you embarrassed," I ask.

"I just feel really helpless, like this."

"Is that a bad thing."

"I don't know. Not exactly, I guess."

I rub the cloth over his inner thighs. His muscles tense. "Maybe I'd better do that."

He takes the cloth from me and quickly washes off the rest of himself. "Can you get me a clean set of clothes?" he asks.

I retrieve a fresh T-shirt and cotton drawstring pants from his bedroom. Still without looking directly at him, I help him get dressed. It's easier than undressing him; I deliberately chose loose clothes that I could slide on without much difficulty.

"Okay, you can look now."

I do. He's flushed, breathing a little more rapidly than normal. My gaze strays to his groin, and sure enough, his pants are tented. "You have an erection," I blurt out. He gulps, but this time, he doesn't apologize. He just stares straight at me.

It doesn't mean much, I tell myself. Males are hardwired to respond to certain stimuli. Even so, I can't deny that it feels good to know that his body still wants me, at least.

I avert my eyes, suddenly self-conscious. "I didn't look," I tell him. "When I was washing you, I mean. I wanted to. But I didn't."

He lets out a tiny chuckle. "Well, I guess I can't blame you for being tempted. I mean . . . all this." He gestures down at his thin body, his legs, still bound up in wrappings and braces. He gives me a lopsided smile. It's strained, and his face is pale and drawn, but it's the first smile I've seen out of him in days.

My gaze lingers on his lips. I think about the night I spent in his bed, the warmth of those lips against mine. And for a moment, I want to.

Then his earlier words echo in my head: *Leave me alone.* A

dull ache fills my chest. Why would Stanley want a kiss from the person who betrayed him?

"Is there anything else you need," I ask. "I could get us some takeout." I'd offer to cook him dinner, but putting bread in the toaster is about the closest I ever get to cooking.

He chews his lower lip. "Thanks, but I'm pretty tired. Can you help me into bed?"

I maneuver him into the chair and wheel him into the bedroom. Once he's settled in bed with the covers pulled up to his chest and a glass of water on the nightstand, I start to walk out.

"Where are you going?" he calls.

"To the couch. That's where I've been sleeping." Using his bed would have felt presumptuous, even if he wasn't there.

"Oh." I have the sense he's about to say something else—or maybe he expects *me* to say something. But what, I'm not sure. He looks away. "Good night, Alvie."

"Good night." I walk out, closing the door behind me. I lean against the wall.

The only reason I'm here now is because I have no other place to go, and because Stanley's still too badly hurt to function on his own. I can't let myself forget that. But I'm glad he let me wash him—that I was able to do something for him, that he trusted me at least that much. Even if he still refuses to let me see him naked.

He's self-conscious about the scars; I know that's part of it. But I can't shake the feeling there's something more.

CHAPTER THIRTY-ONE

The next morning, I brew a pot of coffee and make some scrambled eggs with toast. Or at least, I try. I end up burning the first batch of eggs and have to start over. The second attempt is too runny, but it's edible.

Stanley sits in his wheelchair, holding a cup of coffee, wearing a pair of sweatpants and a button-down white shirt. I helped him into his chair that morning, but he insisted on getting dressed by himself. It took him an hour. I have no idea how he managed it, with his limited mobility. But then, he's had a lot of practice.

"What are you going to do about college," I ask.

"I called the school. Sent them a note from my doctor. They're going to email me the assignments I missed." He picks a bit of shell from his eggs. "I should be able to attend classes again, starting today. If you can drive me."

I nod and pour myself some more coffee. "When."

"Two thirty. I just have one programming class this afternoon."

I wonder, not for the first time, how he affords college on top of everything else. I know he gets some money from his father, but is it enough? Even if his house is paid off—and I'm not sure it is—there's still the electricity, the water bill, the gas, the property taxes . . . not to mention the hospital bills. Maybe his mother had a life insurance policy. Regardless, he probably doesn't have a lot of spare cash.

"If I'm going to be living in your house for the foreseeable future," I say through a mouthful of toast, "I should help with the bills."

"You don't have to do that, Alvie."

"Yes, I do. I'll get another job soon. Anyway, I don't do well with idleness." Already, I miss the animals. And while Stanley will still require some care for a while, he probably doesn't want me hovering around him twenty-four hours a day.

"Well, if that's what you want. . . . Any particular place in mind?"

"Anyplace that will have me. I've been sending in applications. It's just . . ." I poke at the blobby, whitish-yellow eggs with my fork. "I have difficulty with some of the questions."

"I can help you with them, if you want."

I hesitate. "I can't ask you for that."

"I don't mind. There's nothing to be embarrassed about, you know. Job hunting is stressful for lots of people."

"I don't think many people have panic attacks while filling out personality questionnaires," I mutter.

"You might be surprised." His voice softens. "Let me help you."

He sounds so gentle that, for a moment, I wonder. Maybe . . .

No. I can't let myself start to hope again. He probably just wants me out of the house, even if he's too kind to say so.

"All right," I say.

Shortly after, the kitchen table is covered with a sprawl of papers that I printed out from the latest batch of online applications. Stanley picks up one for a burger restaurant. "So which parts are you having trouble with?"

"Everything." My face burns. "The questions don't make sense to me. I left a lot blank, and I don't know if the answers I gave are any good. But I don't know what else to say."

"Let's see. Um—there's this . . . under 'Describe your greatest flaw,' you wrote *bad at talking to people.*" He shuffles through the applications. "And under 'Are you a team player?' you wrote *no.*"

"Well, I'm not."

"I think that's the sort of question you should just answer *yes.*"

I start to rock back and forth, pulling sharply on one braid. "In what sense can I be described as 'a team player.'"

"They're just asking if you're willing to work with others."

"Well, then that's what they should say." I rock faster.

He sets down the paper. "Alvie, it's okay."

I shut my eyes tight. My whole head feels hot. My hand drifts up to my braid and starts tugging again. I stop and sit on both my hands, because I don't know how else to still them.

"You don't have to hide that, you know. Not from me."

I look up, surprised.

"Do that if it helps," he says. "But listen to me. This"—he gestures toward the pile of applications—"is just a mind game invented by corporate bigwigs. These questions don't mean anything. Your ability to fill them out has nothing to do with your worth as a worker or a person. This is just something you have to get through. I guess what I'm saying is, you don't have to be completely honest. They don't expect you to be. It's not lying, per se. It's finding the right words to present yourself in a good light. Everyone does it."

I squint. It still sounds like lying to me. "These people are insane."

"Who?"

"I don't know. Everyone. All these so-called normal people."

"What about me?" He smiles. "I'm so-called normal, right?"

I consider. "You're an atypical neurotypical. I've never liked that word, though. Neurotypical. It implies that there's such a thing as a normal human brain, and I don't think there really is."

"Oh?"

I take a slow sip of my coffee. "The corpus callosum—the stalk of nerve fibers that connects the two hemispheres—is thicker in musicians, particularly those who've studied music from an early age. Certain areas of the hippocampus are smaller in men, and also in people who suffer from post-traumatic stress disorder. Some people have a dominant left hemisphere; others have a dominant right hemisphere. Some people have language centers all throughout their brains, and some have them all clustered on one side. There are even neurological differences associated with different political and religious beliefs. Everyone's brain is measurably different from everyone else's. What does a 'normal' brain even look like. How do you recognize one. How do you create an objective standard by which to judge how *normal* someone's brain is."

"Well, in that case, you're no more or less normal than anyone else, right?"

"Maybe." The world doesn't see it that way, though.

"Let's keep going," Stanley says. He picks up the sheet of paper in front of him and reads: "'If you were a type of beverage, what would you be and why?'"

I wince. "You see what I mean. These questions are ridiculous. How am I supposed to answer something like that."

"Absinthe," he says.

I turn my head toward him. "What."

"I tried absinthe once," he says. "I was about fifteen. My mom and I were at a dinner party with a bunch of people, and I snuck some. One of my few acts of rebellion." He smiles with one corner of his mouth. "It's very strong alcohol. Cloudy green, like jade. It tastes sharp, almost bitter, so some people like to dilute it with water and sugar before they drink it, but I had it plain. It burned all the way down, but it made me feel giddy. Strong and completely weightless at the same time. Like I could fly."

"Wait. So you're saying you'd be absinthe."

"No, I mean—" He clears his throat, ears reddening. "Never mind."

Oh. *I'm* absinthe?

I'm still trying to puzzle out the meaning of this when he continues, distracting me: "Let's see. 'List your five best attributes.' Well, that one's easy. You're smart, dependable, kind . . ."

I want to protest that I'm *not* kind, but I close my mouth, knowing he'll just argue the point, like he always does. Instead, I listen to his voice as he reads.

I'm astounded at how easily he navigates his way through these baffling mazes of questions. It's like some form of psychological jujitsu that he's mastered without even trying. I try to focus on what he's saying, but I find myself daydreaming and just letting his voice wash over me like warm water. I wonder what the inside of his brain would look like, if I could swim through it like a tadpole—if it's filled with complex neurological structures designed for processing questions like *What kind of beverage are you?*

He says that I am absinthe. I still don't know what this means, exactly. But I like the word and I like the way it sounds when he says it.

"Thank you," I say. "For this. It helps a lot."

"Don't worry about it. It's not a big deal."

Even now, when I should be taking care of *him*, Stanley's the one guiding me and easing my fears. There seems to be so little I can do for him.

He hardly ever talks about his own pain. But I know it's there. Every day, in the hospital, I heard it in his voice and saw it in the flat, glassy sheen on his eyes, in the tightness around his smile. Sometimes he cries out in his sleep. He hurts more than most people could ever comprehend, yet still he smiles. And it's not just physical pain he deals with. From what little he's said about his childhood, I know the past still clings to him. Another way we're alike.

I find myself thinking about that first night I spent at his house—the things he said to me. Things he never brought up again.

"So let's see," Stanley says. "This question, 'Where do you see yourself in ten years?' Ugh, I never like answering this one. How is anyone supposed to know that? But they're basically just looking to see if you have goals—"

"You told me once before that your father physically abused you."

He freezes. His expression goes blank, and the color drains from his face. "Jesus," he mutters.

I know, immediately, that I've made a mistake. But it's too late to take the words back.

He takes a deep breath and slowly sets the papers down. "He didn't abuse me. It wasn't like that. He just got carried away sometimes, and—why are we talking about this now?"

I pick at the edge of one thumbnail. "The night after Draco—I mean TJ—after he hit you that first time and broke your arm, I stayed overnight at your house. You said certain things about yourself—that you believed your parents would have been better off without you, that your existence was a mistake. I want to know who put that idea in your head."

He closes his eyes briefly and rubs his forehead. "I was in a bad place that night. I was exhausted and doped up on pain medication. I barely knew what I was saying."

"You seemed pretty lucid."

"Christ, can we just—" He breaks off and lets out a short sigh.

"Look . . . I know I have lousy self-esteem, but that's my own problem. I'm not going to blame anyone else for it. He might be a coward, and God knows he's not going to win any Father of the Year awards, but he's not an abuser. Now, can we drop the subject?"

I lower my gaze. "Okay."

We keep going through applications. I shuffle through the papers, my gaze sliding over the different questions without really seeing them. Stanley tries to sound cheerful when he gives me advice, but I can detect a difference in his tone. I've crossed a line.

For a few minutes, when we were talking about neurology and absinthe, things felt almost normal between us. But now he's withdrawn into himself again.

CHAPTER THIRTY-TWO

That afternoon, I drop Stanley off at Westerly College and watch him wheel across the parking lot, up the ramp to the automatic door. I wait until he's inside before I pull out of the lot.

As I drive, I spot a red-tailed hawk perched atop a telephone pole. He takes flight, wings silhouetted against the pale sky, and I think about Chance.

The last time I saw him was when I dropped him off at the wildlife rehabilitation center. I've had a lot on my mind since then. But it's been too long. I need to make sure he's all right, at least.

The drive to Elmbrooke Wildlife Center takes about fifteen minutes. The receptionist's gaze flits over me without recognition. I wander through the building, which has a comfortable air about it, like a library. I look at the aquariums full of turtles and frogs, the terrariums of birds and lizards.

Outside, in a small wooded area behind the center, there are enclosures with coyotes and foxes and raccoons and a pair of golden eagles. In front of each one is a sign with the animal's name and personal story. Most of them were brought in injured, and for various reasons were unable to be returned to the wild. A cobblestone path winds in gentle curves, dappled with leaf shadows and glints of sunlight.

Near the end of the path, I see a large cage, and in it, a one-winged, red-tailed hawk drinking from a dish of water. He looks up, fixing his bright copper gaze on me. Then he leaps to the floor of the cage and attacks the bloody remains of a rat amid the cedar chips.

I look at the sign next to his enclosure. It's poster board—maybe they haven't had time to make an official one yet—with big letters written in marker. CHANCE, it reads.

I stare at it for a few minutes. Then I turn and walk away, back toward the main building.

Inside, on the counter up front, is a stack of applications. I start to reach out, but something stops me, and I pull my hand back.

The receptionist looks up, arching her eyebrows. She's an older woman, shoulder-length graying hair, small spectacles. "Looking for something?"

My mouth opens, then closes. I clutch one arm. "Those." I point at the applications. "You're hiring." My voice comes out stiff and jerky.

"We're always looking for help. Though I should tell you now, we only hire people who have hands-on experience working with animals."

Before I can lose my nerve, I grab an application and sit down in one of the plastic lobby chairs. The application is one page, double-sided. Sections for basic information, education, and experience. No long, intrusive, nonsensical personality questionnaires.

I quickly fill out the application, then shuffle to the front desk and hand it to the receptionist without looking at her. She could chuck it into the trash as soon as I leave, but I can at least say I've tried.

I expect her to give me a polite smile and say they'll keep me on file. Instead, she adjusts her glasses and says, "Well, you've got the experience. Why don't you come in for an interview on Friday?"

I sit at the table in Stanley's kitchen, poking at a crab Rangoon with a single chopstick. We ordered some Chinese takeout after I picked him up from class.

"You've been quiet," he says. "Is everything okay?"

I roll a bit of sweet-and-sour chicken around on my plate. "I have an interview. At the wildlife rehabilitation center."

"That's great!" He smiles broadly. "It sounds like the perfect place for you."

"It would be." He's right. I should be excited.

His smile fades. "What's wrong?"

"I probably won't get past the interview." My fingers tighten on the chopstick. "Interviews don't go well for me."

"We can practice, if you want. I'll ask questions and you answer."

Still, I don't look up from my plate. No matter how much I practice, I don't know if I'll ever come across as normal. During interviews, people always ask about my interests, but if I talk about my real interests, they think it's weird. And if I start pulling my braid or rocking back and forth, they'll immediately dismiss me.

"Alvie?"

"I just wish I didn't have to hide who I am."

"You know, it might help if you tell them."

The chopstick snaps in my hand. "What."

"I mean . . . it's worth a try, at least."

I drop the broken halves onto my plate and push it away. "How am I even supposed to say it. 'Oh, by the way, I have Asperger's.'"

"That sounds okay to me."

"I shouldn't *have* to tell them. Other people aren't expected to disclose personal medical information in an interview. Would someone say, 'Oh, before you hire me, I should mention I have a terrible case of hemorrhoids.'"

"It's not like that. This isn't something you need to be embarrassed about."

I stare at the mostly untouched food on my plate. My throat feels swollen. How can he say that, after everything I've done? How can he still insist there's nothing wrong with me?

"You know," he says, "I wouldn't be pushing you like this if you didn't want the job. There's no rush. You can stay here as long as you need to."

"But . . ." The words catch in my throat. Is he saying that because he wants me around? Or because he feels obligated?

I'm afraid to ask, but I don't know which answer would scare me more.

It doesn't matter, I decide. I *do* want this job. I want it more than I can remember wanting anything for a long time. So far, trying to hide my condition hasn't worked out so well for me, so maybe I need to switch tactics.

I unwrap my fortune cookie and break it open. *Careless risk brings grave misfortune*, reads the tiny strip of paper. I crumple it in my fist.

My interview is at noon. I try to eat breakfast, but I can't force anything down. Not only would getting this job mean gainful employment, it would mean a reunion with Chance. The prospect turns my stomach into a tangled knot. I sit in the lobby of the wildlife rehabilitation center, rocking lightly back and forth in my chair, waiting to be called. My hand keeps drifting up to tug my braid, despite my efforts to stop it. The receptionist—a college-aged girl with shiny pink lipstick—stares at me. When she notices me noticing, she looks quickly back at the computer screen in front of her. But her eyes stray back to me. People can never seem to stop themselves from looking.

Stanley's sitting next to me in his wheelchair. Sometimes when I was in public with Mama, she would take my hand in hers to keep me from tugging, or else she'd smile nervously at the people around her, as if she was afraid that they would suddenly converge on us and start beating us to death with their fists.

Remembering this just makes me rock and tug harder.

When the receptionist starts staring again, Stanley—to my astonishment—reaches up and starts tugging a lock of his own hair. Her mouth falls open, then she quickly jerks her gaze back to the screen.

He smiles at me, as if we're sharing a private joke at her foolishness.

A door in the back of the room opens, and the woman with gray hair and glasses pokes her head out. It's the same woman who told me to come in for an interview. "Ms. Fitz?"

I take a deep breath, stand, and glance at Stanley. He nods, holding my gaze.

I follow the woman into the back room and sit down across from her. Sweat dampens my blouse, which I just bought the other day. It's stiffer and itchier than the old cotton T-shirts I usually wear. I cut off the tag, but I couldn't get the whole thing; it left one of those little scratchy fringes that rubs against me like steel wool.

"Pleased to meet you," the woman says. "I'm Edith Stone."

"Pleased to meet you," I murmur.

"You worked at the Hickory Park Zoo for eighteen months," Edith says. "Is that right?"

"Yes."

"Did you enjoy the work?"

"Yes."

"And why did you leave?"

Last night I rehearsed an answer for this question, but still, the words come out stiff and halting: "I felt that it was time to move on to something more challenging."

"I have to warn you," Edith says, "if you're looking for a career upgrade, this probably isn't it. We're funded mostly by donations and grants. The people in this center are here because they have a passion for working with animals. The pay will be about what you're used to. Maybe a little less."

I freeze. Suddenly I have no idea what to say. My fingers twitch and clench on the arm of the chair.

Her eyebrows draw together. "Ms. Fitz?"

The space inside my chest shrinks until there's no more than a cubic centimeter to breathe in. I resist the urge to grab and pull my hair.

"Is everything all right?"

I'm ruining this. I know it. Probably I've already lost my chance. My face burns. If I could quietly drop through the floor and vanish, I would.

At this point, there's nothing to lose. "I have Asperger's," I blurt out.

Silence.

"It's a form of autism."

"I see," she says, and I can't read her tone. I don't know if she understands or if she's completely confused. "Will your condition prevent you from performing any job-related tasks?"

"No," I say. "I can do anything you ask me to. But if I seem—different—that's why."

I still can't read her expression. "I called your last employer, Ms. Nell," she says.

My muscles stiffen. Somehow, I doubt Ms. Nell gave me a glowing recommendation. But I force myself to ask, "What did she say."

"She told me that you knew your way around animals, but that you were cold, unfriendly, reclusive, and 'screwy in the head.'"

I lower my gaze.

"She also claims that, after she fired you, you snuck into the zoo and attempted to steal a sign."

My heart lurches.

"Is that true?"

I swallow. My mouth opens, but I choke on the words. I know it doesn't matter, what I say at this point. I'm not going to get the job. "Yes."

Her expression remains calm and blank. "I have to ask—why?"

I raise my head and meet her gaze. "The sign stated that animals don't have feelings. I consider that to be a lie." I stop and rephrase—"It *is* a lie. I know that I shouldn't have tried to take it, but I couldn't stand the thought of people coming in day after day and seeing those words." I pause to take a breath, bowing my head again. "I love working with animals. It's all I've ever wanted to do."

After a few seconds, I force myself to look up. She's grinning. She seems to catch herself, wipes the grin off her face, and clears her throat. "Of course, we can't condone that sort of behavior. Not officially, anyway. But . . . well, if you'll pardon the expression, I admire a woman with balls." At my stunned silence, she adds, "I'm saying I want to offer you a job."

She stretches a hand across the desk. Almost as an afterthought, she adds, "My nephew has Asperger's."

I shake her hand, so dazed that I barely react to the fact that a stranger is touching me.

I am utterly convinced that this is a dream, that at any moment my alarm will go off and I'll realize I have to get dressed and ready for my actual interview. But the floor remains real and solid beneath my feet. Edith's hand is bony, but her grip is firm and steady.

"You can start on Monday."

I'm in a daze when I walk back into the waiting room. Stanley looks at me expectantly. "I got the job," I say.

He hugs me tight and whispers that he knew I could do it.

Before we leave, I take him to the wooded area behind the center, pushing his wheelchair as I walk past the animals' cages. Chance has a real sign now, a shiny plaque with his name and a few brief lines stating that he was delivered by a "mystery benefactor." He's preening his breast feathers.

"He looks very content here," Stanley says.

"You think so."

"Yeah."

We watch him for a few minutes. This probably isn't the place he expected to end up, but he *does* look happy.

When we get home, Stanley wheels over to the kitchen pantry, retrieves a bottle of white wine from inside, and dusts it off. "Want some? I've been saving it for a special occasion. I think this qualifies."

"We're not old enough to drink," I point out.

He grins. "I won't tell if you don't. Though I've got some of that fizzy grape juice, too."

I consider. I've never had alcohol before, or experienced any particular desire to try it—I'm wary of anything that might lower my inhibitions—but it *is* a special day. I feel like trying something new. "Wine."

He gets two long-stemmed glasses from the cabinet and fills them. Then, to my surprise, he removes a candle from the drawer and lights it. "Will you help me carry these into the living room?"

I set the glasses on the coffee table. He grabs the candle and the wine bottle; since his hands are occupied, I push his chair into the living room, and we sit facing each other, the candle flame dancing between us. I take a small, experimental sip. It's more bitter than I expected, but not bad, and it feels warm going down.

In the soft glow, his skin looks smooth and touchable, like he just shaved, and his eyes are filled with candlelight. It's been a while since he's cut his hair. I decide I like it a little longer.

Sitting here with him, it's easy to pretend that things have gone back to the way they used to be. I think about the first dinner we shared in this house, the pancakes he made for me. That night feels like years ago now.

I swallow another mouthful of wine. "In about two weeks, I'll get my first paycheck. I can start saving up money. And then I'll start looking for a new place."

"About that." He takes a deep breath. "I meant what I said. You don't have to rush."

"I don't intend to take advantage of your generosity any longer than necessary."

His eyebrows bunch together, and a tiny furrow forms between them. "Is that what you think you're doing?"

I look away. "If you hadn't taken me in, I'd be sleeping on the streets."

The wine bottle is sitting on the coffee table, so I top off my glass. My thoughts swirl and drift, like a bunch of balloons released on a windy day, and when I grab on to one I lose track of another. I start to take another swig and I'm surprised to find that my glass is empty again, so I pour myself some more.

Stanley grips the glass, the skin around his nails white with pressure. He has barely touched his own wine. "Listen, Alvie . . . I know that for a while, back in the hospital, I acted like I didn't want you around. But that's because I didn't know how to deal with what had happened. I was angry. I mean, you vanished with no explanation. You ignored my calls and my texts. And I kept asking myself—why? Did you hate me that much? Or did I just matter that little to you?"

"That's not what it was like. You know it wasn't."

"I don't know anything. How could I? You never bothered to tell me."

I take another swig. The wine burns going down. I'm aware, dimly, that my guards are lowered and that I probably shouldn't be talking about this right now. But I'm tired of holding everything in; I can't muster the will to care. "I left because it was the only way to protect you."

"From *what*?"

How can he even ask? Does he really not know? "From me. I *hit* you, Stanley."

"You didn't mean to. You lost control—"

"Don't make excuses for me." My throat has constricted to a pinhole, but I force the words out. "Yes, I lost control. And that makes it even worse. Because it means I might do it again. I can't trust myself *not* to hurt you."

"That's ridiculous. It didn't even hurt that much. Besides, shouldn't *I* get to be the one who decides what I can and can't handle? I'm not so weak that I need to be protected from my own choices."

I squeeze my eyes shut and drain my glass. My head droops, and my attention fixes on the carpet. "Maybe you can accept it. But I can't. You deserve better—"

"You're just using that as an excuse. Because you're scared of this."

I grit my teeth. I *am* scared. But so what? That doesn't change what I did. "What if you were the one who'd 'lost control' and punched *me* in the face. Would you think that was okay."

There's a brief silence. "That's different."

"No. It isn't."

His face is flushed—from the wine or something else, I don't know. "You could have called me back, at least. We could have *talked* about it. You didn't have to *disappear*."

I know he's right. I should have. But if I had allowed myself even that much, I wouldn't be strong enough to leave him. "It doesn't matter. It's over now."

"It doesn't have to be. I don't want to give up on this, Alvie."

My eyes refuse to focus; my brain refuses to process his words. I should probably stop drinking. When I try to stand, my legs give out, and I sink back to the couch. "I'm drunk," I murmur.

"I love you," he says.

I flinch. I can't help it.

"Why is it like this?" Stanley whispers. "Why are you so afraid of being loved?"

I open my mouth to tell him that I can't talk about this now. Instead, what comes out is, "Why are you so afraid of sex."

He draws in his breath sharply. In the silence that follows, he doesn't breathe at all. "I'm not . . ." His voice breaks. He covers his face with his hands.

I want to apologize, but the words stick in my throat.

Slowly he lowers his hands. "I'm afraid I'd do it wrong. That it wouldn't be good for you."

"But there's more. Isn't there."

His breathing quickens.

I've gone too far, again. I should stop, pull back. But I can't. "What are you afraid of, Stanley."

He looks straight at me. He's pale, lips pressed in a thin line. "What if I got you pregnant? Things happen. Even when people are careful."

My mouth falls open. I've had the same thoughts myself, but still, I'm caught off guard. I don't know how to respond.

And for a moment, I allow myself to visualize the possibility— a little human kit, a squirming bundle of life with my eyes and his hair. His smile and my nose.

My brain and his bones. "What would we do?" he asks. "What would *you* do?"

What my mother should have done when she was pregnant with me. Rabbits reabsorb their young when they're not ready. In the animal kingdom, abortion is not particularly uncommon. You could say it's kinder. In the wild, young born into unfavorable circumstances—or with genetic defects—don't survive long.

I hear Stanley's words in my head: *I mean, obviously it's better if these things are planned. But lots of kids aren't, and their parents still love them.*

And my own voice telling him, *Love doesn't pay the bills.*

My stomach hurts. I feel like I'm going to be sick. "I don't know."

He looks away. When his eyes move, I see the flashes of blue gray in the dim light. Misty blue, twilight blue. Dark choroids visible through too-thin tissue. "Maybe the wine was a bad idea." He smiles, the muscles of his face stiff. "Let's just go to bed."

CHAPTER THIRTY-THREE

Long after Stanley has gone to sleep, I lie awake on the couch, staring at the ceiling. The mugginess in my head has cleared, but the queasy feeling in my stomach remains. Did we really just have that conversation?

Why are you so afraid of being loved?

I roll over, burying my face against the couch cushions.

Tomorrow, we will have breakfast together. I'll drive him to school, and we'll pretend that last night never happened. I'll seal it away, along with everything else I don't know how to deal with. There's no sense in trying to untangle these feelings when our relationship is already irreparably broken.

You're just using that as an excuse.

I curl into a ball.

He's right. I just keep running, making excuses for myself, because I don't know how to be close to someone.

I won't run away this time. I can't repair the damage, but I can stand my ground and face the consequences of my actions. After everything he and I have been through together, I owe him the truth. All of it. And if he doesn't want to be with me after that . . . well, that's probably for the best.

Quietly I get dressed, pull on my coat, and lace up my boots.

I have to open the Vault, and when I do it I can't be anywhere near him.

I don't know what will happen.

Outside, the world is still and white, cold and clear. I drive and drive, through subdivisions and snow-covered woods, until I see the dark expanse of the lake. I park, get out, and walk, snow crunching under my boots until I'm at the edge of the water. Despite the cold, the lake isn't frozen. It laps at the sand, like hands reaching for me. I close my eyes and see the towering, shadowy doors of the Vault in front of me.

I can't just reach out and open them. They're too well constructed. When I built this place, I made it so that even *I* wouldn't be able to break it open on a whim. But there is a way.

Standing on the shore, I begin to undress. When I strip off my shirt, the frigid air hits my bare skin, raising goose bumps. Ignoring the discomfort, I fold my clothes, placing them in a stack, leaving my car keys on top. I'm shaking hard, and not entirely from the cold. Every instinct is screaming at me to turn and run, run, *run*. The panic is like an alarm bell clanging in my head, drowning out my thoughts.

This is madness. I could get hypothermia. I could die.

But I have to do it. If I don't face this now, I never will.

Naked, I wade into the icy water. It caresses me, wraps around me. My brain is still screaming, but I ignore it and keep wading in until the water reaches up to my chest. My breaths come quick and shallow. The cold eats into me, as though my skin has been stripped off and I'm burning alive.

I take a deep breath and submerge myself completely.

Cold water presses in around me, dark as tar. I open my mouth, and the air escapes my lungs in a flurry of bubbles. Mama's face floats in the blackness, ghost-pale, hair drifting around her in a halo. Her eyes are closed. For a moment, we're weightless.

Then we're plunging down.

My mind is a chaos of static, but my body knows what it wants: it wants air. It wants to live. I claw off my seat belt and fumble in the darkness, my fingers numb with cold, my eyes straining against the black. When I find the car door handle and pull, it won't open. It's like something is pushing back, trying to close it.

Above me I can see a faint light through the water, but it's dwindling. The ache in my lungs has sharpened to pain. My mouth wants to open, but I keep my lips clamped shut, knowing that if I give in to the urge, it will be over. Finally, in a burst of panicked strength, I force the door open.

A cold hand grabs mine, pulling me down. I struggle, kicking out. My nails rake over the thin, gripping fingers, but they won't let go. I claw and kick and pry until finally the grip loosens and slides away, into the blackness.

I kick out against the water and shoot like a bullet toward the surface.

My head breaks through, and I gulp in air. A wave crashes over me, roaring, shoving me back under. The roar fills my ears and drowns out my thoughts. I kick to the surface again, and another wave drags me down, as if the lake is alive. My head breaks the surface and I drag more air into my lungs. Choppy waves break all around me, and foam swirls.

Where is Mama?

Dizziness bursts inside my skull, and my vision blurs. My legs and arms strike out blindly, fighting the water. The shore looks so far away, but I push myself toward it, even as the lake roars around me.

Mama. Where is she?

I remember a hand tugging mine, then slipping away. Slipping down into darkness. Then the memory vanishes, too.

Another wave roars down on me. The rush of water is all around me, and a current pulls at my legs. A bit of information—*the Great Lakes are the only lakes that have currents*—spins through my head like a leaf on the wind. I fight, arms wheeling. The shore is receding. I'm being pulled back and down.

It's hard to see anything, but for an instant I think I glimpse a figure on the shore, beckoning me.

Mama.

When a current has you, you're supposed to swim sideways. Teeth gritted, I dog-paddle, struggling against the pull. The current releases me, and I lunge toward the shore. My head goes under again. More water fills my mouth. My limbs go heavy and weak, but I force them to move. Mama is waiting for me on the shore. She'll take me home, and this will all be a bad dream.

At last, I crawl onto the sand and collapse. A fit of coughing wracks my body, and cold black water floods from my mouth. Weakly I lift my head and look around. But Mama is nowhere to be seen.

My head drops to the sand. I don't know how long I lay there, dizzy and sick, floating in and out of a dull fog.

Two figures stumble into my view. One of them is a teenage girl, laughing. A boy follows her, shoving his hands underneath her shirt. "Brad, stop! Someone will see us!" she gasps.

"Nobody here but us chickens, babe." He peels off her shirt and squeezes her boobs, and they fall to the sand, him growling like a dog while she giggles and squeals.

A weak moan escapes my throat.

Their heads turn toward me. Their mouths drop open.

"Holy shit," the boy says, "is that a kid?"

My vision goes blurry again, and darkness folds around me.

There's a long stretch of nothing, and then a bright white room. For a while, I don't know where I am or what's happening. Doctors drift in and out of the room while I drift in and out of the dark fog in my head. There's something covering my mouth and nose, and my breathing sounds raspy.

I hear a man say: "Amazing that she managed to swim to shore on her own. That takes some strength. She's a lucky girl."

And a woman's voice replies, "I wouldn't say that." A pause.

"Her eyelids just flickered. Is she conscious?"

If the man responds, I don't hear it. I'm already sinking back into the void.

Later, a nurse is looking at the machines around me, writing things down on a clipboard.

"Where is Mama?" I whisper.

She looks at me and doesn't say a word. Her lips tighten, and she quietly leaves.

I remember the car driving over the edge of the pier. I remember a cold hand sliding out of mine and into the nothingness below.

Everything clicks into place. For a moment I can't breathe, can't think, can't move. A blinding red pain fills my whole body, like every nerve is screaming. Then all at once, the pain is gone, the nerves dead and cold.

Alone.

I'm alone.

CHAPTER THIRTY-FOUR

I find myself on the shore, gasping and shivering.

My throat is raw and sore, as if I've been screaming. I don't remember screaming. I should be feeling something, shouldn't I? I've just ripped open my deepest wound, turned myself inside out—but I'm numb.

My clothes are still neatly folded up where I left them. Fumbling, I dress myself, get into the car, and start the engine. I can't feel my feet or fingers, but somehow, I manage to get myself home.

When I open the front door, the lights are on. Stanley is there in the living room, in his wheelchair, his eyes wide, his face pale. "Oh my God. Where have you been?"

I moisten my numb lips. "How long have I been gone."

"Three hours."

I glance at the clock. Four thirty. "Sorry."

He wheels toward me. "Alvie. You're drenched. Are you okay? What's going on?"

The door swings shut behind me, shutting out the darkness

and cold. I know it's warm inside, but I can't feel it. "I . . ." My voice emerges hoarse and cracked. I swallow and try again. "I went to the lake."

His brows are drawn together, forehead wrinkled. "What?"

I take off my coat, walk slowly toward the couch and sit down. My deadened nerves are awakening with searing darts of pain, blasting the fog from my head. I run my hands through my loose, wet hair.

Stanley drapes a blanket around me, takes my hand between both of his and rubs it gently. "Can you feel this?"

"Yes." I watch him rubbing my fingers. "I feel it."

But inside, I'm still numb.

"Alvie." He squeezes my fingers. His voice is gentle but firm. "Talk to me."

I stare into space. This is what I wanted, isn't it? "Mama never knew how to deal with me. She wanted a normal little girl, one she could cuddle and talk to and dress up, and instead she got this silent, broken thing who recoiled from touch."

"You aren't broken."

But I am. I am. Slowly I rock back and forth on the couch. "I never told you how she died."

Stanley doesn't say anything. He just waits.

When I finally speak, my voice is strangely calm. "She drowned herself."

His breath catches.

"It was my fault." My voice sounds strangely indifferent, as if I'm just telling him what I had for breakfast. "In a way, I murdered her."

"No." He grips my hand. "No, Alvie, that's not true. You can't blame yourself for what she did."

I stare at him. My face feels stiff, like wood. Expressionless. I should be falling apart—I've never talked about this with anyone—but there's nothing. It's as if the coldness of the lake leaked into my heart and froze my core.

Stanley bows his head and presses my hand to his cheek. "If I had a child, I could never leave her alone in the world, no matter how much I was hurting."

"She didn't leave me."

His body goes tense. "What?"

I feel my lips stretching into an unnatural smile, though I've never felt less like smiling. "She tried to take me with her."

CHAPTER THIRTY-FIVE

Mama looks at me. Her face is pale and blank, her eyes red rimmed. "I'm so sorry, Alvie."

Everything is broken.

Without those pills . . .

Things were just starting to get better, and now it's all over.

I'm a failure.

I can't keep going . . .

She reaches out. "Come here."

There's something in Mama's face that makes me uneasy. I bite my lower lip, then approach. She pulls me into a hug, and I start to tense up, because it's too tight. I squirm, but Mama just hugs me tighter. It hurts.

At last, she pulls back and smiles at me, her eyes bright with unshed tears. "Go wash up and do your homework, then we'll have dinner."

"I don't have homework anymore."

"Oh." She rakes a hand through her hair and laughs, a little too shrilly. "Right."

I go into the bathroom and wash my hands.

Mama calls me into the kitchen. She's made my favorite dinner, chicken nuggets with macaroni and cheese. She pours herself some chamomile tea and pushes a glass of apple juice toward me.

Her eyes are glassy and a little too wide. When I say, "Mama," she doesn't seem to hear me right away. She stares into space for a few seconds, then smiles vaguely across the table and says, "What's that, honey?"

"Aren't you hungry," I ask. She's barely eaten two bites.

She looks down at her plate and says, "I guess not."

The chicken nuggets are dry and gritty in my mouth.

"I love you so much, Alvie," she says. "I want you to know that whatever happens, it's because I love you. You might not understand, but please believe that."

"Okay." I don't understand at all.

"Make sure you drink all your juice," she says.

I take another swig of my apple juice. It tastes funny, like chalk, and I hesitate.

"Go on."

I look at the juice, which is a little cloudy. Mama is staring at me, waiting, so I keep drinking, and it slides thick and bitter down my throat. I gag a little, but I manage to force it all down.

When the last drop is gone, Mama says, "I don't want you to be in pain."

"I'm not in pain."

She doesn't seem to hear me. She pokes a fork listlessly at her macaroni and cheese. "I never told you much about your father."

Her voice sounds faraway, like sleep talk. "That's just as well, though. I guess I never told you much about me, either. But there isn't much to tell. I've never achieved anything. School, jobs, relationships . . . none of it really went anywhere. And then when I met him, I thought finally, this was *something* . . . but then it was over. It isn't your fault, Alvie." She lets out a small sigh. "It doesn't matter now, I suppose."

Bits of powder slide down the sides of the glass. My vision drifts out of focus, and I blink. My head feels funny. I look down at my half-finished plate of chicken nuggets and macaroni; blobs of orange and brown. My head droops toward my chest, and a thin line of spittle falls from my open mouth and onto my shirt.

What's happening to me?

"I don't want you to end up like him."

"Uhhh." The moan slides out of my mouth, thick, like syrup.

Chair legs scrape the floor as Mama stands. She walks around the table toward me and places her hands on my shoulders. I sway, woozy. I try to ask her what's going on, but all that comes out is another moan.

"Shhh."

She lifts me out of the chair. I hang like a rag doll from her arms, head and limbs flopping as Mama carries me over to the sofa and sits. She hunches over, cradling me in her lap, and holds me tightly as she rocks me back and forth.

My head rolls to one side. Everything is fuzzy. The world spins slowly around me, like I'm on a carousel. Mama strokes my hair.

Usually, she smells like honey and vanilla shampoo. Now a

sour, stale smell clings to her, as if she hasn't washed for a while, and she's clutching me so painfully tight. Her fingers dig into my ribs, like she's afraid I'll float away if she loosens her grip. "I love you so much, Alvie," she says. "Do you understand that?"

I open my mouth, but all that comes out is more drool.

Something is really wrong. If I could just think clearly, I'd know what it was, but every time I try to hold on to my thoughts, they slip through my fingers, like I'm trying to grab wriggly little fish.

I try to form words: *Mama, what's going on?* but my lips and tongue are numb and all that comes out is *uhhh, wuh ruhh.*

She starts singing. It's the song she used to sing to me sometimes when I was little, "My Bonnie Lies Over the Ocean." But now she sings it with my name. "My Alvie lies over the ocean . . . my Alvie lies over the sea . . ." Tears fall on my face. "My Alvie lies over the ocean . . ."

A gray haze closes around me. I'm falling, and her words follow me down.

"Oh bring back my Alvie to me."

I open my mouth to tell her that I'm here. But the gray fog swallows me whole.

For a while, I float.

When I surface from the haze, we're moving. I can hear the car and feel a seat belt across my body. I try to lift my head, but it feels like it's filled with cement.

"Just relax," Mama says. Her voice is soft and faraway. "We're going for a ride. I'm going to take you to your favorite place."

My eyelids are made of stone, but I manage to pry them open

a crack. Mama is driving, her face bathed in the faint glow from the dashboard, her eyes wide and blank. "Everything is going to be okay," she says.

I don't know what's happening. I struggle to put the pieces together, but it's like looking at a jigsaw where none of the edges quite line up. If only I could think. Why can't I *think*?

Within, a small, cold, clear voice whispers, *The juice.* My heartbeat quickens. I have to move. I have to get out of here. I don't know what's happening, except that everything about this is wrong and I have to get out. But my muscles are like spaghetti. It's like that feeling when I wake up in the middle of the night and I'm only half-asleep but my body won't move—*sleep paralysis*—and my eyes won't quite open and my mind is still fogged with dreams, and I think, *Just move one finger*, and I try very hard to move my right index finger, but nothing happens.

Move. Move. Move. *Move.*

I can see out the window. I see the sign that means we've reached the lake. This is the place where Mama usually pulls over and parks. But we keep driving, toward the wooden pier that juts out like a finger over the lake.

And my body still won't move.

It would be easy just to let go and fall asleep. Maybe if I let go, everything will be okay. Maybe I will wake up in my own bed, and this will all be a dream.

As I sink deeper into the warm darkness, her voice follows me: "Whatever happens, it's because I love you."

CHAPTER THIRTY-SIX

Silence falls over the room. Stanley is still holding my hand, but he says nothing. There is no sound except his unsteady breathing.

"She kept saying she loved me. That whatever she did, it was because she loved me." I stare straight ahead. I'm floating, still empty, because if I allow myself to feel anything now, I will shatter. "If that's love, then how can love be good."

He draws in a deep, slow breath. Then he touches my cheek, turning my face toward him. His eyes are vividly blue, wide and filled with tears. "That's not what love is, Alvie."

I stare back dully.

"Even if she *did* love you, what she did that night . . . that wasn't an act of love."

"Then what was it."

His shoulders sag, and he suddenly looks very tired. "I don't know. Fear, maybe? I can't understand why she did it. But I can tell you this much. It was not your fault."

"Yes. It was." The numbness has started to fade. Inside me, something is awakening, and it hurts. "I made her miserable. If I had tried harder . . ." The breath rattles in my chest. "If I'd done things differently, if I'd *been* different, maybe she'd still be alive. And I'm afraid. I'm afraid that I'll always be like this, no matter how I try to be better, that it'll happen all over again, and I—and you—"

He seizes my hand in his, so hard I look up in surprise. "You can spend your life playing guessing games, trying to imagine some other world where you made different choices and everything turned out another way. But there's *no* world where it's okay to drug an eleven-year-old girl, strap her into the seat of a car, and drive into a lake."

"Mama wasn't a bad person." My voice is weak. "She . . . she just couldn't . . ." I trail off. I don't even know what I want to say. "It was too much for anyone, taking care of me."

"What about my parents' divorce? Do you think that was my fault?"

I stiffen. "No. Of course not."

"Then why do you blame yourself for this?"

"That's just . . . different."

"No. It's the same thing. It took years for me to stop blaming myself for everything that happened. And sometimes, I still feel responsible.

"After the divorce, my mom fell apart. She'd always been protective—and once Dad was gone, I was all she had. I wasn't allowed to play outside with other kids. If I tried to sneak out, she would lock me in my room for days. I missed so much school anyway, because of fractures and surgeries, no one really thought it was strange when I didn't show up. Eventually she just pulled me out altogether."

I listen, holding my breath.

"It wasn't all bad. Most of the time, she was kind. Gentle. She gave me everything I needed—bought me books and computer games so I wouldn't get bored, even though I was cooped up in the house all the time. But I felt like I was suffocating. When I told her I wanted to go away to college, she freaked out. Said I was breaking her heart, that I would kill her if I left. But I wouldn't give up. It was the only argument I ever won. Then . . ." He stops. His eyes shine, wet and reflective with tears.

"She got sick, started passing out. She'd known for a while there was something wrong with her, but she didn't go to a doctor, because all the money went to my medical bills. When she finally saw a neurologist, it was too late to do anything. After that, I had to come back. I couldn't leave her. She got worse and worse. She started having these rages, these fits where she ranted at me and threw things. There was this one night . . ." His voice cracks. He stops and takes a breath. "I was taking a bath. She broke into the bathroom, this empty look in her eyes, like she wasn't *there*, and started washing me. All over. Like—like I was a baby, or something. I kept telling her to stop, but it was like she couldn't hear a word I was saying, and I was too scared to push her away. Scared I'd set her off." He sits, shoulders hunched, hands balled into tight fists. "It wasn't . . . I mean, she didn't hurt me. But the next time

I went to my doctor and she asked me to undress so she could see how the latest break was healing, I had a panic attack."

Oh, Stanley, I think. Stanley. Stanley.

"I know she loved me," he says. "And I loved her . . . and my dad, too. I still do. I think it's easier, in a way, when someone hurts you out of hate. It's less confusing. When the ones who hurt you are the people who love you most . . . no one ever tells you how you're supposed to deal with that."

There's a hard, hot ball in my chest. Suddenly I want to go into his mother's room and break all the ceramic figurines, rip apart the flowered coverlet and the rose-patterned curtains. Erase all the pain, all the memories.

"Listen to me." He frames my face between his hands. His palms are warm on my cheeks. "What happened is not your fault. Not even a little. And I'll say that as many times as it takes for you to believe it."

It seems impossible, what he's saying. It seems like a logical fallacy. My mind won't accept it. "If I had never picked up your phone in the park, if I'd never sent you that email, you wouldn't have gone through all this suffering." My voice wavers. "You wouldn't be sitting in this chair, now, with half your body in bandages."

"You're right," he says. "I wouldn't be here. I'd be lying next to my mother in the cemetery."

At first, the words don't sink in. Don't register. Slowly I raise my head. "What."

"After you sent me that email, I changed my mind."

It takes me a moment to find my voice. "Why," I whisper. "Why didn't you tell me."

"I didn't want you here out of pity. I needed to know that this was real."

I can't help it. I kiss him. I feel his soft intake of breath—he tenses briefly, then relaxes into it.

He smiles, tears in his eyes. "I wouldn't give up a single minute of the time I've spent with you. Not even the difficult parts."

I close my eyes and exhale a shuddering breath. My face is still anchored between his hands. "I don't deserve you."

"Stop telling yourself that." His voice is harsh, almost angry, but beneath that, there's a husky throatiness, as if he's close to tears. "I'm not a saint, whatever you think. You deserve to be loved. You deserve to be happy. So please . . ." His grip gentles, and his eyes soften. "Please stop punishing yourself."

I can't speak.

I was so sure that when I told him, he'd be horrified. He'd see me for the monster I was, a creature so detestable that my own mother tried to destroy me. Deep down, a part of me always believed that she was right—that I was better off dead. That my life could never be anything but a mistake. "I'll always be like this, you know."

"Good. Because I want you exactly the way you are."

Two tears slip from my eyes and down my cheeks.

He holds his arms out to me, and I collapse. My hands fist in his shirt. My face presses against his neck, and the sobs pour out—ugly, raw, animal sounds. I can't stop. It's frightening. It hurts, like I'm splitting open and all my insides are pouring out.

He cradles my head against his shoulder and rocks me back and forth.

I cry for a long time. When it's over, I am exhausted, weakened and empty. But it's a clean sort of emptiness. I feel new, like a baby opening her eyes for the first time, looking upon the world in all its strangeness and beauty.

"We didn't have the best luck with family, did we," I say, my voice faint and hoarse.

He lets out a choked laugh. "No."

"If we ever have children," I say, "let's do better."

That night, we share his bed for the first time since I moved in. He clings to me in the darkness. "You'll stay?"

I take his hand in mine and hold it against my cheek. "I'll stay."

His hair shines in the lamplight. On impulse, I touch it. It's short, bristly yet soft, like fur; there's something comforting about the texture. Slowly I slide my fingers through it. His breath catches.

"Is that bad," I ask.

"No. It feels nice."

I touch the back of his neck, where the skin is warm and velvety, and he shivers. When I start to slide my fingers under the collar of his shirt, he tenses, so I pull back and resume combing my fingers through his hair, a slow, steady movement.

I missed this. I missed touching him. His warmth, his scent. The sensation awakens something restless in me, and I want more.

I rest my hand on his thigh.

"Alvie . . ." He gulps

"What's wrong."

"It's not that I don't want to," he says. "I do. Believe me. It's just . . . my legs are still in braces. I can barely move my lower body. I mean . . ." He clears his throat. "*That* part of me is okay, but still. It'll be a while before I'm in any shape for this kind of thing."

"Even if we can't do it the usual way, we can still do *something.* When I did my research—"

"Research?"

Oh, right. I never told him. "I watched a lot of pornography to prepare myself. For the first time, I mean."

"Uh." He won't look directly at me.

"I saw a lot of different positions and methods," I continue.

"Alvie." His voice sounds a little strained.

"What."

"I want our first time to be special." He takes my hand in his. "I really want to do this right. I want to be prepared, and I don't want to be stuck in braces when it happens."

The words frustrate me.

When I first propositioned Stanley, I just wanted to prove to myself that I could do it. I didn't even care if I enjoyed it; I just wanted to feel connected to another human being, if only for one night. But it's not like that anymore. I want *him.* I want to touch him, to feel his skin against mine.

But I remember what he said about his mother—how afterward,

he couldn't even get undressed in front of a doctor.

"I just need a little more time," he whispers.

Stanley has been patient with me. I can be patient, too.

I touch his chest and say, "When you're ready."

He relaxes, and I know I've made the right choice not to push. Still, the frustration remains. We've revealed so much to each other. This is the last barrier between us.

CHAPTER THIRTY-SEVEN

The lake looks the way I remember it—smooth, glassy blue, like a mirror. I pull into the small lot next to the beach.

"You really want to do this?" Stanley asks.

"Yes."

Early-morning sunlight smudges the clouds with pink as I walk across the damp sand. My legs tremble, and sweat pools in the small of my back, despite the crisp, cool air. I face the water. Waves lick the shore.

My mother's body was pulled out of the lake during the investigation, years ago. I learned later that she was cremated, in accordance with the wishes of some estranged relatives I never even met. There is no casket, no headstone. Though she's not here anymore, this lake is the closest thing to a grave she will ever have.

I crouch and place a hand on the smooth, water-polished sand. It's warm, like a living thing. Waves lap over my fingers. Carefully, with one fingertip, I write a name in the sand: CASSIE ELEANOR FITZ.

To me, she was always Mama. I never found out who she was outside of that. I'll never have the chance.

I think back to the days before all the trouble started, when we were just mother and daughter. I am three, maybe four years old. Mama and I are making cookies together. I'm fascinated by the sticky dough, and I keep putting my hands in it and playing with it like clay, getting it on my face and in my hair, and the whole time, Mama is laughing. Later, she wipes my face clean, still beaming. She kisses me on the head and says, "Do you have any idea how perfect you are?"

I'm sure there were difficulties, even back then. I'm sure that I threw tantrums, climbed on furniture, and hid under the bed. But we were happy.

I will always wonder how I could have changed things, if I'd made different choices—if I'd just told her that I'd been taking vitamins instead of antipsychotics, if I hadn't gotten myself expelled, if I'd been able to hug her more often, if I'd found the words to make her understand that it wasn't her obligation to fix me, because it's okay to be imperfect.

Or maybe if I'd seen the truth before it was too late—that my mother was the one who needed help. She'd been wounded inside for a long time, maybe even since before I was born, and she had no one to turn to. What if I had recognized that and told someone that she was depressed—that she'd been drowning long before she drove us both into the lake?

Maybe I could have saved her. Maybe not. We were both children, in a way, stumbling through the dark woods, confused and uncertain, clinging to each other for warmth. Maybe we just lost our way.

I trail my fingers through the shallow water, and a faint ache spreads through my chest, but the tide of anguish I expected doesn't come. I came here to find closure, to say whatever words I need to say to express everything inside me. But in the end, there are only two words.

"Good-bye, Mama."

The waves gently lap away the name in the sand.

Whatever alternate possibilities exist, they are not my world. This is. I look at the blue sky, the sun shining in rays through the clouds, sparkling on the lake. Gulls wheel in the air, brilliant white. The sand is warm under my feet, and I am alive. I stand and walk away from the lake, toward the edge of the beach.

Stanley waits in the car. The sunlight turns his hair a brighter gold.

We drive back. I'm behind the wheel. His hand finds mine and squeezes, then slips away.

"It took a lot of courage to tell me the truth, didn't it?" he asks.

I shrug. "You've been honest with me."

Outside, the telephone poles glide past. A murder of crows flies high overhead, black dots against the clear sky.

His hand drifts to his chest, fingers clenching on his shirt. "I still haven't . . ."

"We have time."

I want to make him understand that the scars don't matter, the pain and fear doesn't matter, because he is my life mate and

I know that in every cell of my body. Nothing will ever turn me away from him. I want to find words to tell him, but no matter how many times I reach for them, the words are never there. There must be another way. I think and think.

And something clicks.

CHAPTER THIRTY-EIGHT

I've never visited a tattoo parlor before. I look at the reclining leather chair, the sample art on the walls, and fidget, crossing my arms over my chest. I feel terribly out of place.

I've prepared myself for this mentally, or at least, I thought I had. Now that I'm actually here, the reality is sinking in, and adrenaline prickles under my scalp. Will I even be able to endure something like this? I have a high tolerance for pain, but pain administered by another person? That's another matter. I imagine sitting there for hours, watching the needle penetrate my skin over and over, fighting the overpowering urge to flee. And of course, I'll be shirtless the entire time.

Already, I want to run. But I've made up my mind. This is something I need to do.

The tattoo artist is tall and skinny, with a goatee and arms covered in lines of Sanskrit. He cocks an eyebrow at me as I sit in the chair. "You eighteen?" he asks.

I'm prepared for this. I'm not eighteen yet, not quite, but I've obtained the necessary paperwork to prove that I'm a legal adult. I show him.

"Okay," he says, but he's frowning. "You already got ink, or no?"

I stare blankly.

"This your first tattoo?" he clarifies.

"Yes."

"And you've thought it through."

"Yes."

He squints at me and says, "You sure you don't need someone's permission for this? Because I don't want to get in trouble."

I'm getting impatient. I wonder if he interrogates all his customers; it seems like a funny way to do business. "There's another tattoo parlor ten miles from here, and three more within a forty-mile radius. If you're going to give me a difficult time, I don't have a problem going to someone else."

He blows air through one corner of his mouth and crosses his scrawny arms over his chest. "Well, it's your skin," he says. "So, you know what you want?"

I pull a piece of paper from my pocket, unfold it, and show him. He takes the paper from me and studies it a moment, his forehead creased. Then he nods. "Where?"

I point at the center of my chest, between my breasts: the place just over my heart. "Here."

By the time I get home, I'm starting to wonder if the tattoo was a bad idea, after all. I've never even asked Stanley what he thinks about tattoos, because these things never occur to me until after the fact.

When I enter the kitchen, he's sitting on a tall stool in front of the stove, stirring a pot of spaghetti sauce. The aroma of tomatoes, oregano, and garlic bread fills the air. He looks over his shoulder at me and smiles. "Hey. Dinner's almost ready." He glances at the clock. "I was hoping to have it done before you got back, but . . ."

"It's okay." I told him I'd be home at eight, since I didn't know how long the process would take. I walk over, lay a hand on his shoulder, and kiss his temple.

It's strange, how natural these gestures now feel.

His face turns toward me, and our lips meet. There's a faint taste of sauce on his tongue; he must have been sampling it.

As we sit down to eat, I keep expecting him to ask me why I was gone for so long, but he doesn't.

"So, how was work?" he says.

I tell him about Kitt, the three-legged fox, and Dewey the crow, who can tie a piece of red twine in a knot using his beak. I tell him about the hexagonal tiles on the cobblestone paths in the wooded area behind the shelter, about the koi pond with the little bubbling fountain. I was worried the fountain would bother me, but the sound of water doesn't seem to affect me as much as it used to.

"You're going to be wonderful there," he says.

"Thank you." I twirl my fork in my spaghetti, conscious of the sore spot on my chest. His tablecloth is off-white and green checkered. I find myself counting the rows of green squares, doing math in my head to estimate the total number of squares on the table. The tablecloth is rough-woven, the fibers thick and visible, a complicated crosshatch of strands overlapping and blending together. It's easy to see them as a seamless whole, when I let my eyes drift out of focus, but nothing is ever seamless or simple if you study it closely.

"Is anything on your mind?" he asks.

I stand. "Come with me."

His brow furrows. He starts to pick up his plate, but I say, "We'll take care of that later." I walk toward the bedroom. He follows me slowly. He's graduated from wheelchair to crutches, but he still struggles getting from place to place.

Once we're inside, I shut the door and face him. He's sitting on the edge of the bed, crutches resting beside him, and I'm reminded of that first night in the motel room.

I'm still wearing my work shirt. Now, I start to unbutton it.

His eyes widen. "What—"

"I got something for you today." My shirt drops to the floor. I undo the clasp of my bra, and it falls. "Don't touch it. It's new." Carefully, I peel off the bandage covering the tattoo.

It took a very long time, and it was agony. Not because of the physical pain, which was bearable. Forcing myself to be still for so long—putting myself at someone else's mercy—went against everything in my nature. I remember sitting, rigid as a board, fingers digging into the arm of the chair, shaking so hard my teeth rattled. The tattoo artist kept smirking at me, as if my discomfort was the most hilarious thing he'd ever seen, and more than once I had to forcibly choke down the urge to kick him. But the result is worth it.

A carnation blossoms on my skin, bright red petals inked over my heart. It's identical to the one Stanley gave me—the one I broke. It's still tender, the skin around it faintly pink, but it's not bleeding.

Stanley's eyes widen. Slowly, he reaches out, but his fingers stop an inch from the flower.

I fidget and tug my braid, resisting the urge to avert my gaze and start studying the carpet. I feel exposed in a way that has nothing to do with my naked skin.

My heartbeats echo through the silence as I wait for him to say something. At last, he clasps my hand against his cheek, then turns his face and kisses the palm. "It's beautiful," he whispers.

The tension runs out of me, leaving me weak and shaky with relief. The last thing I want is for him to look at me when I'm naked and think, *If only she didn't have that stupid red blob between her tits.*

He starts to reach toward it again, then stops. "Does it hurt?"

"A little."

He lightly touches the skin just left of the carnation. The touch is as soft and tentative as the brush of a moth's wing.

His gaze meets mine. "Can you . . . can you turn off the lights for a minute?" He smiles, though I can see the lines of tension around his eyes and mouth. "It's easier for me to get undressed with the lights off."

For a moment, everything inside me goes still. There's a little leap in my chest, a breathless tremor of anticipation. I flip off the light switch.

The rustle of cloth breaks the silence. He's taking off his shirt.

The darkness is thick, tangible; it presses in on me like black fur, and no matter how I strain my eyes against it, I can't see anything.

His fingers curl around my wrist, and he pulls my hand to his chest. I feel the roughness of scars against my fingertips. He's tense, his breathing heavy and rapid as I slide my fingertips lower, feeling the ripples and hard lines of scar tissue. My hands glide over his shoulders, and I trace the length of a long scar running from the base of his neck to the middle of his back. I remember him telling me about how he broke his scapula, how they had to open him and reset the bone surgically; months of agony and immobility, compressed into a line of raised flesh. I trail my fingers lower down his back, and there is another scar. And then another. I touch his arms, and there are more. *Eight, nine, ten, eleven.*

I quickly lose track.

"I want to turn on the lights," I say.

There's a faint *click* in his throat as he swallows. "It's okay. Go ahead."

Instead of the light switch, I turn on the lamp. He's naked, except for his boxers. The lamp's soft amber glow casts pools of shadow in the hollows of his clavicles and between his ribs, emphasizing the thinness of his body. The scars are like a bas-relief sculpture carved on his skin, overlapping lines, some faded and almost invisible, others fresh and bright pink. There are dimples of scar tissue where surgical pins pierced his flesh—rows of them, marching alongside the straight lines of past incisions.

My fingers graze his chest. I trace the scars on his ribs, like

Braille. A history of pain. But without that pain, he wouldn't be who he is: someone with enough empathy to reach out to me, enough courage to love me. "You're perfect, Stanley."

Suddenly he seems very interested in his own bare feet. "You don't have to say that."

I kiss a jagged scar on his collarbone, and his breath shivers in his throat. My lips brush against a scar on his left pectoral. His chest heaves as I kiss another scar, then another. I take his hand in mine and kiss the palm. When our lips meet, I taste salty tears.

His hands slide over my skin. When his palm settles over my left breast, I push into the touch.

I want more. I want to touch him, to feel him respond to me.

My hand drifts down to his boxers, and his muscles tense.

"My legs are still—"

"You won't have to move your legs. You won't have to do anything. Just let me."

He looks baffled. Then his eyes widen as realization sinks in. "You want to . . ."

"Yes."

He closes his eyes and breathes in slowly. He seems to be struggling for control. "Alvie . . ." His eyes open, and he reaches out to touch my face and tuck a few strands of hair behind my ear. "I can't ask that of you."

"You aren't asking," I reply, a touch of impatience in my voice. "I want to." I kneel beside him on the bed, feeling suddenly uncertain. "Do you not want it."

"Of course I do," he blurts out, then bites his lower lip. "It's just . . ." His voice softens. "I want our first time to be more than that for you. It shouldn't be about pleasing me. It should be something perfect, something you can remember for—"

I grip his wrists and pin them down to the bed. "Stanley." He blinks up at me. "For once in your life, stop being selfless and let me suck your cock."

His eyes go so wide I can see the whites all around. "Okay," he says, breathless.

I release his wrists and examine his tented boxers. Carefully, I ease them down, and for a moment, I just look at him.

I'm well familiar with male anatomy, of course. I've seen photos. But this is different. This is Stanley.

My heart is beating fast, my mouth dry, and I realize that I'm nervous. Of course. I've never done anything like this. Before I met him, I'd never allowed myself to get close enough to anyone to even consider it. After opening my mind to him and telling him the darkest secrets of my past, physical contact shouldn't feel so overwhelmingly significant.

Our eyes meet. There's an expression on his face I have no words for. It calms me, somehow, to know that this is just as new for him. I rest my hands on his slender thighs. "Are you ready."

He nods. I swallow a few times, trying to generate some saliva, and lower my head.

He tenses briefly, then relaxes. Surrendering, trusting.

Once I let go of my anxiety, it's not difficult. I lose myself in it, my mind a daze of concentration, noting his responses and adjusting my movements accordingly. I listen to everything; the little hitches and shivers of his breath, the soft, husky groans rising from his throat, the rustle of sheets as he shifts.

Stanley never lets himself relax. Not like this. I didn't realize, until this moment, how much I've longed to see him this way, with all his guards down—not worrying or thinking or distracted by concern over me, not doubting himself or striving to be worthy. Just lost in feeling, in his own nerves. Somewhere deep in my body, there's a pulse, a growing ache. I ignore it, pushing all those sensations into a corner of my mind, leaving the rest of it a cool, efficient computer.

When his eyelids slip shut, I freeze. I need to see his eyes; I need all the available data, to know if I'm doing something wrong. I lift my head long enough to say, "Keep them open."

His eyelids snap up. And I lower my head again.

His muscles tense beneath my palm, then clench. His breathing grows faster. "Alvie," he gasps. "I—I'm gonna—" He cries out.

I pull back, not quite fast enough, and double over in a fit of coughing. Eyes watering, I retreat to the bathroom to rinse out my mouth and drink some water from the tap. When I return, he starts stammering apologies. I silence him with a kiss, then lay my head on his chest. His heart is still pounding. After a moment, it begins to slow. He rests his hand on my back and murmurs, "That felt really good."

My head is buzzing. I feel the way I did after my first few sips of wine, before it started to cloud my head. Light. Pleasantly warm.

I did that, I think. *I made him feel that.*

He reaches out to touch my face, fingertips brushing over my cheekbone. He tucks a lock of damp hair behind my ear. "How do you feel? Are you— I mean—" His eyes move in small flickers, searching my face. "Do you want anything?"

"Like what."

He touches me through my jeans—a light, soft touch.

My heartbeat quickens.

It would be easy to stop now. To retreat, reassess, find my center of control. But I don't want to stop.

Slowly I remove my jeans, then my underwear.

At first he is gentle, almost cautious. I hold still, barely breathing, as he explores me . . . then, gradually, I begin to relax. I find myself arching into his touch, like a cat, my body moving on its own.

The sensations are strange. New. But not bad. There's pressure, some stinging. I squirm.

"Alvie?" he says, his voice low and anxious. "Are you—"

"Keep going."

He does.

For a brief moment, I find myself thinking about the nature show that first gave me the idea to proposition him—the polar bears rutting in the snow, how businesslike and unceremonial it was, and how at the time that had appealed to me because it seemed simple. This is different. I should have known it would be different. His breathless, intent focus, the way he looks at me through wide eyes, as though I am the only thing in his world—I feel *seen.* Every move, every breath, is significant. We are both so vulnerable, so open to each other, and for once, I don't feel the urge to look away.

Stanley, I think. Stanley, *Stanley* . . .

Then everything goes white.

When I come back to myself, I'm lying next to him, his arms around me. There's a sense of weightlessness, as if I'm lifting out of my body, looking down at both of us in the bed.

He holds me tighter. "Are you okay?"

"Yes." My skin is damp with sweat, my head is spinning; it's too much to absorb, too much everything, and for a moment I want my Rubik's Cube, the cool comfort of plastic beneath my fingers, the straightforward simplicity of rows of color clicking into place. Instead, I focus on the gentle pressure of Stanley's arms around me, the heat of his skin.

For now, this is enough.

His hand brushes my leg. I curl against his side, resting my head on his shoulder.

"I love you," he whispers, his lips moving against my ear.

I open my mouth. At first, the words don't want to come out. Even now, my throat closes up, my body resisting through sheer force of habit. Then something inside me relaxes. "I love you, too, Stanley."

He holds me close and tight, his arms a sheltering burrow around me, and buries his face against my hair.

I hear a low, peculiar sound, almost like the cooing of a dove, so soft it's nearly inaudible, and I realize it's coming from my own throat. It's the same sound that rabbits make when they're happy.

CHAPTER THIRTY-NINE

"Are you sure about this?" Stanley asks.

I look around the condo. It's empty, save for the stacks of cardboard boxes labeled BOOKS and DVDs and MISC. STUFF. "I'm sure. Anyway, it's a bit late to be questioning our decision."

The movers will drag in the rest of our furniture tomorrow. For now, all we have is a bed and a TV. And Matilda's cage, which sits on the floor. She's nibbling a food pellet, seemingly oblivious to the change in scenery.

I sit on the edge of the bed and turn my Rubik's Cube over in my hands.

Stanley limps over, leaning on his cane, and sits next to me. "I know that change is a big deal for you," he says. "And I know you liked my house."

"This is closer to Elmbrooke, and to your school. It'll be easier."

A few boxes labeled MOM'S STUFF sit next to Matilda's cage. "What are you going to do with those," I ask.

"Probably donate them to Goodwill."

I nod and look at him from the corner of my eye. "How does it feel."

A smile quirks at one corner of his mouth. "Terrifying. But in a good way." He looks around the condo.

He's been getting a new treatment, a series of injections designed to strengthen the collagen in his bones, and his sclerae aren't as noticeably blue now. But I can still see a faint tinge, like the sheen on a pearl. "Yes."

Sunlight pours in through the picture window in the living room, illuminating the white walls. Everything here feels so bright. It will take some getting used to.

"The kitchen stuff is still in boxes," he says. "Want to go out for dinner? I think there's a pancake restaurant around here."

I nod and slip into my hoodie, and we leave the condo. On the way, we pass a park. It has a small pond, and a bench. "Wait," I say.

He parks, and we get out and sit on the bench, side by side. A pair of geese glide across the water. A rabbit is digging in the grass. She stops and looks up, ears alert and quivering.

We sit, comfortably quiet. Beneath our feet, the winter-brown grass is squishy from the melted snow. A few tender green shoots are visible, pushing their way toward the sun. I breathe in the sharp, cool air. It holds a smell that is familiar yet new.

"It's funny," he says. "I was just thinking, about that phrase from *Watership Down* . . . 'My heart has joined the Thousand.' I know it's about mourning, but to me, that part of it always sounded kind of . . . hopeful. Like it's about becoming something bigger than yourself. About connecting with other people, or the world."

Overhead, the sky arches, blue and clear, and there's a sensation of lifting in my chest—a sense of opening. *My heart has joined the Thousand,* I think, trying out the new meaning. It feels accurate.

I remember the first time I saw Stanley, sitting on a bench in a park just like this. I was upset, I recall, because a stranger had invaded my territory and disrupted my carefully planned routine. I thought about getting up, walking away, and never coming back. I came so close to doing it. But something stopped me. Something—what?

A hint of curiosity. A random pulse of electrical activity in some deep, hidden fold of my brain. The opening and closing of an ion gate on a single nerve cell. The spin of a subatomic particle within that ion gate. Something so small, so seemingly random. And now Stanley and I have a home together. Being with him feels easy and natural—like something that could last forever.

Intellectually I know there is no such thing as forever. Someday we will die and our bones will turn to dust. Someday humankind will be gone and the earth will be ruled by sentient rabbits, or by the machines we leave behind, or by creatures we can't even imagine. And then the sun will go supernova and swallow the earth and all the other planets, and the universe will continue to expand until the bonds of gravity loosen and all things drift away into the darkness, and all stars will go silent and cold, and matter itself will break down into nothingness. Time will end, and there will be nothing but vast, cold, empty space. The atoms that once composed our bodies will be dispersed across unimaginable distances.

But then, subatomic particles are connected in ways we don't understand. Two particles that have interacted physically are bound by quantum entanglement. They will react to each other even after being separated, no matter the distance, linked by intangible cords across space and time.

I tilt my head back, looking into the bright sky, and smile. Stanley reaches for my hand, and I take it, fingers slipping easily and naturally between his. And I find myself thinking of that moment, years ago, when I awakened in the hospital after swimming to shore. I remember the doctor's words: *She's a lucky girl.*

For the first time, I believe it.